Tease

THE TEMPTATION SERIES IV

ELLA FRANK

Also by Ella Frank

The Exquisite Series
Exquisite
Entice
Edible

Masters Among Monsters Series
Alasdair
Isadora
Thanos

The Temptation Series
Try
Take
Trust

Sunset Cove Series
Finley
Devil's Kiss

Standalones
Blind Obsession
Veiled Innocence

The Arcanian Chronicles
Temperance

Sex Addict
Co-authored with Brooke Blaine

PresLocke Series
Co-Authored with Ella Frank
Aced
Locked
Wedlocked

Dedication

To Logan,

Because f*ck. I missed you.

~Tate

Part One

Normal: To conform to a standard; usual, typical, or expected.

Chapter One

"ALL RISE."

THE bailiff's voice cut through the tense courtroom as Judge Wilson emerged from his chambers and took his seat behind the bench. It had been ten minutes since the defendant's attorney had called for a recess, and the time for negotiations was coming to an end as Logan Mitchell got to his feet and buttoned his suit jacket.

He glanced over at Paul Bishop, the tight-assed prick in the horrible tweed suit who had been a thorn in Logan's side for the past seven months. But this time when their eyes met, a smug smile crossed Logan's lips, because what was about to happen was going to be real fucking sweet.

He, and twelve other associates at his firm, had been working tirelessly on a class action suit involving one of the biggest pharmaceutical companies in the country, Berivax, and after his client had taken the witness stand, Logan knew he had this one in the bag—and so did Bishop.

The fight had been hard and drawn out, as one would expect of a giant corporation, but when Bishop leaned down and scribbled a number on a piece of paper, Logan turned to his client and winked. He so had this.

"Please… Take a seat. Take a seat," Judge Wilson said with a wave of his hand.

Everyone in the courtroom complied, except for Bishop, who handed Logan the piece of paper. He took the note and was pleased to see Bishop's frown as he moved back to his side of the courtroom. Logan read over the message then, and barely managed to stop his jaw from hitting the table he was seated behind.

Thirty-five million. Shit. They'd been willing to take fifteen. *But thirty-five? Holy. Fucking. Shit.* Schooling his features, Logan slid the paper over to the woman beside him. He inclined his head once, and as she read the note, her eyes widened. No words were needed.

After months of discovery, depositions, and court dates, this case was finally going to be over, and they'd just received an offer that was well over what he'd been instructed they'd be willing to take. He had just won them the motherlode.

"Okay, you two," Judge Wilson said, looking between Bishop and Logan. "Did you manage to come to some kind of settlement, or am I going to be making a decision for you today? Because either way, we *will* be wrapping this case up before that clock hits four. Do you hear me?"

Bishop got to his feet without sparing a glance in Logan's direction and said, "Yes, Your Honor. We've come to an agreement."

"I'm so pleased to hear it," Wilson said as his eyes shifted to Logan. "And I assume you share this consensus, Mr. Mitchell."

Logan stood once again, and pushed his glasses up his nose. "We do, Your Honor."

"Good. In that case, go and settle it," Wilson said as he looked between them and picked up his gavel. "Court is adjourned."

As he brought the wooden hammer down, calling the session—and trial—to an end, the courtroom exploded in chatter, and Logan caught his client Renate Aleman pushing back from the table to stand.

"You did it," she said, shaking her head. "I can't believe they gave us what we were asking for."

"More," Logan said as he bent to pick his briefcase up off the floor. He placed it on the table and started to load his files inside it. "They gave us *more*. They offered to settle at thirty-five, and that's because of you. You did great up there on the stand, Renate. That's what finally had them caving."

"On that we can agree," someone said from behind Logan. He turned around to see Bishop standing in the aisle of the courtroom with a document in hand and a pinched expression on his face. "You barely had a case until you got her up there."

Logan had to resist the urge to roll his eyes as he reached for the paperwork. "Don't be a sore loser, Bishop.

Your client makes that much money in a couple of hours."

Logan took the papers and placed them inside his case so he could take them back to the office and have everyone sign.

"You know," Bishop said, his gaze drifting over Logan's shoulder to Renate and then coming back to rest on his face, "one of these days you're going to bite off more than you can chew, Mitchell."

Logan shut his briefcase and made sure to lock it before he took it by the handle and looked Bishop directly in the eye. "I don't think so. You see, I'm very careful about what I put in my mouth because it's my motto to always swallow. But you have a good evening, Bishop. I'd like to say it's been a pleasure, but... Let's just leave it at 'see you next time.'"

"Whatever, Mitchell." Bishop turned and walked out of the courtroom, and with all of his belongings packed away, Logan waited for Renate to pass by and then dug his cell phone out of his pants pocket.

Cole was going to pass out when he heard the final number, and Logan would be damned if anyone but him got to deliver the news. As he pushed open the doors to the courtroom, Logan told Renate to head back to the office, where they'd all meet up, and then he called Cole's number and brought his phone to his ear.

It didn't take long, two rings and then, "How'd it go?"

"Well, hello to you too, brother," Logan said as he wove his way through the busy halls of the courthouse.

"Yeah, yeah, hi. So? How'd it go?"

As Logan crossed the polished floor of the main lobby, he chuckled. "Cole, is Jane nearby?" he asked, figuring his brother might need his personal assistant to administer CPR once he found out the figure Berivax had finally settled on.

"She's around. Why? Logan, just spit it out. What number did they come in at?"

Logan pushed through one of the large revolving doors and walked out to the top stair of the courthouse. As the sun warmed him, he took a rare chance to soak it in. Damn, it was going to be nice to slow things down and start getting home at a decent hour again.

"Logan?" Cole said. "What number?"

Logan started down the steps, determined to get back to the office and be done with this so he could meet up with Tate, take him out somewhere fancy for dinner, and then...

"Thirty-five," he said when he reached the sidewalk. Silence met his ear, and Logan allowed Cole a second to process. "Are you still breathing over there?"

"Did...did you just say thirty-five?" Cole asked.

"I did."

The sound of a leather chair creaking alerted Logan that Cole had likely just fallen into his.

"Fuck me," Cole muttered.

Logan checked both directions of the road he was crossing, and then headed over to where he'd parked his car. "I'll pass, if it's all the same to you."

"That's twenty over what we expected," Cole said, ignoring the comment.

"I know."

"Thirty-five..." Cole said again, and the disbelief in his voice matched the feeling Logan had had when he'd opened that piece of paper.

"I know. All I can say is thank God I was sitting when Bishop gave it to me. You should've seen his face." Logan laughed. "This one really burned his ass."

"I bet. He doesn't like you on the best of days, let alone losing to you on something as big as this. Jesus, that's unbelievable."

"It sure is. That's seven million coming our way."

"I...I can't even process it yet," Cole said. "But shit, all those late nights finally paid off, didn't they?"

Logan wasn't so sure about that. As exhilarating as it was to have won today, he was more than aware it had come with a price—and that price was his private life. The hours he'd had to put into this case had been draining, and weekends? They had been nonexistent. And though Tate said everything was fine and that he understood, Logan hated the fact that he couldn't remember the last time the two of them had gone out on a simple date together.

It wasn't only him, either—business at The Popped Cherry was booming, which meant Tate was working nearly every night. And while both of their businesses were thriving, they'd gotten themselves into a routine where they hardly saw each other except when one was crawling *out* of their bed to leave. Not a sight Logan was fond of.

He hit the button on his keychain, unlocking his Audi R8, and slipped inside, tossing his briefcase on the passenger seat. "I don't know about that, Cole. I'm tired. This took a lot out of me." Logan paused and ran a hand over his face before giving voice to the question that was now suddenly on a loop in his head. "Hey? Do you and Rachel ever, you know, get... Ugh, I don't know." He sighed, not knowing what he was trying to say.

"Get into a funk?" Cole asked.

"A funk?"

"Yeah. A routine."

Logan thought about that. "I suppose that's what I'm trying to say."

"Of course," Cole said, as though that was supposed to make Logan feel better—it didn't. "It's part of being in a relationship. I know that might be foreign to you—"

"Bite me."

"But it's normal. People get busy."

"Seriously? That's all you've got?" Logan said, and shut his eyes as he laid his head back against the headrest. "I've never been too busy before."

"You've never been with someone long enough to *get* busy."

"You know, sometimes I really question the reason I ask you anything...ever."

Cole chuckled. "It's because I bring you clarity, and I know you better than almost anyone. Let me guess: you and Tate have been so busy with work that you've hardly had time for one another lately."

"Ugh," Logan groaned. "When you say it like that, we sound so—"

"Committed?"

"Shut up."

Cole's amusement only incensed Logan further.

"It's not a dirty word, you know. With two kids under five, Rach and I have had periods like that. Trust me, I get it. It sucks."

"Well, in this case, it doesn't *suck* often enough. That's the point."

"Logan, you just wrapped up a seven-month case. Tate knows that. Call him, take him out to dinner. Tell him how you're feeling."

Yeah... That was something Logan had never been really great at. Although he'd gotten much better since Tate. Logan ran a hand through his hair and silently berated himself. He knew Cole was right, and hated that he'd let his and Tate's relationship slip into this place where he felt unsure of it. It was the whole commitment thing. He hadn't done that before Tate. And though they shared their lives, and had done so happily for the last four years, after attending their friend's wedding a few months ago, Logan had become acutely aware that that trip away had been the first one they'd had together in a long time.

When had they become so...settled?

Shit. What the fuck is the matter with me? It wasn't like Tate had *said* anything about being bored or upset. But maybe he was thinking it? *No way, that's ridiculous. Even for you, Mitchell.*

"Okay, you're right," Logan finally said. "So, how about you let me go so I can call Tate? A celebration *is* in order, and no offense, I'd rather do it with him."

"None taken. I have a good mind to do the same."

"Well, you can go get your own date. He's mine. Plus, I don't think Rachel would approve."

"You're hilarious."

"Sometimes," Logan said, and started the car thinking of all the things he wanted to discuss with Tate when he finally caught up with him. "I'm heading back to the office to have everyone sign what needs signing, then I'm out."

"Of course. But don't think you're leaving without having a drink first."

"Have a glass of that fancy Macallan waiting for me. I don't plan to stick around for long."

"You got it. And Logan? Great job today, really. You

deserve a fucking raise. Talk to your boss about that, would you?"

"Yeah, I just might do that," Logan said, pulling out onto the side street.

"See you soon."

"See ya," Logan said, and as soon as Cole hung up, he called Tate, set in his resolve that no matter what his bartender was up to tonight, he was coming out.

* * *

"WE NEED THREE bottles of Knob Creek and five of the Silver Patrón, and that's the last of it," Amelia said as she turned to Tate, who was sitting at the end of the bar jotting the numbers down on his spreadsheet.

They'd just finished taking inventory, and were getting ready to open for the happy hour crowd that would start arriving anytime now. Wednesday night—Hump Night—was one of the busiest nights of the week at The Popped Cherry, and as Amelia headed to the end of the bar so she could go and unlock the door, Tate stopped her.

"Hey, before we open, I wanted to talk to you for a minute," he said, and when a frown furrowed her forehead, Tate grinned. "Don't worry, you're not in trouble."

She pushed the bar pass up and came around to take a seat on the stool beside him, bumping his shoulder with hers as she took a sip of her bottled water.

Over the last four years, Amelia had become a good friend to both him and Logan, and at work she was an absolute lifesaver. As part-time manager, she was quick and efficient, and had a personality that drew people in, which resulted in amazing tips and repeat customers, which was why he wanted to talk with her today. Tate had wondered if maybe she'd like to take on a little more responsibility and make a bit more money with some extra hours. One, because she was great at her job, and two, because it would free him up in the late evenings. Let him scale back somewhat.

When he'd first opened the bar, Tate had known he would be putting in late nights and that it would be difficult with Logan's hours to make time for the two of them. But Logan had always been great about coming by after work so they could crash in the loft upstairs. That was until these last few weeks when this case Logan had been working on had gone into overdrive. It was one of the most demanding lawsuits Mitchell & Madison had taken on, and had practically taken over their lives, which had Logan and Tate's schedules all over the place to where they'd barely seen one another. And damn if he wasn't sick of barely getting ten minutes of Logan's time here and there. He missed the hell out of him.

"So what's up, boss?" Amelia asked, her blond ponytail swinging as she placed her arm on the counter.

Tate tapped the pencil he held on the bar and shoved aside those thoughts as he smiled at Amelia. "Nothing bad.

It's just I'm thinking of stepping back a little, and I need to hire someone to take on the later hours and closing up, that kind of thing. And I was wondering if you'd be interested in the position. It'd come with a pay raise, of course."

Amelia twisted the bottle back and forth before saying, "Aww, Tate, I'm sorry. I was actually going to talk to you tonight about giving my two weeks' notice."

"What? Why?" he asked as his phone started to vibrate in front of him. "Are you unhappy?"

"No. Nothing like that," she said, placing her hand on his arm. "I hate doing this, because you and Logan, you're just the best. But I got accepted into nursing school and I signed up to attend full time."

"Oh. Okay, umm, that's not a problem, really," he said, even as he thought about the hole her absence would leave. Amelia knew The Popped Cherry almost as well as he did. Not to mention their easy camaraderie and history. Trying to find someone that fit in even a tenth of the way she did was going to be close to impossible. "I'll put out an ad tomorrow and start interviewing for a full-time manager then. We'll find someone, don't worry." Seeing that it was Logan calling, he picked up the cell and said to Amelia, "Would you mind sitting in on the interviews once they're scheduled, though? Just to get a feel for the people?"

"No. Not at all," she said. "And I'll be available to train them, of course."

Tate smiled and nodded as she slipped off the chair

and headed over to the front doors to officially open for the night.

Okay, well, that was the first thing he'd do tomorrow morning: put out an ad. Or maybe even tonight. He gathered up his clipboard and, as he stood, hit accept on the phone. "Hello, counselor. How'd the big case go today?"

Tate had been eyeing the clock all afternoon waiting to hear the outcome of the Berivax trial, and while he was happy it was finally going to be over, he also hoped all of Logan's hard work had paid off.

"When was the last time we had sex?" Logan's question was so blunt and unexpected it had Tate stumbling over his response for a second, and when he didn't answer, Logan continued, "You don't know, do you?"

The side of Tate's mouth twitched at Logan's disgusted tone. "Well, to be fair, you caught me off guard. I had to think for a minute."

"And now that you've had time to think?"

"Umm..."

"Oh my God. You can't remember," Logan said, and Tate couldn't stop his laugh then. "That's fucking shameful."

"We've just been—"

"Don't say it—"

"—busy." Tate headed over to the door that separated the bar from the tiny foyer and stairwell that went up to their loft, shut it behind himself, and took a seat on one of the steps. "Well, we have been. This case of yours has taken up most of your time, and with the bar hours we just got...busy."

"Yeah? Well, that shit needs to stop. Right now."

Tate leaned his shoulder against the wall and shut his eyes, picturing Logan with his jet-black hair, those piercing blue eyes, and that full, sensual mouth. Tate had barely had time to say goodbye to him this morning, and no matter how much he was laughing it off, Logan was right—this not seeing one another was bullshit. They needed to sit down and work something out, now that Logan's schedule would be returning to something more manageable.

"Agreed," Tate said. "Something needs to change."

"Good. How about we discuss it at dinner?"

Tate winced. "I'm here until one."

"Can't you beg Amelia to stay and come meet me?" Logan asked, and if he hadn't sounded quite so desperate, Tate might not have caved.

"Depends."

"On?"

"What am I going to get if I come to you?"

Logan's voice lowered to a tone that never failed to make Tate hard. "Me. All night. And maybe again in the morning. I'm in a *giving* kind of mood."

Tate swallowed and stretched his legs out in front of himself, suddenly needing a little more room in his jeans. "All night, huh? It's been a while since that happened."

"It has. So come find me and I'll rectify that little issue you're having with remembering our weekend away at the cabin. *That* was the last time my cock was inside you."

"Jesus, Logan." Tate pressed a palm to his erection, recalling the weekend trip they'd made around three weeks ago. Or maybe it was four. *Shit, okay.* They did need to work something out if he was having trouble remembering that. "Let me get things settled here and I'll be at your office in"—he checked his watch—"an hour? Hour and a half?"

"Perfect," Logan said. "I'll be waiting."

"Logan?" Tate said before Logan could hang up.

"Hmm?"

"You never did say—how'd court go today?"

"Oh." Tate could hear the satisfied smile in Logan's voice when he replied, "They settled for thirty-five million."

Tate's mouth fell open, and when he finally managed to shut it again, he said, "Wow, that's… *Wow.* Congratulations. Why didn't you tell me that first?"

"Because there was something more important to discuss," Logan said as though it should've been obvious, and Tate couldn't stop himself from laughing.

"Your priorities are—"

"Spot fucking on for the first time in months. An hour, Tate."

Tate got to his feet and opened the door to the bar, just as eager as Logan was to meet up. "An hour. See you then."

"I'll be here."

And with that, Logan disconnected and Tate went to hunt down Amelia to ask one final favor.

Chapter Two

AS THE ELEVATOR doors opened on Mitchell & Madison's floor, Logan was surprised to see Cole waiting for him in the lobby. He was leaning against the reception desk chatting with their receptionist, Tiffany, as Logan stepped off the elevator and walked their way. Tiffany was the first to spot him, and a bright smile split her lips before Cole turned his blond head and flashed a broad grin. Logan stopped when he reached the two of them, and chuckled when Cole picked up a glass tumbler and handed it to him.

"Now, this is what I call service," Logan said, taking the glass and saluting Tiffany.

"This afternoon I'm inclined to give you just about anything you want," Cole said, and when Logan opened his mouth, his brother added, "I said just *about*—remember that before you issue anything too outlandish."

Tiffany spoke up, sidetracking Logan for the moment. "Congratulations. We all heard the big news."

Logan raised the glass and took a sip of the scotch, then aimed a winning smile in her direction. "Thanks. It was a pretty spectacular day."

"That it was," Cole said, slapping his palm on the

reception desk. "And all of the clients were called to come in and sign, so they should be getting here within the next half-hour. Tiffany, send them in to the conference room when they arrive, would you?"

"Will do, Mr. Madison," she said, as Cole nodded and both he and Logan headed to the double glass doors that led into their law firm.

As they stepped inside, Sherry, Logan's PA, was right there to take his briefcase from him, and Logan couldn't stop his laughter as he looked between the two standing in front of him. "Wow, I should win millions more often. A drink on arrival. Sherry's here to take my things before I'm even two feet in the door. Tell me, do you have Tate waiting naked for me in my office? Because that would really be the perfect way to thank me for the past seven months and the fact that our firm just shot up to the number two spot in Chicago." One of Cole's eyebrows winged up, and Logan pursed his lips. "Is that a no? Okay. Then maybe *when* he arrives, in the next forty minutes or so, Sherry, you could have him escorted to my office so I can take care of that myself."

Sherry had worked with Logan long enough now not to put anything past him, but her deadpan expression had Logan chuckling. "Okay, okay. I'll at least wait until everyone leaves for the night. Better?"

Sherry rolled her eyes and asked, "Are you quite done?"

Logan raised his glass to his lips and swallowed the rest of the scotch down. "Hmm. Damn, that's smooth. It's the good stuff, isn't it?" he asked, looking over at Cole.

"Yes, well, I thought you deserved it until about two seconds ago. I cracked open the—"

"Twenty-five-year-old single malt?" Logan whistled. "I really *did* impress you today. You've been holding on to that like it came from the fountain of youth."

"Damn right," Cole said, raising his own glass. "But if ever there was an occasion for it, this is it."

"There is *more* where that came from, right?"

"Yes, but before you have another, there's someone waiting in your office for you."

Logan frowned, and Cole plucked the empty glass from him and shook his head. "And no, it's not Tate."

"Then have them reschedule. I told you I was done today." Logan looked to Sherry, waiting for her to agree and go tell whoever it was to scram, but instead she said, "I explained you were finished for the day and would be back in tomorrow morning. But he insisted on seeing you and said he wouldn't take up more than five minutes of your time."

Logan looked to Cole, who held up his hands. "Don't look at me. I followed your orders and had your drink ready."

"He said he knows you," Sherry said.

Logan let out a long-suffering sigh. "Does this man

have a name?"

"Yes, of course. Mr. Bianchi."

Logan racked his brain trying to locate or remember anyone by that name. When nothing stuck out, he shook his head. "He's lying. I don't know a Mr. Bianchi."

"Well, he's in your office," Sherry said. "So maybe just go in there, see what he wants, and then tell him to come back tomorrow."

"Thank you, Sherry, for that sage advice."

"That's what you pay me for," she said, and beamed at him before she walked off to her desk with his briefcase in hand.

Logan looked to Cole, who was grinning after her, and then asked, "Why do I put up with her insubordination again?"

"Because *she's* the only one who will put up with you."

Logan slipped his hands into his pants pockets and made his way through several bustling desks toward his office, and called over his shoulder, "You're probably right."

"I am right," Cole replied from behind him. "And come see me once you're done. I'll refill this glass."

"Five minutes," Logan said, as he reached for the door handle and pushed open the door. "Give me five minutes and then I'll—"

Logan drew up short as his eyes landed on the man waiting for him in his office. He was tall and lean, which was emphasized by the charcoal slim-cut trousers he was wearing and the lightweight black turtleneck. But what really caught Logan's eyes were the black-and-blue crocodile monk-strap shoes that matched the messenger bag the man was holding. There was no way in hell he knew this guy, Logan thought, as he walked inside and shut the door. Because he'd never forget someone who wore shoes like—

"Logan?"

As Logan raised his eyes from the bag the man was holding, he saw a face that was both different and altogether familiar staring back at him, and all he managed to say was, "Robbie?"

* * *

THE SUN WAS well on its way to setting when Tate finally stepped into the elevator that led up to Mitchell & Madison. He punched the button for Logan's floor and leaned back against the wall, where he scrolled through his messages, making sure none had been missed on his drive over. When he was satisfied all was good, he reread the text Logan had sent twenty minutes earlier and couldn't stop himself from grinning.

Logan: You coming yet?

And then, before Tate had been able to respond, a second had come through.

Logan: Scratch that. You better not have come yet.

But seriously, are you on your way? This is not the night to be late, Tate.

Oh yeah, Logan was in a mood, and Tate had to admit it was exciting to see this side of his lawyer again. He was more than ready to get this little reunion of sorts underway. When the elevator reached the firm's floor, Tate slipped his phone into the back pocket of his jeans and stepped out into the elegant lobby. Tiffany must've already left for the day, as the reception desk sat empty and the only lights in the entry were the low security lights and the display spotlight that illuminated the Mitchell & Madison sign.

Tate, now a regular around the offices, headed straight through the glass doors to see several people still working at their desks, and the conference room at the back of the main floor lit up with about half a dozen people inside, standing around talking and drinking champagne.

He waved at a few of them, and smiled as he headed in the direction of Logan's office, looking for the man they must've been celebrating tonight, and as he approached, he noted the door was shut. He passed by Sherry's empty desk, about to go ahead and knock before entering, when he spotted Cole walking down the hallway. Tate stopped as the other man waved and took a sip out of the tumbler he held, and then he reached out to shake Tate's hand.

"Hey there," Cole said as Tate embraced him in a jovial hug.

"Hey, yourself. I hear a celebration's in order tonight," Tate said, eyeing the drink in Cole's hand.

"That it is. I've gotta say, Logan really outdid himself this time."

"That's what I heard," Tate said, crossing his arms as Cole took another sip. "I can't even imagine how he must be feeling."

"Pretty pleased with himself, I would say—and tired, apparently," Cole said with a laugh.

"Tired?" Tate asked, not quite understanding.

"Uh huh. Your man is dead to the world in there."

Tate looked at the shut door as though he could see through it, and then turned back to the man he now considered a brother. "You're kidding, right?"

"About him being tired? Or asleep?" Cole asked.

Tate started laughing, the irony of it all not lost on him. Logan was finally free for the first night in months and he was too tired to stay awake past seven. "Of course he's asleep."

"I mean, I probably shouldn't have given him the third glass of scotch. But he was adamant you would drive the two of you to dinner."

"Oh he was, was he?" Tate reached for the handle on the door beside him and shook his head. "Well, let me go and wake Sleeping Beauty and see if he's in any condition to actually eat."

"Tate?" Cole said with a smile. "Don't be too hard on

him."

"Hard on him?" Tate asked, confused. *Why would I be hard on him?*

"Yeah. He's been beating himself up about all the time he's been spending on the case and was worried that you might be getting"—Cole looked slightly uncomfortable—"bored with him."

Tate's hand froze on the door handle as Cole's words sank in. "Bored with him?"

Cole shrugged. "I told him he was being stupid."

"Which I'm sure he loved hearing." Cole's chuckle told Tate he was right, but his words confirmed what Tate had been thinking about earlier today. He and Logan needed to sit down and talk this out, because clearly they were feeling the same but neither was wanting to bring it up. "Don't worry," Tate said. "I'm anything but bored with him. I miss him, that's all."

"That's what I told him, but you know Logan..."

He did, and Logan was always worried about that dreaded word *commitment*, and what it meant to the two of them. "We're fine, I promise. But I think it's time I had a little chat with my lawyer."

"I think so too. He did something wonderful today, and he should feel amazing. He made twenty-one families feel as though their lives mattered. That's pretty special."

Cole winked and raised his glass in salute. "He also made *us* very rich. See you Sunday."

Tate couldn't help but grin as the usually serious Cole waggled his eyebrows and then turned to walk back to the conference room. He was spot-on. What Logan had accomplished today put the man close to sainthood. Tate remembered when Logan had first heard about the case and told him his concerns on taking on the pharmaceutical industry. But when more and more people had come forward with loved ones who had passed due to a faulty drug, Logan had become determined. This became a personal crusade. And though it had taken a slight toll on the two of them, Tate had never been prouder of Logan than he was tonight.

He pushed open the door to the office, and as he walked inside he saw the lamp on Logan's desk switched on, but that was the only light in the room as he shut the door behind him. He glanced around the familiar space, scanning for the man he'd come in search for, and when he landed on the three-seater couch, a slow smile spread across his lips.

Logan was stretched out along the leather cushions with one arm bent back behind his head and the other resting on top of the purple tie he'd worn this morning. His jacket was hanging on the coat rack just inside the door, and his ankles were crossed so that his black Italian leather shoes were propped on the arm of his couch.

Tate's heart warmed at the sight as he quietly crossed the hardwood to look down at Logan, and when he got there, he took a second to really drink in the sight of him. Logan's glasses almost magnified the dark lashes that swept his cheekbones, and the day's dark stubble accentuated those smart-talking lips and chiseled jaw.

God, it wasn't that Tate ever forgot how attractive Logan was. But after years of living with the man, and seeing him on a daily basis, it was easy, Tate supposed, to get used to somebody. To become accustomed to their face.

He crouched until he was at eye level with the sleeping man, and then reached out and brushed a stray piece of hair from Logan's forehead. When Logan didn't stir, not even a little, Tate grinned and rose to place one hand on the arm of the couch where Logan's head was resting, and the other along the back of it. He then bent down to press a kiss to Logan's lips, and a low rumble came from him as he shifted on the couch, instinctively angling his body toward Tate. He slipped his tongue out to trace Logan's lower lip, and as the faint hint of scotch hit his taste buds, the arm that Logan had had bent up and behind his head came down and strong fingers were spearing into Tate's hair as Logan's eyes flashed open.

"'Bout time you got here," Logan whispered, his mouth curving into a sensual smile. "You just missed Mr. Bianchi."

Huh? Who was Mr. Bianchi? At the look of confusion on Tate's face, Logan chuckled. "I'll tell you about him when we go to dinner."

"Okay...but just for the record, I'm right on time," Tate said, and nipped Logan's lip before he raised his head. "*You* fell asleep."

"Hmm. I did, didn't I?"

Tate nodded and brought his hand down from the back of the couch to take Logan's chin between his thumb and forefinger. "You did. Congratulations on your win today, counselor. But I think we should postpone dinner tonight. You're exhausted. You've been working too hard, Mr. Mitchell."

Logan opened his mouth to protest, but Tate shook his head and placed a finger against his lips. "Just say, 'You're right, Tate.'"

Logan's eyes flared at the order, but Tate was sure to hold his stare, having learned early on in their relationship that the only way to handle Logan Mitchell was to give him as good as he dished out. Case in point...

"You're right, Tate," Logan said, and then, quick as a whip, he sat up and took hold of Tate's wrist, tugging him in close so Tate had to brace his palm against the back of the couch again. "Why don't you take me home and put me to bed instead?"

Tate brushed his mouth against Logan's and then straightened to his full height, holding his hand out. When Logan took it and stood, Tate said, "I'm pretty sure the only thing you're going to be doing when we get into bed is sleeping."

Logan frowned, and Tate trailed his fingers down his cheek and smiled. "I like how put out you seem by that notion. But really, let's just go home. You can get a good night's sleep, and tomorrow we'll go out to dinner and celebrate the right way."

"Are you sure you don't mind?" Logan asked, placing a palm on Tate's chest.

"I'm sure," Tate said. "Plus, it's been a while since I've spent an entire night with you. Call me selfish, but I want you functioning at full capacity when...you know."

The light that sparked Logan's eyes was full of devilry as he smoothed his palm down the front of Tate's t-shirt to the hem and asked, "When...*what*?"

Tate's focus shifted to the tip of Logan's tongue as it flirted with his top lip, and when Logan's fingers grazed against the bare skin of his abs, Tate took in a shaky breath before reaching down to halt Logan's hand. "When I finally have your full attention."

Logan leaned in so his cheek was resting against Tate's and whispered in his ear, "You have it now."

"Stop it." Tate chuckled and turned to look Logan in the eye. "There's a conference room full of clients three doors down from us, and you need a full night's sleep. So quit teasing me."

"But it's so much fun," Logan said. "And it's been so long since I had the time to follow through in a way we'll *both* remember."

It really had been, and Tate was enjoying this teasing side reemerging from Logan as the burden of the past months melted away, but...

"One more night won't kill you."

"It might."

Tate took Logan's hand in his and shook his head. "It won't. Now grab your things. The quicker you sleep tonight off, the quicker you can take me out to..."

"Spiaggia?" Logan suggested.

Oh, nice. He really is in a celebratory kind of mood. Tate and Logan had been talking about Spiaggia with Rachel the last time they'd been over at her and Cole's for dinner. The both of them had raved about a dessert there that was, according to them, to die for. "That Italian place?"

Logan stopped by the coat rack to put his jacket on, and then he picked up his briefcase and said, "Yes. That's the one."

"But that place is booked solid, from what Rachel said."

"It is, but Rachel has connections."

Of course she does, Tate thought. Rachel and her brother, Mason, knew all the ins and outs when it came to the foodie scene in Chicago, since their restaurant, Exquisite, was one of the top dining experiences about town.

"So how about it?" Logan asked, reaching for Tate's shirt and walking forward until he could kiss him lightly on the lips. When Logan pulled away, Tate made a grab for him, but Logan smirked. "Sorry, that's all you get for now. Don't want to be accused of *teasing* you."

Tate's eyes narrowed on Logan's sinfully handsome face. "You fucker."

Logan chuckled and opened the door, and as he walked out with Tate following behind, he called over his shoulder, "Not tonight I'm not."

Tate couldn't keep the ridiculous grin off his face at the smartass comment. It was so inherently Logan, and it wasn't until right then that he realized how starved he'd been for his company, and tomorrow night he was going to be sure to let him know.

Chapter Three

"TO ALL OF your hard work finally paying off," Tate said
as he turned to Logan and raised his wine glass.

The twinkling lights of the art deco chandeliers
reflected off the glass of Merlot the sommelier had just
poured for Logan, as he angled his head toward the man
seated beside him in one of the plush booths of Spiaggia.

Logan swirled the contents of his drink, letting the
aromas blend together as he took in the way the candlelight
from the table flickered over the bronze hue of Tate's skin.
"I'll drink to that," Logan said. "And to your patience
throughout the months of prep and these last crazy weeks
leading up to trial."

Tate inclined his head, their eyes never wavering
from each other, as they each took a sip of their wine. The
night sky had enveloped the Windy City around an hour
ago, and the large windows that flanked their side of the
restaurant showcased a breathtaking view of Lake Michigan.
Not that either of them seemed to care as they sat there
enjoying, for the first time in months, a night out with no
interruptions.

Tate placed his glass back on the table as Logan took

another sip, closed his eyes, and hummed, savoring the smooth flavor.

"I assume you approve?" Tate asked, his raspy chuckle drawing Logan's gaze.

As Logan lowered his glass, he allowed himself the pleasure of giving his date a thorough once-over. He had had to go to the office early that morning to get all the paperwork sent off for this case to finally be over, and the two of them had agreed to make the dinner reservation for tonight at eight. So, once Logan had gotten home and ready, he'd waited for Tate, who arrived a short time after.

His date for the evening had quickly showered and changed and then stepped out of their bedroom, and it had been all Logan could do not to tell him to turn the hell around and get back in there, because Tate looked...well, "fucking gorgeous" about summed it up.

With his curls brushing his forehead, ears, and collar of Tate's light blue dress shirt, Logan's fingers itched to spear through them and mess them all up as his eyes shifted to the sleeves Tate had casually rolled up his forearms. Around his neck, he wore a black tie with tiny white polka dots that was being kept in line by an elegant silver tie bar. But that wasn't what had Logan's mood going from the relaxed vibe he'd eased into at the thought of a night out to *not* so fucking relaxed. *Oh, no...* That had everything to do with the finely checkered charcoal and white vest and pants set that fit Tate's lean torso and long legs in ways that made

Logan's cock hard and his desire to peel him out of the outfit the only thing on his brain.

"I do approve," Logan said, finally answering Tate's question. "It's not too...sweet."

"No?"

"No. It has hints of a sweet sophistication but an underlying raw earthy quality." Logan winked. "It's got spice."

Tate laughed and raised his own wine back to his lips. He took another sip, and as he swallowed Logan followed the path the wine took down that strong throat. Then Tate placed his glass back on the table and picked up the menu. "You got all that from a sip of your wine? I'll never understand you people."

Logan reached for his own menu and flipped it open. "You *people*?"

The side of Tate's lips quirked, but he didn't take his eyes off the choices in front of him. "Yeah. You fancy wine-tasting people."

Logan scoffed. "You're a bar owner. You should *be* one of those people. It always astounds me that you're not."

"I mean, I like a glass of it," Tate said, and then looked at the bottle on the table. "Or a couple of glasses. But all the tastes and flavors... I'll leave that to your discerning palate."

"I do have very particular tastes."

Tate's eyes crinkled at the edges. "Are we still talking

about the wine?"

"Of course." Logan looked back to his menu before
he did something crazy like pull Tate across the table and—

"What are you thinking of having?"

You, was the first thing that popped into Logan's
head, but he shoved it aside, determined to have this night
the way it should be had. That meant dinner, conversation,
and then—

"Logan?"

Logan cleared his throat and studied the menu
before looking up at Tate, who was watching him with an
expression Logan figured matched his own. The heat and
desire swirling in Tate's eyes told him loud and clear that
there was no way the man currently focused on him was
bored or unhappy.

No siree. That look said something else entirely. Then
Tate leaned over and brushed his lips against Logan's,
and…yeah, okay, maybe they should've gotten the physical
part of the night out of the way first, because keeping his
hands to himself right then was one of the hardest things
Logan had ever done.

When Tate sat back and brought his menu up to read
through his choices once more, Logan tried to remember
how to breathe.

"So, what are you thinking?" Tate asked again.

"Give me a minute. I'm trying to remember *how* to
think."

Tate smirked, and Logan shifted in his seat.

"How about you sit back and let me order for you?" Tate said. "It's not like I don't know what you like. And tonight *is* supposed to be a celebration in your honor."

"Oh, I like the sound of that," Logan said, and shut his menu, curious to see if Tate would pick what he had decided on.

"I'm pretty sure I know what you like."

"Really?"

"Yep. I know you very well, Mr. Mitchell," Tate said, as Sergio, their waiter, stopped by their table with his hands clasped behind his back.

"All right, gentlemen. Have you made your choices?"

Tate nodded, turned toward the waiter, and pointed to the menu. "For an appetizer, can we please have the Polpo?"

Score one for Tate. The octopus with the sunchoke, blood orange, and jalapeño had been exactly what Logan had been looking at.

"Certainly, sir. And for your mains?"

Logan already knew that Tate would pick the—

"Gnocchi for me, thanks," he said.

"Ahh yes, with the black truffle and ricotta. That's one of my favorites," Sergio said, and then turned in Logan's direction. "And for you, sir?"

"I believe my fate lies in his hands tonight," Logan

said, aiming a smile up at Sergio. Yes, he'd let Tate direct this portion of the evening. But later...

"Oh, very well." Sergio looked back at Tate, who pointed to the menu and said, "He'll have the Bistecca alla Fiorentina. Cooked medium rare."

"That's a great choice. The porterhouse with the truffle hollandaise is one of our most popular items," Sergio said, taking the menus from Tate. "You picked well. I'll go and get your orders in and they should be out soon."

As their waiter left, Logan looked over to see Tate take a slow sip of his wine before placing it back down and asking, "Well, how'd I do?"

Logan scoffed. The smug fucker grinning at him knew damn well he'd just nailed it, and that confidence made Logan love Tate even more. Never had he expected when they'd first met that four years later Tate would be the one person who knew every single thing about him. Including, apparently, the exact meal he would pick for himself at an upscale Italian restaurant.

And what exactly did that mean? That he'd become too familiar? Too...predictable? A shiver raced up his spine at the thought. *God forbid.* "You were spot-on."

Tate lounged back in the booth and raised an arm to rest it along the seat, then he winked. "Told you I know you."

"That you did."

"Just like I know you're sitting there wondering what

it means that I *do* know you that well."

"No, I'm not."

"Yes, you are." Tate chuckled. "It just means that I pay attention. It *means*, Logan, that whenever I'm with you, I'm watching to see what you like and what you don't. And not just when it comes to eating."

Logan's mouth opened, and then he cleared his throat and said, "Is that right?"

"It is. But it's been a while since we've gone out to dinner, so I wanted to make sure I still had it."

Logan barely contained a groan as Tate's fingers flirted with the hair on the back of his neck. "Oh, you've still got it. Trust me."

Tate's eyes lowered to his mouth, and when he said, "Good," Logan had a feeling they had definitely moved on from discussing Tate's ability to pick out his meal.

* * *

TATE COULDN'T KEEP his damn hands to himself as he sat in the restaurant inches away from the one man who never failed to make his heart thump and his cock hard.

Logan looked unbelievably hot tonight. Not that that was anything new, but *damn*. No one wore a suit the way he did. He was in all black, from his leather shoes, to his pants, to the pressed dress shirt he'd left open two buttons down so that Tate kept catching a glimpse of his chest. And with his coal-colored hair styled as preferred—*neatly parted to the left*—Logan looked like a wicked, dark promise of sex and sin wrapped up in a polished shell. A shell that Tate knew firsthand housed a filthy side unlike that of anyone he'd ever met.

As Tate continued to run his fingers up and down the back of Logan's neck, Logan shut his eyes and arched back a fraction into his touch, and Tate said, "God, I've missed you."

Logan turned his head, and when he opened his eyes, Tate said, "We need to talk about this, work out our schedules. Because I'm sick and tired of only seeing you for a handful of minutes here and there each day."

"I know. I'm sorry. This case was—"

"Important," Tate said, and removed his fingers so he could reach for the hand Logan had resting on the table. "I'm not just talking about you. I'm as much to blame as you are for our ships-in-the-night routine."

Logan frowned. "No, you're not. Your hours never changed. Mine did."

"I know. But my hours are hardly conducive to a normal life."

"We both knew that when you bought the bar," Logan said. "That's why the loft is so handy. It allows us to meet up and stay in the same place the nights you work until closing."

That *had* been the arrangement, and it had worked

perfectly for the first three years. He could be on hand as much as was needed, and as a new owner, Tate had wanted to do everything in his power to make sure The Popped Cherry ran smooth and was a success.

But that want had been realized. During the week, the bar was a hot spot for the young and middle-aged business crowd, and on the weekends, it was packed to the walls with anyone and everyone. He couldn't have been prouder, and a lot of that success was due to Logan helping him in any way he was able to, and being one hundred percent supportive and understanding of the dream Tate had wanted to fulfill. Even when that had meant long nights and staying at the loft above the bar. But now it was time for them. Time to let their success enhance their lives, not hinder it.

Tate sat forward and looked at the man beside him. "I want to hire a manager for the bar."

Logan was about to respond, but before he could, Sergio appeared and placed their appetizer on the table between them. They each served themselves a plate, and then Logan said, "Isn't that what Amelia is? Did she do something wrong?"

Tate laughed as he put his napkin in his lap. "Like what?"

"I don't know. But why else would you fire her?" Logan picked up his fork and pointed it at him. "Did she hit on you?"

"No, she didn't hit on me."

"Hey, it's not that strange of a question."

Logan was joking, of course, and Tate rolled his eyes.

"She was the part-time manager, yes. But I'd been thinking about hiring on someone full time. I offered her the position but she's going back to school next semester and handed in her two weeks' notice instead."

"That bitch," Logan said with a smile as he put his fork down and brought his napkin to his mouth. "Didn't you tell her that education rots the brain?"

"Says the lawyer at the table."

"Hang on, let me get this straight. You want to hire a full-time manager so…?"

"So I can get into bed at a decent hour with you."

The expression that crossed Logan's features was a mix of surprise and pleasure. Tate could see that Logan was happy about what he'd just said, but was also unsure if it was what Tate really wanted. It was.

"Are you sure?" Logan asked as he picked his knife and fork back up.

"I am." When Logan took another bite of his food and glanced at him, Tate smiled. "Business is doing great. The staff are all reliable and well trained. It runs like a well-oiled machine, minus the fact I'll have to train a new person. But Logan, it's time."

Once Logan's plate was empty, he sat back and contemplated Tate with narrowed eyes. "And you're not just doing this because of what's been going on recently? Because that was a one-off—"

"Was it?" Tate asked, genuinely wanting to know if Logan's taste of the big cases, the glory, had made him want more of it.

"Yes, it was. I was just telling Cole how exhausted I am." Logan shook his head. "I sound like an old man."

"Thirty-seven is not old."

"Shit, don't remind me," Logan said, wincing. "But the truth is, this case sort of stumbled its way into my lap. It started with Renate and then snowballed."

"But now more people with similar cases will seek you out. Are you sure you don't want—"

"Tate?"

"Yes?"

"I'm sure. I don't want that. Yes, it was an incredible feeling sticking it to Berivax and Paul Bishop in his horrible tweed suit. Actually..." Logan leaned over and fingered the hem of his vest. "Is this tweed?"

"It is."

"Okay, I've changed my mind. Not all tweed is horrible, this is really..." Logan seemed sidetracked as he played with one of the four black buttons running down the center of Tate's body.

"Logan?"

"Oh, right." Logan sat back and removed his hand. "It was a once-in-a-lifetime case. One I don't wish to repeat anytime soon. But Cole and I need to talk about a few things regarding the business, and then we'll sit down with you and Rach. But trust me, I don't want that to become the regular."

"Are *you* sure?"

"Yes. You aren't the only one who missed this. Missed *us*."

"Glad to hear it," Tate said as their plates were cleared away, and Logan reached for the bottle of wine and refilled each of their glasses. "So, okay, if you're not going to be working any more crazy-big cases, I won't work past…eleven."

"Someone else will close for you?" Logan asked.

"Yes," Tate agreed. "And every other weekend off."

Logan's eyes widened. "Are you serious?"

"As a heart attack."

"So Monday through Friday you'll be home before midnight, and every other weekend off?"

"Yeah. That's the plan. Is that all right with you?"

Logan appeared completely gobsmacked, and when he finally recovered, he said, "In all the time we've been together, I've never had you on the weekends."

"Now that's not accurate. I'm pretty sure you've had me on every day of the week at some point."

Logan's lips curved. "True," he said, and then took Tate's hand. "You really mean it, though, don't you?"

"Yep. We'll be just like normal people." As soon as

the word *normal* left his tongue, Logan frowned and Tate
interlaced their fingers. "There's nothing wrong with being
normal, you know."

"I never said there was."

"You don't have to. It's written all over your face.
There are certain words that make your warning bells go
off." Tate laughed. "And that's one of them."

"You don't know what you're talking about," Logan
said, and freed his hand.

"Yes, I do. Remember, I *know* you."

"Oh yeah. Then what are the others?"

Tate was about to answer when Sergio arrived with
their main course, so he waited while their plates were
placed in front of them, and then he turned to Logan and
said in much the same manner one would check off a
checklist, "Settled. Domestic. And committed."

Logan held Tate's gaze for one, two, three seconds,
and then reached for his wine and swallowed it down. A
loud laugh leaving Tate. *Ahh, there's my little commitment-
phobe.*

"Eat your damn food, Tate."

That only made him laugh harder. Because while
those three words made Logan nearly hyperventilate, Tate
knew that Logan loved him more than anyone ever had or
would. He'd proven it time and time again in his actions,
even if the words still freaked the guy out.

But, for now, Tate would let him think on it and eat

his dinner, content in the knowledge that whether Logan wanted to admit it or not, he was extremely pleased with the new *normal* that was about to become their lives.

* * *

THE ENTIRE WAY through dinner, Logan could feel Tate's gaze on him. After their little discussion, he had decided it best to keep quiet for a while. He was caught somewhere between fucking ecstatic that he would finally be able to plan things to do with Tate on the weekends, and having an anxiety attack over the fact he liked the idea of the two of them finally settling down. *Jesus*, that even sounded weird in his head.

As he finished the final mouthful of his steak, Logan rubbed a hand over his stomach and sighed. "That was delicious."

Tate was still finishing off the last couple of bites of his gnocchi, but he nodded in agreement.

"I can't believe we've never been here before."

"I know," Tate said, tossing his napkin by his plate now that he was done. "The food was amazing."

"It sure was."

Just as they settled back against the cushioned booth, Sergio arrived at their table and looked at the empty plates. "I see you've both finished."

"Yes. Thank you," Logan said. "We were just saying

how delicious dinner was."

"That's what we like to hear," Sergio said as he stacked up the plates and then dug a small menu from the pocket of the long black apron he had wrapped around his waist. "Do you have room for dessert?"

"Oh God," Logan said, and looked over at Tate, who'd taken the menu.

"Yeah, let us take a look and see what you've got." Sergio smiled. "Take your time."

As he rushed off, Logan said, "You're ambitious."

Tate waggled his eyebrows as he scanned the menu and then turned it Logan's way, pointing. "That's what Cole and Rachel were talking about."

Logan read the description of the Torta Opera. An Italian-style opera torte with salted caramel gelato, namelaka, and gold leaf accents. *Yep, that sounds right up Cole's alley.*

"Share a piece?" Tate suggested.

"Sounds good to me," Logan said as Tate turned the menu back to himself, then, right before he closed it, he spotted something, opened his mouth, and then shut it again before looking over at Logan.

When Tate didn't say anything, Logan asked, "Something wrong?"

"No," Tate said, and shook his head. "I just saw bianchi on the menu and it reminded me of something you said last night. That I'd just missed a Mr. Bianchi when I got to your office."

"Oh," Logan said, remembering his own surprise from the brief meeting he'd had yesterday. How had he forgotten to tell Tate about that? "When I got back from court yesterday, Sherry said someone was waiting in my office for me, and you'll never guess who it was."

Tate frowned. "Who?"

"It was Robbie."

Logan could see the wheels turning, and then Tate said, "Sucks-like-a-Hoover Robbie?"

And Logan lost it, a booming laugh leaving him before he could stop it. "Yes," he said, trying to control his hilarity at Tate's blunt recollection of a certain barista. "That Robbie. Except he goes by Robert now."

"Robert," Tate said, still trying to put all the pieces together. "Robert Bianchi?"

"Yes, and he's..." Logan paused as he tried to think of how to say what he was thinking.

"He's *what*?" Tate asked before Logan could come up with anything, and the slight edge to Tate's voice made Logan laugh all over again.

Boy, does he have the wrong idea. If only he could stop laughing long enough to tell Tate so. Finally getting himself under control, Logan said, "He's changed a lot since we last saw him."

"Changed? How?"

Logan pictured the well-dressed man who'd been

waiting in his office and said, "He's...grown up, I guess."

"That's not very specific," Tate said. "And what is he doing looking you up?"

Logan scooted over on the seat until their thighs bumped, and then placed a hand on Tate's leg under the table. "I forgot how pissed off you used to get over Robbie. Hmm, maybe I'll keep talking about him."

"I thought his name was *Robert* now?"

"It is," Logan said, and placed a kiss to Tate's cheek. "You should see him. I almost want you to stop by in the morning so you can."

"Stop by? So, he's coming back? What does he want?"

"A lawyer," Logan said. "Well, *he* doesn't need a lawyer. His cousin does, and he said the first name he thought of was—"

"Yours," Tate said. "How nice."

Logan's lips twitched, and he couldn't stop himself from playing with Tate a little. "I thought so. It *was* nice to know I left such an impression on the young man." The frown on Tate's face morphed into a scowl, and Logan continued, "He's a lot more subdued now than he used to be, though. I didn't even recognize him until he turned around. The platinum hair's gone, and so is the eyeliner, and he was wearing the most outrageous shoes I've ever seen."

"Glad you took such a long look at him," Tate said.

Logan opened his mouth to inform Tate that he'd

only spent five minutes setting up a meeting for Friday and then sent Robbie on his way. But before he could, dessert arrived and they were thanking Sergio, who also placed the check on the corner of the table and told them there was absolutely no rush.

Logan bit back a grin at Tate's stiff shoulders but decided it was time to forget about everything other than why they were there. This discussion could wait until tomorrow. Tonight was about them reconnecting, and what better way to do that than— *Hmm…touching*, Logan thought, as he slipped his hand down the inside of Tate's thigh and watched him shift in his seat.

"Logan," Tate said, but Logan didn't care. He was on a mission now, and that mission involved getting his man home, naked, and under him.

"Yes, Tate?" He angled his entire body toward Tate's side so he could lean in and nuzzle his nose against his curls. He pressed a kiss to Tate's temple as he slipped his hand higher on his thigh and whispered, "I'm done with food for the night."

He heard a soft groan leave Tate, and when he turned his head to face him, Logan flattened his palm over the erection Tate was now sporting and licked his lips. "There's something else I want in my mouth instead."

With a nod, Tate reached beneath the table to still Logan's wandering hand. "Go and pay, then, so I can get myself under control enough to walk out of here."

Logan's entire body heated at the gruff order, but then he was sliding out of the booth with the check in hand. It was clear both he and Tate were of the same mindset. They didn't want to wait around for the time it took Sergio to come back to their table, and suddenly neither of them were interested in the exquisite dessert sitting untouched on their table.

"Don't make me wait," Logan said, as Tate stared up at him. "If you're not at the front door in five minutes, I'm coming back to drag you out."

Tate's eyes sparked at the words. "I'll be there in four."

And Logan left to pay the bill.

Chapter Four

TO SAY THE cab ride home was an exercise in restraint would be an understatement. As if the two of them had come to some kind of arrangement when they'd left Spiaggia, they each sat in the back of the cab in silence as it wove its way through the city toward home.

Tate was situated with his back half against the seat and half against the door, so he could keep an eye on Logan, who had one hand on his thigh drumming out an impatient rhythm, and the other oh so casually resting on the back of the seat. But there was nothing casual in the way Logan was watching him.

When they'd slid inside the vehicle around five minutes ago, Logan's eyes had invited him to come closer, but Tate had only just managed to get his body to cooperate so he could walk from point A to point B. There was no way he was going to let Logan get his hands on him again until he was somewhere he could do something about it. So for the moment, that meant he'd have to settle for the intense eye fuck Logan was subjecting him to. And hell if that wasn't just as dangerous to his peace of mind as Logan's hands, mouth, or words.

The lights from the city glittered and reflected off the

glasses that framed Logan's heavy-lidded eyes as he trailed them all over Tate. And when Logan caught the direction of his gaze, he scraped his teeth along that full lower lip, and it was all Tate could do not to dive across the back seat so he could lay Logan out flat on it.

The arrogant expression that crossed Logan's face did nothing to bank the fire he'd just lit, as the cab finally pulled to a stop at the front of their building and Tate realized he had to actually move. As a chuckle left Logan, he pushed open the passenger door and climbed out as Tate reached into his back pocket, pulled out his wallet, and paid the cab fare. Then he got out of the car and found Logan waiting for him.

With his jacket buttoned and his hands in his pants pockets, Tate knew right then that Logan was having just as much trouble keeping his hands to himself as he was. He tugged the hem of his vest into place, and when Logan caught his breath, Tate slipped his hands into his own pockets and strolled toward him. *Oh yeah, he's as on edge as I am.*

"Something wrong?" Tate asked, as he stopped opposite Logan just outside their lobby door.

Logan leaned in, careful not to touch him, and said in a ball-tingling voice, "Yes. We're still standing *outside.*"

Tate grinned as he stepped around Logan and opened the door for him. "That's not my fault. You're the one who lingered."

As Logan went to walk by him, he stopped, looked Tate dead in the eye, and said, "I wasn't lingering. I was making notes in my head."

Tate narrowed his eyes, but followed Logan over to the elevator, which, thankfully, opened immediately. They each got in, taking opposite sides, the silent agreement still in place. Then Tate pressed the button to their floor and said, "Notes?"

Logan nodded, his eyes once again dipping down to what Tate was wearing. "Yes," he said, shoving off the wall. "I was making notes on the best way to get you out of this sexy fucking outfit you're wearing tonight."

The modicum of self-control Tate had managed to keep throughout the cab ride vanished at Logan's words, and as he pushed off the wall to reach for him, Logan took two steps back.

"Oh no. Not yet," Logan said, his eyes darkening with all kinds of illicit intentions. "You put the no-touching rule into play."

"No, I didn't."

The elevator dinged as it hit the floor, and Logan winked. "Yes, you did. Now you get to *wait* for it."

As Logan left the elevator, Tate palmed the erection Logan had teased to attention by merely being in his breathing space. Then he stepped out into the hall and went in search of the man who was without a doubt going to make this night one he wouldn't soon forget.

* * *

LOGAN HAD JUST placed his glasses on the table by his side of the bed when he heard the front door shut. He smiled at the loud slam, knowing that Tate was on a mission and didn't care about anything other than getting in the same vicinity as Logan. And he was right, because only seconds later, Tate strode through their bedroom door and scanned the space until he spotted Logan.

Logan had tossed his jacket over the arm of the couch when he'd gotten inside, and as he held Tate's stare, he unbuttoned his cuffs and tugged his shirt out of his pants. Tate walked farther into their room, and when he stopped at the foot of their bed and reached for the buttons of his vest, Logan said, "No. Don't do that."

Tate's fingers stilled. "No?"

"No," Logan said, as he removed his wallet and tossed it on the table. "I told you, I made notes."

"Can I at least take my shoes off?"

"If you make it quick."

Logan did the same, and then he walked barefoot around to the end of the bed, where Tate was waiting for him. "It's been a long time since we got into bed at the same time. Even longer since we spent the night tearing up *these* particular sheets."

"It has been."

Logan touched a finger to the top button of Tate's vest. "Let's make sure that never happens again."

"Deal," Tate said, his voice a raspy promise.

"Good. Now that that's decided, how about you turn around and remind yourself what our bed looks like? Because you're about to become intimately reacquainted with it when I fuck you in it all night."

Tate's jaw bunched, and Logan knew he was biting back either a curse or a groan. *Hell, probably both.* He knew he was. "Turn around, Tate."

Tate did as he was instructed and pivoted so he was facing the bed with his legs slightly spread, and Logan moved so he was standing directly behind him.

Tate's broad shoulders and trim waist were framed beautifully by the snug vest, and thanks to the cut of it, the hem rested right at his lower back, showcasing the matching pants, which hugged the curve of his ass in a breathtakingly intimate way.

Logan took a step closer and placed his hands on Tate's shoulders before nuzzling his nose into the thick curls sweeping the collar of the shirt.

"God," Logan said. "I've missed being with you like this." Tate shuddered, and Logan raised his head as he smoothed his hands down Tate's back. "Missed talking with you. Laughing with you," he said as he took hold of Tate's waist and pulled him back against himself. "Just *being* with you."

Tate relaxed against him, letting his head fall to the side, and the second Logan's mouth connected with the warm skin of his neck, a groan rumbled out of Tate's throat.

"Mhmm, you've missed it too. Haven't you?" Logan said, and trailed his fingers along Tate's black leather belt until they reached the square metallic clasp.

"Hell yes," Tate said, as Logan freed the buckle and unbuttoned the top button of Tate's pants. "Missed you so goddamn much."

Logan nipped at Tate's lobe and then whispered in his ear, "Never. Again," before he pulled one end of the belt and slid it free. It dropped to the hardwood floor with a *clunk,* and then he was unzipping Tate's pants and tugging his shirt from its restrictions.

"Never," Tate agreed, and then his breath caught as Logan reached inside his pants and boxers to wrap his fingers around Tate's erection. "Jesus...*fuck.*"

Logan hummed from the sublime pleasure he got from finally having his hands back on Tate. "I'm going to put my lips on every inch of you tonight. Then I'm going to sink my cock back inside you where it's dying to be."

Tate's hips punched forward, his agreement loud and clear, but Logan wanted the words. Wanted to *hear* what Tate wanted. "Is that okay with—"

"Yeah. But..." Tate's words faded as he grabbed the arm Logan had wrapped around him. Logan stilled his fist as Tate's fingers dug into his forearm, and the sound of

Tate's heavy breathing was the only noise now in the bedroom.

"But?" Logan asked.

Tate turned his head, his lust-laden eyes finding Logan's, as he took in a shaky breath and said, "If you don't stop that, I'm gonna come before you get my fucking clothes off."

Logan licked his bottom lip and slowly released his hold. "Well, we wouldn't want that now, would we?"

Tate's eyes flicked to Logan's mouth. "No. I'd much rather come somewhere else."

Fucking hell, there was no way Logan was going to last if Tate kept talking like that. So he stepped around in front of Tate, took hold of either side of his face, and crushed their mouths together.

Tate opened to him immediately, and Logan sank his fingers into Tate's hair, twisting them around the silky texture. The hand Tate had on his arm came up to rest on Logan's chest, and when his fingers curled around the material of his shirt, Tate tugged him in as close as they could get with their clothes on. Logan growled as he gave his tongue to Tate, who sucked on it, and then Logan slid his hand down to the back of Tate's neck to hold him in place so he could get a more thorough taste of him.

"Logan..." Tate panted when he tore his mouth free. His lips were swollen and wet, and when he slicked his tongue along them, Logan reached for the buttons of Tate's vest, understanding exactly what he wanted. Tate went to undo Logan's shirt then, but he was quick to put a stop to it.

"Uh uh. I'll take care of that," Logan said, just as the vest parted and he ran his fingers down the length of Tate's tie, removing the silver tie bar. "Let's work on getting you naked first."

Tate's mouth curved as he lowered his arms to his sides. "Don't let me stop you."

"Not a chance in hell of that happening," Logan said, and made quick work of the tie, tossing it to the floor.

The buttons of Tate's shirt were next, until it and the vest hung open, exposing a wide strip of mouthwatering skin. Logan placed his palms on Tate's chest and slowly slid them up to his shoulders, moving in to scrape his teeth along Tate's jaw as he pushed the material down his arms and then finally to the floor.

His fingers went to Tate's pants then, and Logan flirted with the edge of the material before his wandering hands went to either side of Tate's hips. He sucked on Tate's earlobe, and when a muttered curse left him, Logan raised his head, smiled, and then gripped either side of his pants as he lowered down in front of him, removing the remainder of Tate's clothes.

* * *

NOW NAKED, TATE waited with his hands fisted by his

sides and a raging hard-on courtesy of the fully clothed man getting back to his feet. When Logan was finally standing opposite him again, he said, "Get on the bed, Tate."

Tate's eyes shifted over Logan's shoulder to their wide king-sized with the stark white sheets, navy-blue pillows, and white duvet. Then he looked back to Logan and asked, "Back or stomach?"

"Oh, you're going to end up on both. But for now, let's start with your back."

Tate couldn't stop himself from stealing a kiss before he walked around Logan and said over his shoulder, "Bring it on."

As he moved to his side of the bed and pulled the covers down, Tate heard Logan unbuckle his belt, and by the time he'd climbed to the center of the mattress and was reclining to his back, he saw Logan over on his side with his shirt unbuttoned and a bottle of lube in his hand.

Logan tossed it on the mattress, and when he placed his knee on the bed, the tails of his shirt shifted and Tate's eyes trailed down to where Logan had unsnapped and unzipped those black pants he still wore. *And fuck if that isn't the hottest invitation to sin ever. God.*

Tate reached down to wrap a fist around the root of his cock, needing some kind of pressure there or he was going to lose it before the real stuff even began. But it had been so long, and even *longer* since he'd really had the time to enjoy this side of Logan, that having all of that potent energy directed at him was like a lit match being tossed on a barrel of gasoline.

A couple of seconds later, Logan was across the bed and stretching out along the top of him. Tate took hold of Logan's waist as he pushed one of his legs between Tate's naked ones, and then rested his forearms by either side of his head.

"Not going to take these off?" Tate asked, as he moved his hands to the material still covering Logan's ass.

"I will. But right now, they're the only thing stopping me from already being inside you. And I told you, I'm going to make you wait."

Logan ground his hips down, and when his covered erection grazed the top of his naked one, Tate groaned.

"See…doesn't that feel good?" Logan asked, a smirk crossing his devious lips.

Fuck yes it feels good, Tate thought. So damn good that he grabbed Logan's ass and used him as an anchor, as he thrust his hips up and rubbed all of his naked skin against Logan's hard body.

"*Fuck*, Tate," Logan said on a ragged breath.

"You asked," Tate teased. "I was just answering."

Logan lowered until his entire body was resting on top of Tate, and then his eyes lit with challenge. "I'll have to remember that for next time."

Tate rocked against the heavy weight of Logan's frame and ran his hands up under his shirt. "You do that—

*Damn...*that feels..." Tate's train of thought vanished as Logan began to bite along his jaw, and the material of his pants abraded his inner thighs and—*fuck yes*—his balls.

"Yes, Tate?" Logan asked.

Tate squeezed his eyes shut, trying to get his lust in check. But the chuckle that left Logan told him he wasn't going to have a hope in hell at controlling anyfuckingthing. Least of all the man who was now kissing his way down his body.

* * *

LOGAN LICKED AND sucked his way down Tate's chest, ribs, and muscled abs, and when he was finally situated between his spread thighs, he raised his head to look up at the man staring down at him.

Tate had clamped a tight fist around the base of his cock, and when Logan licked his lips, Tate stroked his hand up the length of his engorged shaft and swiped his thumb across the broad head of it. Then, with his scorching eyes trained on Logan's, Tate extended his arm, and Logan was right there taking hold of his wrist and sucking his thumb between his lips.

Gorgeous fucker knows exactly how to make me lose my mind, Logan thought, and when Tate removed his hand and placed it behind his pillow, plumping it up so he could see better, Logan had to take a moment.

He shut his eyes and counted back from ten, and once the desire to *attack* was somewhat banked, Logan reopened them to look at everything that was only inches from his face.

Tate's muscled thighs were splayed wide, his cock was being leisurely worked by its owner, and his heavy balls were pulled up nice and tight, close to his body. Logan turned his head and placed a kiss on Tate's inner thigh, and then trailed his tongue up to the crease of his leg. Tate shoved his hips up, trying to get closer to his mouth, but he wasn't about to be rushed. He slipped his hands under Tate's ass and held him in place as he repeated the same move on his other leg, and then he licked across one of Tate's balls, making him curse.

Logan raised his head to see Tate's fingers flexed around his dick and his other hand down by his side curled around the sheet, and the sight he made was a fucking glorious one. He looked like a man who knew he needed to hold on to something, because what was about to happen next was going to drive him crazy. *And he isn't fucking wrong.*

Lowering his head again, Logan nuzzled into Tate's groin and pulled him a little way down the bed so he could drag his tongue up the length of his erection. Tate moaned and let go of himself to reach for Logan's hair, and when his fingers found purchase, he took hold and directed his mouth exactly where he wanted it.

Logan swallowed Tate between his lips and reveled

in the way he thrust in and out, over and over, and when Tate placed a foot on the bed and really started to fuck the mouth surrounding him, Logan shut his eyes and let him have whatever it was he wanted.

"Logan…if you don't… Fuck. *Fuck*," Tate said, his fingers fisting Logan's hair as his bent leg slid back down to the mattress and he brought his other one up and over Logan's shoulder so he could shove deeper into his mouth.

Logan growled at the viselike way Tate had wound himself around him, keeping him exactly where he wanted him with his strong leg, as guttural sounds ripped out of him. Then, as Tate's hips began to move at a rapid pace, Logan slipped a long digit between his ass cheeks and pressed against the tight hole he couldn't wait to get back inside of.

Tate's fingers clenched, and his cock shoved to the back of Logan's throat, and then he was coming as he shouted out Logan's name.

* * *

FUCK YES, WAS all Tate could think. *I sure as hell have been missing* this. But before he even had a chance to bask in his orgasm, Logan raised his head, licked his well-fucked lips, and flipped Tate over.

Everything moved at warp speed then because, before his body could even begin to recover from the first rush, Logan was right there revving it up for round two.

Now flat on his stomach, Tate grunted as Logan came back down over him. But this time around, the shirt and pants were removed, and finally, Logan's erection was leaving a sticky trail along his backside. With his hands planted by Tate's head, Logan's hot breath over his ear was a seductive caress, his thick cock an erotic promise of what was about to happen next.

"I don't know about you, Tate. But I'm not feeling very *settled* right now…are you?"

Settled? Fuck no, he didn't feel settled. And as his words from dinner came flooding back, Logan burrowed his nose under the hair at the nape of Tate's neck and scraped his teeth along his shoulder, making Tate shudder.

Tate saw Logan reach for the bottle of lube and bucked back into the wall of hard muscle he could feel pressing him down into the mattress. The friction of the sheet against him felt out of this world as he unbelievably began to stiffen again.

"That's it…I know you've got another round in you. Don't you?" Logan said, right before a slippery finger flirted down the crack of his ass.

Tate bit the pillow under him as Logan probed for entry, and when he found it and his finger pushed inside, Tate couldn't keep his hips still. He jacked them back, and when Logan's teeth sank into his shoulder, he cursed, and Logan did it again.

Tate drew one of his legs up on the mattress, spreading himself wider for the man on top of him, and when Logan finally slipped *two* fingers into him, Tate squeezed his eyes shut and reached under himself to stroke his cock.

"Hmm," Logan said as he licked the teeth marks Tate knew he'd left on his shoulder, and the slow, methodical way Logan continued to stretch him, getting him ready, had him hard all over again.

"God, Logan... I *need*—" Tate's words morphed into a curse when Logan's fingers found and massaged that bundle of nerves that never failed to make his toes curl, and then Logan was pulling them free and hauling Tate up to his hands and knees.

Tate felt one of Logan's hands on his shoulder holding him in place as the head of his erection knocked against his hole. Then Logan stilled where he was before he slowly began to ease inside of him.

That was when Tate heard him say, "Does this feel *domestic* to you?" Then Logan gripped his shoulder and jammed his hips forward until his cock was lodged balls deep inside.

* * *

THERE REALLY WASN'T anything that felt better than the way Tate's ass squeezed Logan's cock when he tunneled it inside. Of *that* Logan was positive. Well, unless he counted the way it clung to him on the withdrawal.

But as Logan kneeled behind Tate enjoying the heat of his body and the exquisite way it surrounded his shaft, he concentrated on not exploding before he even dared to move. He flexed his fingers into Tate's hip as he looked at the smooth expanse of his back, and then Logan repositioned his hand to cup the back of his neck.

Logan licked his lips as Tate groaned and let his head fall forward. Then, as Tate rocked back, trying to get him to move, his curls tickled the back of Logan's hand and he finally gave Tate what his body was begging for.

Logan muscled him down so Tate's torso was angled in a way that his cheek was against the pillow and his ass was hip height. Like this, Tate was most certainly in a submissive position. But when Logan pulled out and then propelled his hips forward, there was nothing subservient about the forceful way Tate shoved back to take him inside. And fuck, there was no way Logan wasn't about to take him up on the invitation he was issuing.

With a rough shove, Logan followed Tate down onto the bedding, jamming his hips against the delicious ass that was more than happy to be on the receiving end tonight.

Tate cursed and Logan growled, as he delivered hard, quick thrusts into Tate's leanly toned body, and Tate was right there with him, one hand gripping the pillow under his head and the other snaking down to get himself off. Logan reached up and took hold of the pillow also, and he put his other hand on Tate's hip, holding him in place.

This was what they'd both needed. What they'd both craved. And the furious way they moved atop their bed was a testament to the fact that while they may have both been busy these past few months, weeks, and days, never had their attraction subsided. Never had their love.

There was nothing settled or domesticated about them or this reunion, and as Tate shouted out Logan's name for a second time that night, Logan felt his own orgasm coil and then explode in a rush as he came deep inside the man whose body he was certain had been made to be a part of his.

Chapter Five

"WHAT? NO GREETING at the door today, Sherry? Well, that didn't last long," Logan said the following morning as he came to a stop by his PA's desk. She looked up from what she'd been working on and peered at him over the edge of her glasses.

"No greeting, period," she said. "You're late."

Logan's mouth opened, but before he refuted her claim, he looked at his watch. *Shit.* "It's Tate's fault."

"I'm sure it is," she said as she got to her feet and came around her desk to take his briefcase. Logan handed it over and took the manila folder she held.

"What? You don't believe me?" he asked.

"If the choice is between something being your fault or Tate's…then my money is going on it being *your* fault. Tate is such a lovely young man."

"That's not very nice."

"Mhmm," she said, even as her lips curved. "Cole is waiting for you. And remember, you have a meeting scheduled for—"

"Nine. I know. If the staff meeting runs over, come get me, would you?"

"Of course," she said, and reached down to pick up the coffee cup on her desk. After she handed it to him, Logan took a sip and sighed. *Ahh, perfection.* Sherry had gotten into the habit, from early in their relationship, of having a steaming cup of French press waiting for him on arrival. He'd often told her that if he wasn't so taken with Tate, he just might be tempted to steal her from her husband. "You better get going before Cole comes looking for you."

"Right," Logan said, and when he lowered his mug, he grinned and turned it around so the words faced her. "How is it that you think a man who gave me *this* particular mug is lovely?"

Sherry read the words: **Blow me. I'm *hot*.** scrawled in white across the black ceramic mug, and then raised her eyes back to his. "You have a meeting. Shoo."

"That's not an answer."

"I have work to do," she said with a waggle of her fingers, and Logan narrowed his eyes on her.

"Fine, but we're not done here."

"I'd be disappointed if we were," she said, and then walked into his office with his briefcase and the mail from yesterday.

With a smile on his face, he headed down the hall to find Cole, and when he got to the shut door of his office, Logan knocked twice and stuck his head inside. "Ready, slacker?"

Cole glanced up from his computer, and when he spotted him, he nodded. "Good morning to you, too."

"What? No comment about my being late? Damn, I need to take advantage of this."

As Cole got to his feet, he buttoned his suit jacket. "I figure you deserve a week's reprieve for good behavior."

"Ahh, I see. In other words, your hot wife can't keep her hands off you since you told her about the fantastic settlement I reached for the firm, and you *not* giving me hell is your way of saying thank you."

Cole picked up his binder and walked across the office to him. "I assure you, I do not need your help getting laid."

"Yes, but telling her the firm won seven mil didn't hurt, right?" Cole shoved him in the arm as they both stepped out into the hallway. "At least tell me you used protection. Two rugrats under five is enough already, don't you think?"

"What I think," Cole said, "is that you're ridiculous."

As they reached the door to the conference room, Logan put his palm on the handle and stopped. "I'm right, though, aren't I? The seven million didn't hurt."

Cole chuckled. "No. It certainly didn't hurt. What about you?"

Logan pushed down on the handle. "Oh, don't worry, Tate can't get pregnant. We don't need to use protection."

He laughed as Cole rolled his eyes, and then the two of them stepped into the full conference room.

Over the last three years Logan and Cole had hired on a couple of new attorneys, and under Cole's careful guidance, their family law team was one of the most sought after in the city, and with Logan winning this pharmaceutical case and focusing on the corporate and commercial side of things, they both knew the firm was set to explode with new business, which meant it was time to do some major hiring.

It was also time to talk to Tate and Rachel about an idea they'd been sitting on for the last few months, something they'd both agreed they would bring up at their family dinner this Sunday now that the Berivax case was over. For now, though, it was time to go over where they were this month.

"Good morning, everyone," Logan said as he walked to the front of the room and tossed the manila folder on the table.

Everyone in attendance gave him a round of applause before Cole laughed and raised a hand. "Okay, okay. That's enough. Let's not give him another reason to think he's better than the rest of us."

A chorus of laughs rang out as Logan took a sip of his coffee then placed his mug on the table and rubbed his hands together. "As you already know, Mitchell & Madison had an extremely good day on Wednesday, which means things are likely to get a little crazy around here. We expect business will pick up tenfold when word spreads. That means there are going to be some changes happening in the next few days, weeks, and months."

As excited chatter started up around the room, Logan slipped his hands into his pants pockets and looked to Cole to continue speaking.

"First off," Cole said, "we expect all hands to be on deck. We want to keep our clients happy so if, and when, new potential clients ask around about us, they hear nothing but glowing reports. That means if your client calls, big *or* small, you answer your phone. If they want to know where you're at with their case, you give them a detailed breakdown. And if they merely call to ask what they should eat for dinner that night, you give them at least three choices. Got it?"

As everyone nodded, Logan flipped open the folder he had on the table and looked at the packets Sherry had printed out for him. They were the résumés of several first-year associates that he and Cole had decided it was time they took a look at. This way they could groom them over the next few years and end up with some really fantastic lawyers in the company.

They'd narrowed the pool down to four, and it was time to get them in for an interview to see if any were what they were looking for in person.

"Angela," Logan said, addressing the brunette two

seats up from where he was standing. She was one of the family law attorneys who'd been with them for two years now. "We'd like you to give these four a call and set up interviews with them. Cole and I picked who we like on paper, and now we want you to tell us who we should see in person."

"No problem." She took the folder from him and placed it in her leather binder.

"Good," Cole said. "Okay, so, those of you who need to be elsewhere, you're free to go right now. But as for the rest of you, let's go over current cases that are open, this month's billable hours, and the end-of-year functions taking place that you are *strongly* urged to attend."

As a chorus of groans filled the air, those who needed to get to court or on the phone exited the conference room, and as others took their seats and flipped open their notepads and laptops, there was a knock on the door, and Logan looked over to see Sherry.

"Your nine o'clock is here."

Logan's eyes moved to the clock on the wall, and he grabbed his mug and said to Cole, "You got this? I've got a meeting."

Cole nodded. "I think we'll manage. We still on for Sunday?"

"Of course. We're bringing the meat."

Cole looked unsure as to whether he was serious or not, and then Logan clapped him on the back and said,

"Your wife told us to bring steaks for grilling."

"Ahh. Gotcha. Go on then, get out of here. I've got this. But I'll be leaving at two. Lila's got a doctor's appointment."

"Give those two gorgeous girls of yours a kiss for me. And tell Thomas I want my Hot Wheels back this weekend."

"Good luck with that. He takes those things everywhere."

Logan chuckled, thinking of his nephew's face last Sunday when he'd brought his vintage collection of cars over to Cole and Rachel's. "Then maybe he'll let me play with them."

"Maybe. If you're nice."

"We'll be there around one," Logan said, and with a final wave, he was out the door and heading down the hallway to his office.

Sherry was back behind her desk at work, and as he walked past her, he said, "Can you hold my calls until I'm finished in here?"

"Of course."

"Except for—"

"I know," Sherry said with a soft smile as she went back to typing.

It was a given that if Tate called he was to be put through immediately. But Logan always made sure to clarify, especially after Tate's accident when they'd first started dating. He always made sure to be near a phone, and was always mindful of having his cell charged. There was no way he'd *ever* miss an important call again.

And speaking of things from years ago... Logan opened his office door, and when his nine o'clock appointment turned in the seat, Logan still couldn't believe the man staring back at him was Robbie.

With the platinum gone, Robbie's hair was now a chestnut color with caramel highlights threaded through the long strands, and the short cut to the sides enhanced a face Logan remembered, but was shocked to find had matured over the years. Robbie was an attractive guy, and this new look he was sporting suited his twenty—*shit, how old is he now? Twenty-nine? Yes*—twenty-nine-year-old self.

The eyes focused on Logan narrowed, and when Robbie stood as though he wasn't sure he was allowed to be there, Logan shut the door.

"Mr. Bianchi. So nice to see you again." Logan crossed his office floor, and when he stopped opposite Robbie, he lowered his eyes and fidgeted with his hands.

"Thank you for seeing me."

The almost shy response was so unlike the man Logan remembered that he couldn't help but poke a little. He held his hand out, and when Robbie's head snapped up and he blinked several times, Logan felt a sliver of unease race up his spine.

Something was off there. Just as it had been the other

day when they'd scheduled the meeting. This wasn't the outgoing Robbie he remembered. Instead, he appeared timid and skittish. Scared of Logan, and his own shadow.

When Robbie seemed to realize that Logan posed no threat, he reached out and shook his hand, and, trying to ease the tension in the room, Logan threw a joke out there.

"I promise I don't bite," Logan said, but then he remembered Tate's shoulder from last night and added, "strangers."

Robbie didn't so much as smile as he withdrew his hand and once again looked away.

What in the world is going on with him? Logan thought, as he slipped his hand into his pocket and really checked out Robbie.

In his black pants and polo shirt, the only thing that hinted of the loud personality Robbie once had were the red polka dots splattered all over the polo. It was almost unbelievable that the withdrawn stranger standing in front of Logan was the same guy who'd once come home with him and—

"I'm sorry if this is inappropriate. Me, coming here to your office."

Robbie spoke softly, but it had Logan snapping out of his walk down memory lane long enough to say, "No, it's fine. You just look..." As Logan searched for the right word, Robbie stared back at him with wide eyes, as though he had no clue he appeared so completely...*changed.* "Different. You look different."

Robbie chewed on the corner of his lip and again lowered his eyes, and Logan suddenly found that he hated that. He hated that Robbie appeared *intimidated* by him. But what could he do? It wasn't like he knew Robbie well. Hell, he hadn't seen him in years. So, it was probably just best he stuck to what he *did* know—his job. After all, that was what he was there for.

"Okay then, Robbie. How about you take a seat here," Logan said, gesturing to the chair Robbie had been occupying. "And we can talk a little bit about your cousin."

"Robert," Robbie corrected, and then took a seat as Logan headed around his desk and sat in his leather chair. "I go by Robert now, and yeah…uhh, okay. Vanessa. She's in trouble. A lot of it. And I'm not sure we can even afford—"

"Robbie—sorry, Robert," Logan said, his eyes trained on the man who was twisting one of his hands around his other one. "Don't worry about money right now. Just tell me what's going on and I'll tell you my thoughts."

Robbie grimaced but nodded. "Okay. She was arrested Wednesday night, around an hour before I showed up here. The police had a search warrant for my nonna's house because of Vanessa's brother, Jared. They'd been trailing him for months."

"Why?"

Robbie rubbed his hands over his face as though he were tired, and then aimed his eyes straight at Logan.

"Drugs. Cocaine."

Logan winced. "Using or selling?"

"Both. They were after Jared, but he disappeared. Vanessa knew about his drugs in the house—she'd told him over and over to clean his act up and get that shit out of there, but he wouldn't listen, and when the police showed up, she didn't want Nonna to get in trouble, so she went to Jared's room and was trying to hide them."

Shit, that wouldn't look good to the police. And Logan had a feeling what was coming next.

"When the police got to her, she was holding the drugs and looking guilty as hell. They arrested her immediately and charged *her* for possession with intent to distribute."

Yeah... This wasn't good at all. But depending on her age, maybe... "How old is Vanessa?"

"Seventeen."

"Damn it," Logan said, and Robbie flinched.

"It's not good, is it?"

"No. It's not." Logan picked up his pen, scrawled the facts down on his notepad, and then let out a breath. He wasn't about to sugarcoat shit, even with Robbie acting the way he was. His cousin was in a whole lot of trouble, but until Logan spoke to her and listened to her side of things, there was no way he could ascertain whether they had a fighting chance.

On paper it looked bad, really fucking bad, but if she

really was innocent, then maybe he could get the prosecutor down to a lighter sentence. At least he hoped so, because the alternative if this went to trial and she was found guilty was years—and a lot of them. "I assume bail was posted and paid for?"

Robbie nodded.

"Okay, so she's at home right now?"

"Yes. The judge set the hearing for Thursday morning. But the lawyer they appointed was..." Logan waited in the silence of the office as Robbie tried to find his words, and then he shrugged and said, "He wasn't you."

Robbie continued, "You always said you were the best. I thought if anyone could help her, it would be you. But..." Robbie looked around the elegant office. The wide wall of floor-to-ceiling windows behind Logan, the bookcases with law books lining one side of his office, and the leather couch on the other, and then his eyes came back to Logan's. "I'm not sure we can afford you."

Logan tossed his pen on the notepad and got to his feet. As he walked around his desk and came to a stop in front of it, he leaned his ass back against the wood and looked down at Robbie. "Don't worry about the money. I want to meet with her. Can you get her down here at the same time on Monday morning?"

Robbie nodded. "Yes. I can do that."

"Okay. Let's start there." Logan crossed his arms as he continued to study Robbie, and noticed the dark lines under his eyes. "Are you...okay?"

Robbie let out a breath and stood, and once again Logan found himself baffled by the man in front of him.

"I will be, now that I know you're going to help."

"I'm going to listen," Logan corrected. "And then we'll see."

"Vanessa's a good girl. She doesn't deserve this. Any of it."

"Then it's good she's got you looking out for her, isn't it?"

"I guess."

Logan pushed off the desk and put his hand out for Robbie to shake once more, and this time when he took it, Logan tightened his fingers. When Robbie looked at him with a question in his eye, Logan asked again, "Are you sure you're okay?"

"Yeah, I'm just a bit stressed. That's all."

Logan didn't believe for a second that that was all that was going on. But if Robbie didn't want to talk, who was he to force him? Then he had an idea, and before he knew he was going to, Logan said, "Ever heard of The Popped Cherry?"

"I have. Been in there a couple of times."

Obviously when Tate and I haven't been there, Logan thought. "Why don't you stop by tonight?" When Robbie frowned, Logan said, "Tate owns the place. Well, technically we both do, but he runs it."

"Tate? That guy with the curly hair?"

Logan chuckled. "Yes. One and the same."

Robbie looked like he wanted to say more. But then he shook his head. "I don't know..."

"Really, you should stop by. We'll both be down there. I think Tate would get a kick out of seeing the, ahh, new, well, you."

Robbie appeared to think it over some more, and again Logan got the feeling something else *other* than his cousin was bothering him. There was a time when Robbie would've jumped at the chance to hang out with the two of them. In fact, he'd begged them both on several occasions.

"I'll see," Robbie said.

"Okay... If you decide to come, you know where we'll be." When Robbie merely nodded, Logan decided it was time to move on. "Sherry will call you later today to confirm the Monday meeting. So give her your cousin's details and we'll get right on this and see where we can go from here."

"Thanks again, Logan."

"Don't thank me yet. I'm not sure there's much I can do."

"It's the thought that counts."

"Then come see us tonight and you can buy me a drink."

"Yeah, uhh, maybe." The noncommittal smile Robbie gave told Logan he wouldn't be seeing him later that night, and while that would've once pleased him, it now...troubled him.

"Fair enough," Logan said, knowing it wasn't his place to push for anything more. "I'll see you later then, *Robert.*"

Robbie's cheeks flushed at his full name being said, and as Mr. Bianchi left the office, Logan could almost picture the infatuated barista he'd once known and realized he kind of missed him.

Chapter Six

"WHAT CAN I get you tonight?" Tate asked, stepping up to the counter, where a blond man in a business suit was standing with his back to him, facing the Friday night crowd. It was nearing the end of happy hour at The Popped Cherry, and the place was wall to wall busy with the steady stream of customers that the beginning of the weekend always commanded.

The man turned at the sound of Tate's voice, and when his face came into view, so did a wide, friendly smile.

"Morrison? Tate Morrison?"

Tate catalogued the brown eyes, the crooked broken nose, and the wide shoulders of the ex-quarterback and realized he was staring at his sister's high school sweetheart.

"Scott Thompson. Well, this is a surprise. How you doing, man?" Tate said as he placed a black napkin with the bar's red and white insignia of two cherries and the name on the counter.

"Good. Good. Shit, man, how long's it been since I've seen you?"

Tate braced his hands on the counter and grinned, thinking back. "Hmm. At least ten…eleven years, right?"

Scott ran a hand through his hair and nodded. "Yeah, at least. I was still dating your sister, and you were with Diana. Man." Scott laughed. "That girl was all about you when we were in school. Constantly mooning over Jill's older brother. Then I heard she up and married you."

Oh hell, Tate thought, as the image of his ex-wife popped into his head. And while he and Diana had settled their divorce on amicable terms years ago, it still made him uncomfortable to think about. All of that anger and all of the hurt that had come from that time in their lives had reached an explosive end when they'd gotten one helluva wake-up call in the form of him lying in a coma in the hospital.

God, the memory of that still gave him chills. But it wasn't the memory of Diana and her concern that caused his palms to sweat and his pulse to trip—it was the reminder of the agony Logan had to endure during that time.

"That was a long time ago," Tate said, and tried for a smile. "We aren't together anymore."

"No shit?" Scott said, and then took a seat. "Sorry to hear that, man."

"Hey, things happen. We grew apart, that's all," Tate said. "So, can I get you something?"

"Oh yeah. Umm, a Sidecar and a frozen margarita, thanks."

"You got it," Tate said as he placed a tumbler on the bar and started the Sidecar. "Give me one sec, and I'll have that margarita for you."

"No problem," Scott said as Tate turned to the back counter for a margarita glass and the blender.

As he mixed the tequila, lime juice, and Cointreau with ice, he tapped his fingers on the wood surface while the whir of the machine drowned out everything else. It wasn't until he felt the warm pressure of a hand on his waist that he even noticed Logan had come up beside him.

"Good evening," Logan said, as he sidled in close and pressed a kiss to his cheek.

Tate smiled and leaned into the intimate gesture. "Evening. When'd you get here?"

Logan rested against the back counter as the blender stopped and Tate grabbed the margarita glass.

"Around five minutes ago. I was on my way upstairs to drop off my stuff, but when I saw you standing here, I couldn't pass up the opportunity to say...*hello.*"

Tate hummed in the back of his throat as Logan's fingers trailed across the small of his back. "Is that what you're doing?"

"Mhmm."

"Well, while you're saying *hello,* pass me a lime wedge, would you?"

Logan picked up a piece of lime and handed it over. "Is Amelia around?"

"Yeah, she should be. Why?"

"I thought you might like to come upstairs and help me get more...comfortable."

Tate chuckled. "That's a new way of putting it."

"I have no idea what you're referring to. I just want to get out of these clothes."

"Oh, I'm sure you do. But before you head upstairs, there's someone I want you to meet," Tate said, even as Logan's gaze drifted to his lips. "Would you focus, please? You can kiss me in a minute, when I'm helping you get comfortable."

Not in the least bit repentant for having been caught, Logan said, "Promise?"

"Promise." Tate licked his lower lip, and Logan said under his breath, "Fucking tease. Okay, who am I meeting?"

"A friend from school. Well, he was Jill's boyfriend for a few years, so he kind of became a permanent fixture around the house." Tate could see the wheels turning behind those intelligent eyes he loved, but before Logan said anything, Tate got in first. "The sooner you meet him, the sooner we can be upstairs getting you out of these clothes."

One of Logan's eyebrows arched. "Well, I can't argue with that logic."

"Good," Tate said, and then picked up the margarita as the two of them turned around to face Scott, and the expression on the man's face almost had Tate's feet faltering.

Confusion, judgment, and distaste was stamped all over Scott's features as his gaze flicked from Tate to Logan. It was obvious he'd witnessed the exchange between the two of them and didn't approve, and a twinge of hurt had Tate's spine stiffening, as his heart ached over the lack of acceptance in Scott's eyes even as he tried to shove it aside.

The crazy thing was that it hadn't even occurred to him that it would be an issue. He'd been with Logan for so long now he never thought twice about the fact that some people might have a problem with it. But he supposed maybe it should have. Especially with people from his past who'd known him when his life had been much...different. His own mother and sister were a terrific example of that.

But the difference between then and now was that he didn't give a flying fuck one way or another about what others thought of him and Logan.

This was their life.

This was their place.

And if someone, friend or stranger, had a problem with that, then they could damn well leave.

As if Logan had some sixth sense when it came to him, Tate saw him glance his way and raise a questioning eyebrow.

I fucking love that about him, Tate thought. *Always checking that I'm okay.*

But Logan had nothing to worry about. Tate shook his head once, indicating he was fine, and then took the final steps he needed to be back opposite Scott Thompson.

"Here's that margarita," Tate said, as Logan stopped beside him. "And hey, I wanted to introduce you two. Scott, this is my boyfriend, Logan. We run this place together."

Logan held his hand out, and as Scott's eyes dropped to it, he slowly pushed off the stool and got to his feet. Tate felt his hackles rise at the blatant dismissal, and as Scott's eyes continued to ping-pong between the two of them, Tate had had enough.

"There a problem?" Tate asked.

Scott said nothing as he fished his wallet out of his back pocket and tossed two twenties on the bar. Tate looked at the money, and, not wanting things to escalate, was about to take it and just walk the fuck away, figuring that was the best course of action. But then, well, Scott spoke.

"No problem. I just remembered a rumor I heard a few years back. Gotta say, Morrison. I shoved it aside thinking it was bullshit, but seems it was right all along. You really are a faggot. No wonder Diana left you."

Tate's hands curled into fists, and he reminded himself not to let his temper get the better of him. This wasn't the first time he'd been at the end of such a close-minded comment, and it definitely wouldn't be the last. That didn't, however, mean he had the same kind of control over Logan.

"What the hell did you just say?" Logan barked, and it was as though his question made time stand still. The buzz of the crowd seemed to instantly dissipate, and the only sound Tate could hear was the thumping beat of the music now keeping time with his heart.

Scott's eyes found Logan's, and when Scott's lip

curled up in a cruel sneer, Tate knew he needed to do
something, but was momentarily frozen.

"I said, I don't blame his wife for leaving him, since
apparently he likes to suck dick."

Before Tate could get the message from his brain to
his body to move and hold Logan back, Logan had launched
himself across the counter, taken hold of Scott's shirt and tie,
and yanked him, with surprising force, halfway across the
bar.

"Likes and *excels* at it," Logan said through gritted
teeth. "And soon you will too, since you'll be sucking on a
fucking straw for food once I get through with you."

Finally kicking his ass in gear, Tate grabbed hold of
Logan's arm. "Logan," he said, trying but failing to get his
attention. Logan wasn't in any kind of mood to listen.

"Your type are all the same," Scott said. "You think
you can just go around shoving your disgusting
relationships in our faces and expect us to all say nothing."

Jesus, Tate thought. *Am I really hearing this shit?* Scott
needed to shut the hell up or Logan was going to break his
face, and it looked as though he'd have help from some of
their customers, who'd gathered around to watch the
commotion going on. But evidently Scott was as stupid as he
was ignorant, because the fucker just wouldn't shut his
mouth.

He aimed his hate-filled eyes at Tate and spat, "No
wonder your mother doesn't show her face at church

anymore…" That particular comment was like a sucker punch, and Tate released Logan's arm to grip the counter and hold himself up from the blow of it. "Too ashamed of her queer-ass son and who he's fucking to—"

Before Scott could finish his sick diatribe, Logan's arm pulled back and then sprang forward until his fist connected with Scott's jaw.

"*Logan*," Tate shouted, and grabbed hold of Logan as he brought his arm back again, no doubt for round two. Then Tate caught Logan's eyes, and the wild fury swirling there had Tate muscling him away from the bar so Logan had to release the asshole he'd just knocked square in the jaw.

As Scott stumbled over the stool, grabbing hold of his face, Tate turned on Logan and pinned him in place with a determined look. "Stop."

Tate watched as Logan's eyes darted over his shoulder to where he could hear someone coughing, and when Tate rounded back to see the entire bar staring at Scott, who was now staggering to his feet, Tate walked as calmly as he could to the counter and said, "Get the hell out of my bar."

Scott rolled his jaw around as though testing it wasn't broken, then said, "Hope you know a good lawyer, Morrison. If anything's broken, I'm gonna sue you faster than you can blink."

Oh, Tate knew a good lawyer, all right. One who had

just clocked Scott in the jaw, which, in Tate's opinion, made him the best fucking lawyer around.

"You know what," Tate said, crossing his arms, "I'm not that worried. Pretty sure you'd need a witness and I don't think you're going to find one in here."

"Are you an idiot? Everyone in here just saw what he did to me. You," Scott said, pointing to Hoyt, one of their regulars, who'd just sat down at the end of the bar. "You saw that asshole hit me. Didn't you?"

Tate looked at Hoyt, who shook his head and raised his beer to take a sip. Then he placed it on the counter and said, "I don't remember that. I saw you spoutin' off your worthless mouth…"

Tate's lips tugged up in a smirk at Hoyt's answer, and then he directed his attention back to Scott. "See. It's your word against ours. And your word doesn't mean shit. Now, I won't tell you again. Get out of my bar."

"Fuck you," Scott said, and Logan was right back to shoving his way forward past him.

There was nothing Tate wanted more than to jump across the bar and take a swing at Scott himself. But this was their place of business, and he didn't think it would look good if one, or both, of the owners were hauled off in the back of a police car.

So Tate placed a palm on Logan's chest, holding him back. Then he let his eyes roam over Scott and said, "I didn't think you were into that. But even if you were, you aren't man enough for that honor. Now get the fuck out, before I personally throw you out."

With a final curse, Scott shoved his way through the audience he'd attracted and headed toward the exit. Tate could feel Logan's chest heaving under his hand, and when he caught Amelia's eye where she stood in the surrounding crowd, she said, "I'll make sure he leaves."

Tate nodded and watched as she followed after Scott, before trying to settle his nerves and flashing a smile at their curious onlookers. "All right. Show's over, folks," he said.

Some raised their glasses in triumph while others they knew cheered them on, and when Tate turned to Logan, he could still see the anger stamped all over his partner's handsome face.

"You need to go upstairs," Tate said, knowing Logan needed some space to calm himself down, because it sure wouldn't happen if they started arguing with each other.

Logan's eyes glittered with annoyance, and Tate knew it was from the order he'd just issued. Adrenaline was riding Logan now, and Tate needed him the hell out of such a public place.

"Tate—"

"Go upstairs and settle the fuck down. Once you have, come back and see me. Got it?"

And before Logan could answer one way or another, Tate headed down the bar to serve a customer taking her seat, wanting to put this ugly altercation behind him.

Chapter Seven

WHEN LOGAN HAD gone upstairs, he hadn't done so with the intention of staying there. But when he entered their loft and looked around the space that had been one of the biggest draws for him and Tate, he'd headed straight for the liquor cabinet to pour himself a glass of whiskey.

That dick in the bar—*what was his name? Scott? Really, who the fuck even cares*—had ruined his mood, night, and good goddamn week. And Tate sending him upstairs to cool off wasn't helping his current frame of mind either.

Snatching up the bottle of Jameson, he headed into the living room with a glass and some ice. The loft wasn't large by any means, but over the years the two of them had made it a cozy place for them to crash—and by cozy, that meant a fully renovated kitchen directly off to the left, with all-black marble, wooden cabinetry, and stainless steel appliances. The original hardwood floors had been polished and refinished, and had large rectangular rugs under the leather couch and coffee table. And they'd both agreed to leave the exposed brick as it was, because it added character when in contrast with the wall of windows that made up the other side of the space.

However, none of that was what he loved most. *No.* His favorite area was up the ten winding steps that led to a balcony that hung over the kitchen. That was where their bed was.

Up there, it was as though they were as far away from the world as they could possibly get. But tonight, it felt as though it had been invaded. It felt like that motherfucker had come into their home and tainted it with his hatred, and that made Logan want to kick someone's ass. Well, more so than he had already.

Fuck, it wasn't often that he let people get under his skin. He was an expert at not giving a shit about what others thought of him. But when someone went after Tate? When someone had the audacity to judge him, to judge what they shared? Not much could hold him back—except Tate himself, that was, who'd quite pointedly sent Logan's ass upstairs. So, that was where he'd stayed. Now there he was with a bag of ice on his knuckles, and several drinks in him, and somehow three hours had passed.

As the heavy firehouse door slid open and Tate stepped inside, Logan glanced over his shoulder to see a scowl plastered on Tate's face, and then turned back to down his drink.

"Why didn't you come back downstairs?" Tate said.

Logan sat forward on the couch, put his empty glass on the table, and got to his feet. "I wasn't quite sure I'd be welcome," he said as he flexed his fingers and dropped the

Ziploc bag on the table.

Tate's eyes slid to the bottle and glass, and then came back up to lock with Logan's. "You drunk?"

"I'm... Not quite yet."

"But that's the goal?"

"It'd crossed my mind," Logan said as he headed into the kitchen, thinking the likelihood of continuing on his current path was now over and he might as well drink some water.

Once he'd gotten himself a bottle from the fridge, he moved so he could lean against the counter as Tate came over and rested back against the fridge's double doors.

"What's going on here?" Tate asked.

Logan took a swig of water and then shrugged, thinking it might be best if he just slept his mood off. His emotions were still primed and on edge—and not in a good way.

"I missed seeing you downstairs," Tate said as his gaze wandered over Logan. "Sitting there. Watching me. I'd been looking forward to that all day."

Logan twisted the bottle between his fingers but remained silent, knowing if he did open his mouth, this wasn't going to end well.

He was pissed. Pissed at what that asshole had said. Pissed that Tate hadn't let him check that he was okay after the horrible things that *had* been said. And he was pissed that *he* was yet again the reason some jerk-off thought they had permission to disrespect the amazing man currently staring him down, waiting for a response.

"Hey?" Tate said. "You need to let this go. Everything's okay now. He's gone."

And that was when Logan finally decided to speak up. "Shouldn't you be downstairs closing?"

"Amelia's doing it tonight. I wanted to come and find you. Now would you please start talking? What's going on with you?"

"Was just thinking."

Tate cocked his head to the side. "About?"

Logan placed the water bottle down and shoved his hands into the pockets of his jeans. "What happened earlier."

"Yeah, I got that much. Which part are we talking about here? The beginning or the end?"

"How about we go with option C—all of the above," Logan said as he shoved away from the counter, ready to head upstairs and go to bed. But as he walked by, Tate reached out and took hold of his wrist.

"Logan, talk to me."

Logan told himself to just let it go. Told himself to just kiss Tate and drag him up to bed and work out this leftover aggression he was feeling. But he'd never really been one to take advice—even his own. "So now you want to hear what I have to say? You didn't seem all that interested earlier." Tate frowned, and Logan raised an eyebrow. "Am I wrong?"

"I told you to come back once you'd cooled off. I could see how pissed you were."

Logan wrenched his arm free and turned on Tate.

"Damn right I was pissed. Can you blame me?"

"No," Tate said, taking a step forward until Logan was caged in against the counter, placing his hands on Tate's chest for balance. "Of course I don't blame you. But taking it any further wasn't going to do either one of us any good. It happened. The same as it has before, and likely will again. But we deal with it and move on. Especially if, and when, it happens at work."

"It shouldn't ever fucking happen."

"No, it shouldn't," Tate said, and reached out to circle Logan's wrists. "But it did. And I hardly think our customers wanted to see either of us handcuffed."

Logan was practically vibrating from his outrage at the injustice of it all. Why shouldn't he be able to stand up for himself, for Tate, if he fucking wanted to?

But then Tate brought Logan's right arm up so he could inspect his knuckles. "I hate that you hurt yourself," he said, and Logan closed his eyes and let out a sigh as Tate pressed his lips to the abused and swollen flesh, the fight in him slowly subsiding.

"I don't know, Tate. Maybe it'd just be better if I didn't come in during your work hours."

"To your own bar?" Tate said, raising his head and

looking Logan in the eye. "To *our* bar? You own this place as much as I do. One of our homes is above it, for fuck's sake. You can't be serious."

"I'm dead serious. One of the reasons I don't let you anywhere near a courtroom is because—"

"Stop talking."

"Excuse me?" Logan said, getting sick and tired of being cut off tonight.

"I said. Stop. Talking."

Logan's eyes narrowed on the irritated expression that had crossed Tate's face, but instead of heeding the warning, he continued. "I don't let you in there because I get distracted and it affects my job. I don't want my being at the bar to be the cause for some customers to leave or to start fights with you."

The muscle of Tate's jaw ticked, and he shook his head.

"What? It's true," Logan said. "If I hadn't come up to you when I did—" He didn't get to finish his sentence, though, because Tate let go of his hand and stormed into the living room to pour himself a glass of whiskey.

Fucking hell. I knew this would turn into an argument.

Logan kept his eyes on Tate as he brought the glass to his lips and downed the alcohol, and then he slammed the tumbler on the table and turned to walk back to Logan. The fulminating look from a second ago was still there, but when Tate stopped in front of Logan, he said, "Come with me."

Logan watched in silence as Tate walked over to the stairs, and when he got to the bottom, he looked over his shoulder to where Logan still stood.

Okay…guess he's not gonna ask twice, Logan thought, and headed over to where Tate was waiting, and was shocked when he held his hand out and said, "What you just said. You can fucking forget it."

"Forget…?"

"Not coming to the bar. Come on, Logan, it's not like you to let someone get under your skin like this."

Logan narrowed his eyes. "It's not *me* I'm worried about. I don't like how it makes *you* feel."

"And how do you think it makes me feel?" Tate said. "Please tell me, because obviously you have it all worked out."

"Pissed off. Uncomfortable."

"Of course I'm uncomfortable. I wanted to do exactly what you did and beat his ass for what he said. But instead, I have to play nice. I have to keep a level head and keep that place running. That's enough to make anyone uncomfortable."

"And is that the *only* reason you're uncomfortable?" Logan said without even realizing he'd been going to ask. It wasn't that much of a shock, really. This concern. This worry. It wasn't a new one for him, that was for sure. But it was one that was always there, niggling away at some recess of his mind whenever someone was anything other than accepting of them.

Does Tate still think this is all worth it? Does he think that I'm worth it?

"Ahh. I see," Tate said. "Now we're getting to the real reason for you stewing up here. Aren't we?"

Logan glared him down, and Tate, the bold fucker, held his stare and took a step forward until they were toe to toe.

"So what if we are?" Logan said. "You've been pushing at me since you walked in that door tonight."

"You're right. I have been. But you still haven't said what's really on your mind. Have you?"

Logan was the first to admit he was horrible at expressing himself, and even worse at arguing his point when it came to Tate. He always managed to somehow put his foot in his mouth, so he tried to avoid it as much as he possibly could.

When he remained stubbornly silent, Tate took his hand again and said, "Come with me."

As Tate started up the stairs, Logan trailed behind until they reached the landing that housed their bed, and not much else. Tate stopped and pivoted so they were face to face, with only the slivers of moonlight filtering through the large windows, and then he stepped in close enough that he could touch their lips together.

"Go on," Tate whispered, and a shiver skated up Logan's spine. "Ask me."

"Ask you what?"

"The question I can see in your eyes," Tate said as he cupped either side of Logan's face, making him hold his stare.

"And what question is that?"

"The same one I see each time someone questions *me* about us," Tate said in a tone that dared Logan to deny it. "Ask me."

Logan searched Tate's expression, and the raw honesty he saw there finally had him lowering his guard and voicing his greatest fear: "Do you ever regret it?"

* * *

AND THERE IT is, Tate thought, as one of his curls fell forward and Logan automatically moved to brush it back from his forehead. For a man who claimed he wasn't sweet and said the wrong things, Logan always managed to take the wind right out of Tate's sails in moments like these. He wasn't even sure Logan was aware of what he was doing. But the look of absolute devotion in his eyes as he fingered the strand of hair put into words everything he was unable to say out loud. And Tate loved that this was a side of Logan that was all his.

"*It?*" Tate asked, recapturing Logan's attention.

"You know which *it* I mean... Me. Us. This."

Tate bent his head until his forehead was resting

against Logan's. "There's only one thing I regret. And that's that I didn't meet you sooner."

Logan's breath caught, and when his entire body trembled, Tate took hold of the back of his neck and pulled him forward. As their lips met, Logan opened immediately, letting him inside, and as soon as he got the taste of Logan on his tongue, Tate groaned and tightened his grip, holding Logan in place so he could devour the mouth now consuming his own.

Tate closed his eyes, allowing the wave of emotions to crash over him as he reached for Logan's shirt next, and when it became clear what he was about to do, Logan tore his mouth free and raised his arms so Tate could pull the fabric off him. Tate tossed it to the floor and then went to work on his uniform as Logan removed the rest of his clothing, and by the time the both of them were naked and climbing beneath the sheets, Tate was desperate for the feel of Logan's body pressed alongside his.

With the shadows dancing over their skin, the two of them stretched out on their sides, their legs tangling as their mouths reconnected, and Logan's fingers threaded through his hair, causing a groan to emerge from the back of Tate's throat.

Christ. He loved being with Logan like this. It was everything. It was what he lived for, and as Logan's cologne enveloped him, Tate closed his eyes and let his senses go into overdrive.

He basked in the man destroying him and then reviving him with every touch and sound he made. Then Tate rolled Logan to his back and hovered over him.

As he looked down at the man under him, Tate stroked his fingers through the thick strands of black hair on the pillow and said, "When are you going to understand that nothing anyone says to me will ever change how I feel about you?" As Logan's blue eyes glistened, the depth of his vulnerability had Tate lowering his head to kiss his temple. "I love you, Logan Mitchell. That's never going to change."

Logan wrapped his arms around him, cupping one hand at the back of his neck, and Tate took another inhale of the intoxicating scent—the cologne he'd given Logan for his birthday. It was masculine and woodsy, yet had a floral undercurrent that enhanced the dark, sultry blend. And on Logan, it was downright potent.

"God, Tate," Logan said, as he smoothed his hands down his back to his waist, and when Tate raised his head to look at him, Logan shut his eyes, but Tate wasn't about to have that. What he was about to say next he needed Logan to hear, understand, and believe.

"Look at me," he said, and when Logan's eyes opened and found his, Tate traced a finger down his jawline. "After all this time, you still don't realize how important you are to me. And you need to. This, what we have, is the reason I wake up in the morning. And Logan?"

Logan swallowed once, and his nostrils flared.

"Yes?"

"I will never leave you. I can't even imagine what that would be like. I don't ever want to."

Logan's eyes darkened as Tate stared at him, and just when Tate thought he would stay silent, Logan said, "Never, huh?"

A slow smile curved Tate's mouth as he lowered his head and bit Logan's lower lip. "Not. Fucking. Ever."

Logan's answering smile was so damn rewarding that Tate would've gone through tonight over and over again just to see it before he fell asleep. But luckily for him, that wicked grin was one Logan offered up to him on the regular, and it was a more than welcome sight tonight.

He nestled in between Logan's thighs and kissed him once more before he laid his head down on the broad chest beneath him. The storm had finally passed, and as the tension in the room faded into the shadows, he felt a hand smooth over his hair as the steady *thump thump thump* of Logan's heart lulled him to sleep.

Then, right before he drifted off, Tate heard Logan whisper, "I love you so damn much. I can't believe there was ever a time when I didn't."

And if Tate had his way, Logan would *never* know a time like that again.

Not. Fucking. Ever.

Chapter Eight

BY THE TIME Sunday rolled around, things were back to normal, and by normal that meant they'd spent Saturday lounging around the condo catching up on the shows Logan had missed over the past few weeks and doing not much else. And today they were making the sixteen-mile commute from downtown Chicago to the northwest suburbs, just as they did every Sunday.

"Wait a minute," Logan said, glancing at Tate out the corner of his eye. "You're telling me that I should just *demand* Robbie tell me what's going on with him?"

About halfway to Skokie, Logan had remembered the reason he'd wanted to talk to Tate on Friday before the shitstorm had broken out. And after explaining the weird vibe he'd gotten during his meeting with Robbie, Tate had suggested he use his biggest weapon—*himself*—when it came to the ex-barista.

"Yeah. The Robbie I knew could barely remember his own name when you were around," Tate said.

"And your answer is for me to charm him?"

"No. No," Tate said, around a chuckle. "You don't get it. Let me see if I can explain this better for you."

"Plain English usually works. I'm not an idiot, you know."

"I know. But you have no idea the effect you have on people." Logan frowned as Tate squeezed his thigh. "You're fucking hot."

Logan rolled his eyes. "Be serious."

Tate started laughing loudly. "I am. It's that simple. You, Logan Mitchell, are sexy. I used to always think of you as sex on legs."

"Used to?" Logan asked, only mildly offended.

"Still do," Tate said, flashing him a grin. "But when we met, I was so damn confused by you. I didn't understand why I couldn't get you out of my head. Then I'd get so angry when you'd constantly show up. And even when I wanted you to go away... God, I loved looking at you. You're..." Tate's words lingered as he let his eyes rove all over Logan.

"Hard as hell now," Logan said, shifting in the driver's seat.

"Well, I'm just trying to explain that you have a very commanding presence," Tate said. "It's one that Robbie used to trip all over himself to get close to. The next time you see him, sit him down, and *make* him listen to you. I guarantee the second your attention is focused on him and *you're* asking him questions, he'll tell you anything you want to know."

Logan thought about that and shook his head. "I think you're a little biased."

"Logan?"

"Yes?"

"Trust me on this. I thought about you even before you touched me, and considering I was adamantly straight, I'd say that's one hell of a presence."

Logan eyed him as he exited the highway and licked his lips. "Tate?"

"Hmm?"

"Stop talking now. We're about to be in the company of minors, and I'd rather do that without a raging hard-on."

"Okay," Tate said. "But the next time you see Robbie, treat him the way you used to, not carefully or differently. See how he responds."

Logan nodded, and decided that tomorrow, when he saw Robbie, he'd see how he was going to play it out. He reached down and placed his hand over Tate's in a familiar move, and when Tate interlaced their fingers and brought them to his mouth to kiss his bruised knuckles, Logan looked over and said, "Thank you."

He wasn't sure which part he was thanking him for—maybe both the advice and the kiss—but when Tate grinned and said, "Anytime," Logan sighed and looked back out at the road, thinking he had to be just about the luckiest man on the planet.

As he took several turns and drove past the *Welcome to Skokie* sign, Logan looked at the familiar homes lining the streets.

A couple of years ago, when Cole and Rachel had found out they were expecting their second child, they'd made the decision to move out of the city and head for the suburbs. A decision that Logan took great delight in busting Cole's balls over to this day. He still couldn't believe his brother had gone from Mr. Cool and Controlled to this warm, domesticated father-of-the-year type. But hell if that role didn't suit him. He'd never seen Cole happier than when he was around his wife, son, and daughter, and as Logan finally pulled into the driveway of the Madison's two-story colonial home, evidence of the family who lived inside was littered all over the front lawn.

As he and Tate shoved open the car doors and got out, Logan spotted a blue bike with training wheels lying on its side on the perfectly cut grass and smiled. Beside it was a soccer ball, and over by the garden that lined the path to the front door was a small pink bucket with a shovel beside it. It looked like the Madisons had been out enjoying the warm August day.

Logan headed around to the trunk and took several of the grocery bags Tate handed him, and couldn't help stealing a kiss from the man whose eyes were hidden behind his Aviators.

"What was that for?" Tate asked with a grin as he reached up to shut the trunk.

"Do I need a reason?"

"Not ever."

"Glad to hear it," Logan said as he ran his eyes over the cargo shorts and white shirt that Tate wore. His hair was a stylish mess that somehow suited him, and the stubble lining his jaw was a little thicker today, and made Tate look casual and sexy in an effortless way.

"You ready to head inside out of this heat?" Tate asked.

"Sure am. After you," Logan said, and stepped aside, but Tate flashed him a crooked grin and said, "Oh no. After you. I'd rather come from behind today, if that's okay with you."

Logan lowered his sunglasses down his nose. "You did not just say that to me when I finally have myself back in a somewhat decent state. You do realize we have to spend the afternoon in a house with a two-and-a-half-year-old and four-year-old."

Tate chuckled and kissed his cheek. "I do. And I did. I would say I'm sorry, but you're looking really hot in those tailored shorts and shirt all tucked in and proper."

"Proper?" Logan looked down at his white Bermuda shorts and navy-blue polo. "There's not one proper thought currently in my head."

"I know," Tate said. "That's what makes you even hotter. Now get inside, Uncle Logan. I can already see someone waiting for you."

Logan turned around and looked at the glass front door that was obviously locked, and Tate was right. There, waving so hard his little arm just might fall off, was Thomas Madison.

As the two of them headed up the paved walkway, Logan took in the fair-haired boy with hazel eyes who was the spitting image of Cole, and marveled, as he always did, that he was getting a glimpse of what his brother must've looked like when he was the same age.

When they got to the two steps leading up to the front door, he could hear Thomas shouting excitedly through the glass. "Uncle Logan! Uncle Tate!" And then Rachel appeared, a yellow sundress swishing around her as she hurried down the hallway to unlock the door.

As it swung wide, Thomas charged outside, like a horse from a starting gate, and launched himself at Logan. His arms wrapped around Logan's legs as he hugged him tight and beamed up with a bright smile, his eyes twinkling.

"Hey there, big guy," Logan said, as Rachel reached for the bags he was holding. Once his hands were free, Logan picked Thomas up and gave him a big bear hug. Thomas growled and squeezed him back as Logan kissed him on the cheek. "Are you bigger than you were last week?"

"Nooo," Thomas said, and shook his head. "You say that every week."

"Because it's true," Logan said as he stepped inside and kissed Rachel's cheek. "Isn't that right, Mom?"

Rachel smiled at him as she pushed her black hair

with purple highlights behind her ears. "Sure is. See,
Thomas, if you keep eating your vegetables, soon you'll be
taller than Logan."

Thomas scrunched his nose up, looking doubtful.
"Will I be as tall as Daddy?"

"If you eat your veggies, you just might be," Logan
said, and put Thomas on his feet. "Between you and me, I
think he's shrinking." As he ran a hand over the back of
Thomas's head, Logan moved aside so Tate could greet
Rachel with a kiss.

"Hey there, Rach," Tate said, as Rachel wrapped an
arm around his waist and leaned into his side.

"Hey yourself. You're just in time. Cole was finishing
up feeding Lila, then he'll be ready to head out the back and
fire up the grill."

Thomas took hold of Logan's hand and tugged on it,
leading him up the hallway, which was lined with photo
after photo of the Madison clan and their extended family.

As they passed by, Logan saw the image of Rachel
with her brother, Mason, when they were kids, and right
beside it the one of them just last Christmas. Both of them
were laughing, their heads tipped back, and they looked the
very picture of happy siblings. Above that image was one of
Rachel and Cole, arms wrapped around one another, lips
touching, and again she was all smiles, even as Cole's lips
were barely tipped up in a smirk. Knowing Cole, he'd
probably said something he shouldn't have—something his

wife clearly appreciated.

Under that one was Thomas as a baby, and directly beside it Miss Lila, and then farther up was the entire Madison clan for last year's Christmas card. Logan remembered receiving it in the mail and thinking how perfectly cheerful they all were.

Cole and Rachel sitting on the bricks surrounding their fireplace with Thomas on Cole's knee and Lila in her mother's lap. Pure joy shone from their eyes. It was enough to make even his heart swell.

Then, just as they reached the end of the hall, he spotted the gift that he and Tate had given Rachel last month for her birthday. Tate had thought of it, of course, and Logan remembered the tears in her eyes when she'd unwrapped the framed photo of them that had been taken at their friend's wedding back in May.

Both in suits, the two of them looked sharp. But it was the moment they'd been captured in that Rachel claimed made the image so powerful. Tate was standing behind Logan with his arms wrapped around his waist, and Logan was looking at him over his shoulder—he remembered it perfectly. He'd been bitching about having one of the grooms' bow ties flung into his drink, and Tate had kissed his ear and said, "Cheer up. I promise to blindfold you later with *my* tie. Not throw it in your drink." And the resulting look between them was a scorching expression from Logan, and a hell of a wicked smile from

Tate as they stared each other down.

That night had brought up some interesting emotions for him when Tate and Ace, one of the grooms, had joked about how they'd pair their names if they were to ever get married. But Tate had quickly squashed any discussion on that, insisting it was all a joke. So it wasn't that shocking some of the telltale signs of all that love and matrimony was evident in the photograph.

You can practically feel the love between you two here, Rachel had said when she first looked at it. And she was right about one thing: that night, when they'd gone back to their hotel room, love had definitely been felt.

"Logan? Tate," Cole said, and Logan tore his eyes, and thoughts, off the photograph. "You're here."

Thomas had released his hand and run through the living room to the kitchen where Cole was sitting at a table in the breakfast nook, and beside him in her high chair was the little miss—Lila.

With her thick ebony hair in pigtails, her chubby pink cheeks were made to be kissed as she raised her hand and waved. Logan stared at the picture the three of them made gathered around the kitchen table. Cole at the head, Lila to his left, and Thomas tapping Cole on the shoulder.

So cozy. So homey. And when Cole looked down at Thomas and laughed at something his son said, Logan thought, *So happy.*

He took Tate's hand in his, and they walked over to

where the three sat as Rachel headed into the kitchen. As they got closer, Lila, who'd been watching her brother and father, looked up and spotted Tate.

Her blue eyes widened and she immediately raised her arms, saying, "Unca Tate. Unca Tate." Basically, her little heart melted—much the same way Logan's did whenever he saw Tate.

Awesome, Logan thought, *I pretty much have the exact same crush a two-and-a-half-year-old girl has.*

"There's my girl," Tate said, and let go of Logan's hand to head around the table to where Lila was now practically bouncing in her highchair. Logan laughed as he walked into the kitchen, stopping behind the island.

"Is she all done here?" Tate asked Cole, who had a small plate in front of him with a half-eaten triangular sandwich on it.

"Yeah, she's done. And honestly"—Cole chuckled at his daughter, who was wriggling in her chair—"I'd almost be scared to deny her what she so clearly wants."

"Unca Tate," she said again, and when Tate reached for her, she giggled. "Lift!"

And just like everyone else in that room who'd met Tate, Lila immediately welcomed him with open arms.

Chapter Nine

LILA MADISON WAS a total heartbreaker, and just about the cutest thing Tate had seen. He scooped her out of her highchair and brought her close for a hug and kiss. With her pigtails held up by pink ribbons that matched her dress, the little girl who grabbed his cheeks and smacked a kiss to his lips stole his heart a little more every time he saw her.

When she pulled back and looked over her shoulder to see everyone watching her, she started to giggle, and then turned back to do it again.

"You know, little miss, you're lucky I'm not jealous by nature," Logan said, which had Rachel snorting and saying, "Sure you're not."

When Lila pulled away a second time, Tate shifted her around his body so she was resting on his hip, and he could see Rachel placing an open Corona on the counter in front of Logan.

"Thanks," Logan said, glancing at his sister-in-law. Then he looked over at Tate and saluted him with the bottle. "Plus, it would be in poor taste to be jealous of someone who clearly has such *fantastic* taste. Who wouldn't want to kiss Tate?"

"True," Rachel said, joining Logan at the counter. "There is something about him."

Cole coughed, which had his wife looking in his direction. "Is that right?" Cole asked as Thomas started to drive a Hot Wheels across the breakfast table.

Logan raised his beer, took a sip, and then nodded. "Yeah... It's the hair. There's something about those—"

"Ow," Tate said as Lila grabbed a tiny fistful of said hair and tugged on it.

Logan laughed as Rachel winced, then Lila tugged again and announced, "Pretty curls."

Tate reached up to try and pry her fingers free, but Lila had a tenacious grip. "Uhh, Logan," Tate said, walking over toward the two in the kitchen. "A little help."

Logan put his beer down and came around the end of the island to where Tate stood with Lila, and looked between the two of them. He smiled at his niece and then placed a hand on Tate's shoulder and leaned in to press a kiss to her cheek.

As she laughed, Logan took hold of her iron grip and said, "Aww, come on now, hon. I'm the only one that gets to pull Tate's hair like that."

When Logan straightened and waggled his brow, Tate rolled his eyes, but Lila let go, clapped her hands, and pointed to her cheek.

"Again!" she said.

"A true Madison," Logan joked, and then leaned in

to give her another kiss. "Demanding and not afraid to go after what she wants."

Rachel looked over at Cole, whom Thomas was now climbing all over like he was a jungle gym, and said, "Thomas, why don't you take your sister into the family room and watch *Peppa Pig* for a little while so Daddy can help Mommy get ready to go and grill?"

Thomas froze halfway up Cole's back and frowned, and the fierce expression on such a young face was almost comical. "I want to help grill."

"And you can," Rachel said. "But first Daddy and I want to talk to Uncle Logan and Uncle Tate. I'll come and get you when the men head outside. Okay?"

"That sounds serious," Logan said. "Sure I can't go watch the pig too?"

Tate snorted, and Thomas looked between him and Logan with narrowed eyes, as if he didn't trust what he was being told, before he slid off his dad's lap and trudged over to where Tate was putting Lila back on her feet.

Thomas held his hand out for his sister, and when she smiled and took it, Tate had an unexpected flash of Jill when they'd been kids and the way she used to follow him around everywhere.

God, where did that come from? Tate thought, as he watched the two little ones head off toward the family room, Thomas steady on his feet as he guided the less-than-steady Lila. *Scott Thompson, that's where it came from.* Bringing up his damn family. Actually, *not* his family, since his mother had disowned him when he'd started dating Logan, and Jill had followed her lead. At least he still had a relationship with his dad. A good, solid one.

"Hey," Rachel said, coming over and handing him a beer. "You okay?"

Shoving the memory aside, Tate took the frosty bottle from her and nodded. "Yeah, I'm good. You've got some great kids there."

She looked over at the two small figures disappearing into the family room and then smiled at him. "I agree. Come on," she said, looping her arm through his elbow and leading him over to where Logan was taking a seat at the table with his brother. Tate pulled out the chair beside Logan, and once he was seated, he looked over at Cole, who pushed back from the table so Rachel could take a seat on his lap.

"Why do I suddenly feel like I'm about to get in trouble?" Logan asked.

"Because you have a guilty conscience," Cole said, as he wrapped his arms around his wife.

Rachel slung her arm around Cole's shoulders and nodded. "It's true. You do," she said, and Logan turned his head to look at Tate.

"Did you tell them?"

Tate knew Logan was referring to his altercation at the bar on Friday night. But he hadn't said a word, so he shook his head. "Nope. I don't know what this is about, so any guilt you're feeling is your own."

Logan aimed a *very funny* glare at him before he looked back to Cole and Rachel, who were now staring at the two of them, waiting for an explanation of some sort.

"Oh, fine," Logan said. "I got into a fight at the bar on Friday night and punched someone."

"You what?" Cole said, as Rachel sat up and said, "Oh my God."

"In his defense," Tate said, "the guy deserved it. And it broke up soon after that."

"Logan, you can't just go around punching people," Cole said.

"Gee, thanks, Dad," Logan said.

"What did the guy do?" Rachel asked, and Logan took a swig of his beer and said, "See. That's what you should be asking, Cole. I wouldn't just *hit* someone."

"I know that," Cole said, and sighed. "Well, what did he do?"

"He was being an asshole," Logan and Tate said at the same time.

Rachel frowned, and as soon as she did, her eyebrows drew down into a deep V and Tate started to laugh.

"What?" she said, the frown becoming even more pronounced.

"I just realized where Thomas gets his fierce look of

consternation from."

Cole hugged Rachel back against his chest. "She is
fierce when it comes to protecting those she loves. This is
also her *don't even think about it* look."

As they all started to laugh, Tate put a hand behind
Logan's chair and ran his fingers absently over the line of his
shoulder. Man, he loved this family. Right from the get-go
Rachel and Cole had taken him in and welcomed him as
though he were already part of them, and as they sat around
the table talking about last week's big win for the law firm,
he still couldn't believe how fortunate he was to be able to
call this amazing group of people *his* people.

"So, okay. Spit it out. What do you two want?"
Logan asked.

Tate leaned over on his seat so he could press a kiss
to Logan's temple. "Very subtle, Logan."

"Excuse me, I know when I'm being buttered up for
something."

"He's not wrong," Cole said. "We do want
something."

"See?" Logan said.

Tate's lips twitched, and he couldn't stop himself
from kissing the know-it-all. "I see."

Logan turned back to the two at the end of the table.
"Okay, what is it?"

"Well," Rachel said, "we were wondering if you
were free next weekend."

"Yeah, we don't have any plans," Tate said. "Why?"

"Oh good," she said, flashing an overly enthusiastic smile at them. "You know how it's my birthday this week? Well, Cole wants to take me away for the weekend and, uhh, we were wondering if you guys would mind taking the kids for the night."

There was a three-second pause and then Logan said, "Like…the whole night?"

A booming laugh left Cole, and Tate couldn't help but join in, and when Cole finally settled, he said, "You should see your face."

"I mean, it's not an unreasonable question," Logan said, then aimed a glare over his shoulder at Tate. "I'm glad you're so amused."

"I'm sorry."

"Yeah, you really look it. But have you thought about what this entails?" Logan asked, and then he looked back to the laughing parents. "Have you two? Are you really willing to leave your children in our care for an entire night? I don't even know what to do with a kid after they've been fed."

Rachel slipped off Cole's lap and walked over to wrap an arm around Logan's shoulders. "Oh, we totally trust"—she paused and looked over Logan's head to meet Tate's eyes—"Tate."

Tate bit back a laugh and ran a hand over Logan's leg under the table. "We'd love to," he told Rachel. "And I'm sure we'll manage. It's not like we haven't taken them off your hands for an afternoon before."

"Exactly," Logan said. "An *afternoon*. Not an entire night. What if we break them?"

Cole stood and headed into the kitchen. "If you break them, I'll kill you. I thought that was laid out in the contract the first time you took care of them."

"Very funny," Logan said.

"Seriously, though," Rachel said, "other than Mase and Lena, who are both working, there is no one we trust them with more. And it's time. They love the two of you, and honestly, I really need a night away with my husband."

Tate nodded, accepting on Logan's behalf, knowing that Logan would always be there to take care of his niece and nephew, no matter how uncomfortable he might be about it. He loved those kids as though they were his own.

"We'd love to. Wouldn't we, Logan?"

"Sure we would. But I have one condition," Logan said, and Rachel cocked her head to the side. "You don't come back from this night pregnant. Two kids I can wrap my head around minding. Three...I'm leaving the state."

* * *

SEVERAL HOURS LATER, steaks had been consumed, drinks had been shared, and Rachel's salted caramel chocolate tarts had been devoured. Logan was surprised they could actually walk from the back patio to inside with as much food as they'd all eaten, but somehow they managed.

As they headed into the comfort of the living room, Rachel and Cole took the kids into their playroom, Thomas declaring he was going to make the biggest Lego castle any of them had ever seen, and, of course, Lila was right there alongside her big brother to help.

Logan sat on one side of the large love seat facing the fireplace, and when Tate wandered his way, he placed his arm along the back of the cushions in open invitation. Tate took him up on the invite in a second, sitting beside him so damn close their legs were practically glued from hip to knee.

"Hmm..." Logan said, and Tate shifted and placed his lips to his jaw. "What's that for?"

"No reason," Tate said. "I'm just happy."

"So I see."

Tate placed a hand on Logan's chest and smoothed it down over his polo shirt. "Yep. I'm very happy."

Logan took Tate's chin and bent his head to steal a kiss. His intention was to keep it nice and light, knowing that Cole and Rachel would be along as soon as they had the kids occupied. But Logan should've known better. The second he got the taste of cinnamon gum and Tate on his tongue, the word *nice* left his vocabulary.

He slipped his tongue past Tate's lips, and when Tate moved on the couch so his front was flush against Logan's side, the fingers he had on Tate's chin traveled down his neck. Logan clasped the back of it, and Tate smirked, clearly about to shift away from him, until Logan brought his other hand up to grab hold of his shirt, keeping him in place.

The warmth he'd seen in Tate's eyes earlier turned molten then, and as Logan's gaze swept down to the shiny lips he wanted either back on his or wrapped around his cock in the next five minutes, he was trying his hardest to think of a good excuse to have them up and heading for the door ASAP.

"Sorry about that, guys," Rachel said as she walked into the living room, and then came to an abrupt halt, which made Cole run into her. "Uhh...sorry. Are we interrupting something?" she asked, as she took in the picture they made on her couch of Tate practically lying over Logan's lap, while Logan had his hand balled in Tate's shirt like he wanted to rip it off him.

"Yes," Logan said, just as Tate pushed away from him and said, "No."

Cole grumbled something about them at least waiting until they got home. But Logan tuned him out the second Tate resituated his ass back against the couch close enough so he could wrap an arm around him.

"If you can contain yourself for five minutes, Logan, maybe we could finally talk to Tate and Rachel about the idea we've had," Cole said.

Logan let out a put-upon sigh. "Why couldn't you

have brought this up before Tate decided he couldn't keep his hands off me?"

"Is that what that was?" Tate asked. "You were the one holding on to me."

"Hey, you were telling me how happy I make you then rubbing all up on me. How else am I supposed to take that?"

Tate shook his head, but the smirk on those fantasy-inspiring lips let Logan know this was one conversation that would be revisited the minute they got home.

Logan looked back to Cole and nodded. "Okay, if it's only going to take five minutes then I think I can manage. Any longer than that and you can forget it."

Rachel took a seat in her favorite spot. It was a reading chair by the fireplace, and they all knew better than to go anywhere near it.

Then Cole sat in his recliner and said, "As you both know, over the last couple of years the firm has been doing extremely well, and with Logan's big win this week, Mitchell & Madison is set to—"

"Explode," Logan ended for him. "Our firm is about to be featured everywhere, which will likely have clients calling from all over. Some who want to bring us their business, and those who want to make sure they'll remain with us no matter what."

"Okay," Rachel said, as her eyes moved between the brothers. "What are you two thinking? Because as long as

I've been married to Cole, you have never sat me down for a business meeting."

Cole glanced at her and then looked at Logan, who nodded, as though agreeing it was time to tell them. "For the last couple of months Logan and I have been discussing scaling back a little, slowing down enough that we can enjoy ourselves. Me, with you and the kids."

"And me, with Tate." As Logan said the words, he brought his arm down so he could take Tate's hand in his. "This past year has been insane. This case took up nearly all my time, and while I love my job, there's something— actually somebody—who I'd rather spend my time with."

Tate's crooked grin just about melted Logan's heart, and when he managed to tear his eyes off him to look at Rachel, she was sitting with her hands over her chest.

"That's so sweet."

"Oh God. You're not going to cry, are you?" Logan asked.

She gave him a *die now* look, and Logan looked over at Cole, indicating he should start talking again.

"Anyway, here's what we've been looking into, and we want you both to know we will only do this if you are one hundred percent okay with it. The floor above us in the building has come up for lease. It's been vacant for the last seven months, and Logan and I have been tossing around the idea of expanding."

"Wait a minute," Rachel said. "How would

expanding help you slow down?"

"Well, that's the biggest thing we want to talk to you about," Logan said, and then looked at Tate. "We want to bring in a third partner."

"Wow," was all Tate managed, and Rachel said, "Really?"

Cole nodded. "Really. We've thought about it for months now, and whoever we bring in would not be a name partner; the firm will remain Mitchell & Madison. But they will take on a third of the caseload and give Logan and me more time to spend with our families."

"Oh my God," Rachel said, and slumped back in her chair. "I'm in shock."

"This is a little bit of a surprise, guys," Tate said. "Are you sure this is what you want?"

"Yes," Logan said. "We've been talking about it for a while. But we wanted to wait until after the Berivax case to make the final decision. We wanted to make sure we could afford it, first off. Because not only would we hire on this new partner, but we want to get a couple of first-year associates, and basically we'd put our offices upstairs with the conference room and several of the other senior attorneys, and have everyone else where we are right now. We want Mitchell & Madison to be one of the top firms in Chicago. But to do that and keep our sanity, we need to hire more attorneys and a partner with a fire under their ass."

Rachel and Tate both nodded at that, and Rachel

said, "I assume you both have someone in mind?"

"We do," Cole said, and when his lips pulled into a smirk, he said to Logan, "I'll let you tell them."

Logan chuckled and looked between the two waiting for an answer. Finally, he said, "We're going to call a priest."

Chapter Ten

TATE WAS STILL trying to process everything from tonight's reveal at the Madisons as he and Logan headed toward their front door. It wasn't that he didn't think it was a fantastic idea to hire on more staff. But another partner? *That* was unexpected.

"You'd really be okay with bringing in a third person with you and Cole?" he asked, finally voicing the question he'd had since he found out what the two brothers were thinking.

Logan glanced over his shoulder and flashed him a reassuring smile. "Yes, I really would. I mean, we aren't just going to hire anyone. We vetted him. And this is someone Cole and I have both worked with, so we know we can trust him. Plus, he's the best criminal law attorney I've ever seen. And we want the best."

"This priest guy?"

"Yes. His name's Joel Priestley. He's located in L.A. right now, but we've had a few conference calls with him to see if he'd be interested in relocating if offered the right incentive. Another reason we wanted to wait until the Berivax case was either won or lost."

"Ahh, right," Tate said, coming to a stop behind Logan at their door. "Well, if it's what you both want, I see no problem with it."

Logan inserted the key and nodded. "Like you said about the bar and hiring help, it's time. Cole has a family, I have you, and we're in a position where we can afford to do it. So, it's the perfect opportunity."

Tate agreed, and thought about the two brothers he'd first met at his old job in After Hours, and then again in their conference room the day he'd arrived to sign his divorce papers—that was the same day he'd first kissed Logan. *Damn, that seems like another lifetime ago.* He remembered being so pissed off at the two of them that day, and now here they all were discussing their business as a family.

Both extremely proud men, Cole and Logan were often considered arrogant by those they met, including Tate at first. But over time, he'd come to realize it was an arrogance that was well deserved. The Mitchell and Madison brothers were extremely intelligent, and two of the hardest-working men Tate had ever met. They'd taken an inheritance from a father both of them had reason to detest, come together on their own to form an unshakable relationship, and built one of the most sought after law firms in Chicago. It was impressive by any standards, and Tate hadn't wanted to question their intentions; he just wanted to make sure the decision was one both men were a hundred percent happy with.

As Logan walked through the front door, Tate followed inside to the hallway that had been swallowed up by the darkness of the night. He went to reach for the light switch, and as he did he heard a loud thump, and then Logan cursed.

Flicking on the light, he spotted Logan bent over, rubbing his shin where he'd obviously just hit it against a case of wine that had been delivered yesterday. He bit down on his lip trying not laugh and because, *damn*… Logan had one of the best asses he'd ever seen, and those shorts he was wearing were stretched across it perfectly.

Tate walked up behind him and ran a hand over the seat of the white material, and Logan straightened to look over his shoulder.

"This place is getting too fucking small."

"It is," Tate said, then he stepped around Logan and kissed his frowning lips. "You've got to be careful. Want me to kiss it better?"

One of Logan's eyebrows rose. "I'd rather you kiss something else. But if that's my only choice…"

"It's definitely not your only choice." Tate nipped at Logan's lower lip. "Actually, it's not your choice tonight at all."

"Is that right?" Logan said as he swayed forward, reaching for the material of Tate's shirt, his shin clearly forgotten. "In that case, let me shower first. I want all options *available* to you."

As Logan's teeth found his jaw and his hand found his cock, Tate groaned in the back of his throat. He'd wanted to undress Logan since they'd arrived at the Madisons that afternoon. And he'd told himself that once he got Logan alone tonight, he was going to be the one to do the taking—and he would be damned if Logan rushed or turned the tables on him. No matter how much he wanted to drop to his knees for him right then.

"Okay. Shit..." Tate said, pulling away and running a hand over his eager erection. When Logan bared his teeth in a wolfish grin, the look was so smug it made Tate want to shove him against the wall and teach him a lesson. But that wouldn't work; he wanted this to be longer than five minutes. He wanted to lose himself in the man who'd now walked past him and was heading across the living room.

As he watched Logan go, he fought back the impulse to immediately follow. "I'll be there in a minute. I just want to get a drink of water." *And calm my dick down so I can take my time and enjoy you.*

Logan reached for the hem of his shirt and pulled it up his torso and over his head. When he reached the door of their bedroom, he faced Tate, bundled the material, and tossed it at him.

"Don't make me wait too long," he said as he undid the button of his shorts, and Tate let his eyes roam down to Logan's hands.

Of course he thinks he's running the show tonight. Time

for a reality check. Tate brought Logan's shirt up to his nose and inhaled. *Jesus, he always smells unreal.* When Logan cursed, Tate looked over and caught his gaze—it was blazing. Logan looked ready to cross back to him and fuck him where he stood. But before he could do that...

"I'm going to hang on to this," Tate said, and Logan's eyes narrowed slightly. "You better go take that shower. You're on my time tonight. And Logan? You're going to wait until I'm good and ready to take you. Got it?"

Logan touched the tip of his tongue to his upper lip as though in deep concentration, then gave the smallest of nods. "Oh, I got it."

"Good. Then I'll see you soon."

As a final *good luck trying to resist this,* Logan shoved his shorts down his hips and kicked them at Tate, before he turned around and walked bare-assed into the bedroom, calling out, "Yes. You will."

* * *

LOGAN WAS IN AND out of the shower in record time, and as he finished running the towel over his hair, he took in several breaths, trying to calm his thudding pulse. After that bossy fucking order and the tone with which Tate had issued it, he was finding it difficult not to get himself off before he saw him again just so he wouldn't ruin whatever Tate had in mind for him.

Tossing the towel on the floor, Logan ran a hand through his hair, sweeping it back from his face, and then headed out of the en suite fully expecting to find Tate in their bed, or at least the bedroom—but he was nowhere in sight. The lamp on the bedside table had been switched on, but other than that, the duvet and pillows remained untouched, and when he looked over to the doorway, he saw that all the lights out in the living room had been switched back off.

"Come out here."

Tate's authoritative voice drifted through the air of the condo and found Logan, and when he looked down his nude body to his engorged cock, he thought, *Yeah…a controlling Tate does this to me every damn time.* With a sure stride, he headed out of their bedroom to see the balcony curtains had been left open so the lights from the city illuminated the space, and there, sitting on their couch, was the man issuing the orders tonight. Tate's feet were bare, but beyond that he still wore all of his clothes—something that would soon be rectified, if Logan had any say in the matter.

As Logan walked across the room, his feet sank into the plush rug they'd purchased a year or so ago, and Tate's eyes tracked him. Beside him on the couch was a bottle of lube, and when Logan stopped in front of him, he saw that Tate held the shirt he'd tossed at him earlier over his lap.

"You're a little overdressed for the occasion, aren't you?" Logan asked.

Tate said nothing as his eyes roved over him, and the perusal felt like an actual caress with the way it made Logan's dick throb. Then Tate moved the shirt aside to reveal his shorts were unzipped and pushed down enough that his flushed cock was on display, pointing up toward its owner.

He's been using my shirt to get himself off? That perverted fucker. God, I love him.

"Jesus, Tate," Logan said, fisting his own dick as he took a step closer like he was hypnotized, and when Tate raised the shirt to his nose and inhaled what Logan could only imagine was *his* cologne and Tate's pre-cum, he almost lost it.

Fuck, that's hot. So. Fucking. Hot.

Logan aimed his eyes down at Tate's erection and said, bold as ever, "I want that."

Tate tossed the shirt aside, wrapped his fingers around his length, and stroked. "Where?"

Logan raised his eyes to Tate's and managed, "Huh?"

"I said, *where* do you want it?"

Logan swallowed at the ragged tone of Tate's voice. "Anyfuckingwhere you want to put it."

"That's a generous offer."

"What can I say," Logan said, as Tate spread his legs so he could step between them. "I'm in a very generous mood."

Tate punched his hips up, shoving his cock through his fist, then aimed a filthy look up at Logan. "Glad to hear it. 'Cause I'm in a bit of a selfish mood, and I feel like using you—all night."

Fine by me. Logan dropped to his knees and placed his hands on Tate's upper thighs as he peered up at the man who seemed determined to drive him crazy. "Start with my mouth," Logan suggested, reveling in the switch of roles, enjoying the game he knew they were about to engage in and both win. And when Tate released his straining length to reach for the back of his wet hair, Logan grunted at the fingers spearing through the strands.

With Tate's eyes locked on his, Logan waited for whatever instruction he was about to issue next, and, as always, Tate didn't back down. He told Logan exactly what he wanted, and hell if Logan didn't get off on knowing he'd been the one to teach Tate exactly what that was over the past four years.

"I want to feel the back of your throat against the head of my cock. And I want to see that feral fucking look that hits your eyes when you do it."

God. Damn. It. There was something to be said for finding your exact equal when it came to sex. Logan had always known he was a deviant. He'd always been curious by nature and open to trying anything to get as close as possible to the person he was with. But then Tate had come along, and that need to be one with another had been ratcheted up about one thousand times.

There wasn't anything he wouldn't try with Tate, nothing he wouldn't do to please him, and while that may seem crazy under normal circumstances, the absolute need and compatibility they shared was so in tune with one another's desires that Logan never once questioned it. He merely accepted it as part of who they were.

Tate tugged on his hair, and Logan didn't need any more urging to move than that. He was up on his knees and tracing his tongue along the veiny underside of Tate's length, and the guttural sound that filled the air had Logan dipping his head down to do it again. Tate's fingers flexed, and when they twisted so he could direct Logan exactly where he wanted him, Logan moved one of his hands from the thigh he was braced on and used it to shove Tate's shirt out of his way.

As he swirled his tongue around the glistening tip of Tate's cock, Logan dug his other fingers into the thigh under his palm, and then he opened his mouth and swallowed Tate to the back of his throat.

"*Jesus*. Logan," Tate growled, but Logan didn't let up. He'd been given an order, and hell if he wasn't about to follow it. He moved his lips up and down, and then aimed his eyes at Tate per the request, and without him having to say a word, Tate got the message. He thrust his hips up, shoving between Logan's lips to the back of his throat, and Logan was in danger of coming without one touch to his aching dick.

Tate's Adam's apple bobbed and his jaw clenched, and the physical reaction followed by a curse had Logan repeating the move until Tate's head fell back against the cushion and he was pumping his hips up and down.

Logan shut his eyes and continued to suck, enjoying the salty taste hitting his tongue until he knew Tate was precariously close to not being able to hold back, then he removed his lips and looked up at the man he knew he would never get enough of.

With his white shirt unbuttoned midway down his chest, Tate's tanned skin peeked through. The bottom of the material was crumpled to shit after the way Logan had been fisting it, and was shoved aside to reveal Tate's open shorts and plump cock, now wet and slick from Logan's mouth. His hair was all over the place, and Tate's lips looked swollen from where he'd been biting on them to hold back his groans.

Damn, he's a sight, Logan thought as he sat back and clamped a fist around his cock, trying to calm himself.

As Tate's eyes slowly opened, his lips parted and he slicked the tip of his tongue over the top one, and Logan thought he'd just about die if he couldn't kiss him in the next few seconds. Then Tate scooted to the edge of the couch and raised a hand. He crooked his finger at him, and in an instant Logan was on his feet and stepping forward.

Logan's cock jutted out toward Tate, who took his

hips between his hands and guided him as close as he could get him. It was Logan's turn now to push his fingers through Tate's hair as he pressed a kiss to his right hip.

"Tonight," Tate said, his warm breath ghosting over Logan's taut skin, "I want you in my lap." When Tate found and held his stare, the depraved glint that entered his eyes made Logan swallow. "I want to watch your face when your ass swallows my cock and you ride me."

"Shit," Logan said. "You're really asking for it to—"

Tate chose that moment to suck the tip of Logan's erection, making him forget the word he'd been about to say.

A rush of air left Logan's lips, as Tate then released him and sat back on the couch with a smirk so he could shove his shorts off. Once they were gone and he was left naked from the waist down, Logan was on him in a heartbeat, moving to straddle his lap.

As his knees flanked either side of Tate's hips, Logan's bare ass rested on those strong thighs he'd been hanging on to earlier, and he reached for the couple of buttons left holding Tate's shirt together. Once he had them undone, he parted the material and ran his fingers down Tate's chest and abs to where that phenomenal cock was being worked, and with their eyes connected, Logan wrapped his fingers around Tate's and whispered, "Let me."

As Tate removed his hand, Logan replaced it with his own, then leaned in and gently nipped at Tate's jaw. "You better get your fingers in me soon, Tate, if you want tonight to happen in the order you specified."

Tate's hands smoothed up Logan's sides and then back down to cup his ass, and with a rough tug, he brought Logan's body flush to him.

"Bossy fuck," Tate said.

"As if you're not," Logan said. "You want it as bad as I do. Your cock is making a fucking mess all over my hand." Then he brought his fingers up and licked them clean, before taking hold of Tate's chin and claiming his mouth in a fierce and filthy kiss.

Chapter Eleven

EVERY SINGLE TIME, Tate thought, as he tightened his hold on Logan's hips. *He destroys any control I have. Every. Single. Time.* Logan was just that sexy.

As Tate parted his lips and Logan slid his tongue inside, the tangy taste of his own cum had him moaning. Logan was gloriously naked as he sat astride him, and there was something about having him totally uninhibited and out of his usually polished getup that was always such a turn-on. He was rolling his hips in a rhythm that was utterly mind-blowing, and that was one of the main reasons Tate *loved* taking him like this. The man had hips that could move in the most sinful way, and there was nothing more erotic than when he did it while Tate's cock was buried inside him.

Tate brought one of his hands down between them to wrap it around both their erections, and Logan was right about the mess they were making, but it wasn't only him. Logan's cock was leaving a sticky trail all over the damn place with every punch of his hips, and as Tate stroked them both, Logan flattened his hands on his chest and tweaked his nipples.

"Fucking ouch, Logan."

Logan laughed a raspy, sensual laugh and twisted his fingers again, and the bite of pain had Tate clenching his fist around their cocks.

"Oh… Look at that. I think you like that little bit of *ouch*. Get your fingers in me, Tate." Logan panted as he stared down at him, and Tate blindly reached for the lube.

Once he'd poured some into his hand, he wrapped his arm around Logan's waist and slipped his middle finger down between his ass cheeks. Logan pushed back against the probing digit, and when the tip breached his tight hole, he gripped Tate's shoulders and said, "Deeper."

Tate took Logan's lips in a demanding kiss as his finger slid all the way inside and he used his other hand to spread Logan wide.

"*Yes*," Logan said as he ground down over him. "More. Give me more."

Two fingers pushed inside then, and as Logan took them, Tate widened and stretched him, the snug fit of his body a raw, hot promise of what was to come.

Logan kissed the hell out of him as he writhed over his lap, and their cocks made the stickiest mess Tate had seen and felt on either of them in a long time. It was as though they hadn't had sex in months, years, decades…not days. But Logan felt unbelievable in his lap, and judging by the rapt expression on his face, Logan agreed.

"Yes… So *good*…" Logan said against his mouth, as he ran his hands up the back of his neck and pulled on the strands of hair so he could lick a path up Tate's Adam's apple. "God, Tate. Get *in* me."

The demand was followed by Logan kissing his way down his neck as he shoved his shirt as far out of the way as he could manage. Tate slowly removed his fingers and grabbed the lube, coating his palm so he could reach between them and slick up his cock while Logan continued to suck and kiss the base of his throat until a biting sting hit and Tate knew that Logan had just left a goddamn bruise.

As Logan tongued the spot he'd just marked, the sound he made was somewhere in the middle of a growl and a snarl, and so fucking possessive that Tate's climax raced to his balls and took a tight hold of them.

He'd wanted Logan like this tonight. Wild. Untamed. And thinking only about how to get that next release. It was hot. It was arousing. And when Logan raised his head and aimed a savage smile his way… *Yeah, he almost made me come.*

"So," Logan said, as Tate smoothed his hands down his sides to the small of his back. He dipped his fingers between Logan's ass cheeks, and when Logan bucked forward, Tate let free his own grin. "How do you plan to *use* me first?"

Tate spread Logan apart and urged him up on his knees, then he took hold of his cock and aimed his eyes up at the devilish blue ones looking down at him. "Sit."

With his hands braced on Tate's shoulders, Logan slowly lowered himself until—*fuck me*—he settled down over the top of him. Tate reveled in the sensation of Logan's ass swallowing him to the root, and once he was fully seated, he said, "You're going to ride me."

* * *

TATE'S STARE WAS direct and full of arrogance, and it made Logan's entire body feel alive. Tate looked like he wanted to pound him into next week, and if the sharp punch of his hips was any indication, Logan was right.

Sprawled back on their couch like some kind of corrupt king, Tate's eyes were stormy, his mouth pure sin, and his shirt was shoved off his torso as Logan sat naked astride his pulsating cock.

"I am, am I?" Logan said, and his voice was so hoarse it sounded as though it was being scraped over sandpaper. Tate lowered his eyes over everything on display for him, and then shifted his hips a little as Logan took one of his hands from Tate's shoulder and grabbed a fistful of his hair.

"Yes," Tate said, and Logan noted the tic in his cheek, as though he were trying to hold himself back.

"How do you want it?" Logan said as he slowly rolled his hips.

Tate's fingers dug into Logan's waist, and his lips pulled tight as he tried to keep a handle on himself.

"You want it nice and slow?" Logan asked, and then

leaned forward and said against Tate's mouth, "Or do you want it hard and fast?"

Tate's eyes narrowed and he sat up slightly, causing his erection to bump against Logan's prostate.

"*Fuck*," Logan said, and Tate let out a low chuckle.

"I don't care how you do it. I just want to watch you drive yourself crazy on my dick."

Logan put both palms on Tate's hairless chest and shoved him back into the couch—done sitting idle. "That's what you wanted all along, isn't it?"

"Mhmm," Tate agreed as his hands plumped Logan's ass, rocking him gently. "But you get extra defiant when you're told what to do, so I was just priming you."

"You fucking tease."

"Call me what you want. But for God's sake—" Tate never finished his thought, though, because Logan moved his hips over the top of his, causing him to drop his head back to the couch and moan.

"Oh fuck yes. Like *that*, Logan," Tate said, and then Logan fisted his hair and yanked him forward so he could take his mouth in a blistering kiss.

He could feel Tate's fingers slipping between his ass cheeks as he guided him up and down, and Logan reveled in the way Tate controlled his movements but left the pace and everything else up to him.

So he wants to watch, does he? Logan thought, as he placed both of his hands behind himself, bracing them on

Tate's knees. And the view he offered Tate then was as explicit as it was sensual. *Then I'll give him a show.*

His body was bowed back, his neck arched, and as he rode the steely length inside him, Logan couldn't get enough of it. Tate's hands were traveling all over his hips and thighs, and then finally he started to stroke him as he moved on top of him, and the act, position, and feelings flooding Logan were so fucking intense that he had to shut his eyes for a moment so he wouldn't come.

"Logan… *Christ*, you're sexy," Tate said, causing Logan to open his eyes and focus on the man he was losing his mind over.

When their stares collided, there was no way Logan could stay where he was. He needed to get closer to all of that. Shifting on the thighs he was balanced on, Logan leaned forward and placed his hands on the back of the couch on either side of Tate, and once he had a firm grip, he really started to move.

His ass surrounded the hard length inside it like a glove every time he rose and then settled back down. It felt unreal, and when Tate sank his teeth into his shoulder, Logan reached down with his hand and clamped a fist around his cock.

"*Yes*," Tate growled against his neck. "Goddamn. So fucking hot, Logan. Do it. Let me watch you."

Logan frantically worked himself as his hips and ass moved over and around Tate. He lowered his forehead to

Tate's as his breathing came in rough pants, but it wasn't until Tate said, "Come on me," that Logan lost it.

Tate jammed his hips up, once, twice, and Logan's orgasm hit him with the impact of a train. It slammed into him and he grabbed Tate's shoulder as he came all over his own hand and Tate's stomach, his ass clenching around the rigid length still lodged deep.

Before he could think about that, though, Tate was on the move. With a hand on his ass and back, he had Logan laid out flat on the couch and was over and in him with no time to spare. Several curls flopped forward on Tate's sweaty forehead as he began to tunnel into him, and Logan wrapped his legs around Tate's naked ass and held on.

This wasn't going to take long at all, and, feeling the devil on his shoulder, Logan swiped his fingers over the mess on Tate's stomach and then brought his fingers to Tate's mouth, *and yeah*...that dirty fucker sucked them inside. Tate's eyes darkened as Logan licked his lips, and then he threw his head back and shouted as he came hard, calling out Logan's name.

Logan *loved* when the two of them were together like this. Rough, hard, and raw. It was passionate and sensual all at once. And with Tate, it was everything.

Several minutes later, when he could actually find the energy to speak, he ran a hand over Tate's hair and said, "I think it's safe to say we were both well used tonight. Don't you think?"

Tate raised his head and grinned, and Logan couldn't help but reciprocate.

"I think so," Tate said. "I think it's also safe to say I am now very, *very* happy."

Logan laughed at the reminder of that earlier conversation, and kissed him. "You are, aren't you?"

"Happy?"

"Yes."

"More than I ever thought possible."

Logan ran a finger over the mark he'd left on Tate's neck and sighed. "Good. You'd tell me if you ever weren't, wouldn't you?"

Tate narrowed his eyes on him. "Of course. You'd tell me too, right? If you weren't happy."

"Yes," Logan said, and then traced Tate's lips with the tip of his finger. "But Tate?"

"Yeah?"

"I think it's physically impossible for me to be around you and *not* be happy." When Tate chuckled and fingered his chest hair, Logan asked, "What's so funny?"

"Nothing. I'm just always amazed that after your mouth has been so unbelievably dirty it can then say the sweetest things."

Logan angled his head to press a kiss to Tate's lips. "I could say the same thing for you. But since we're both so dirty, why don't we go and have a shower before we head to bed?"

Tate climbed off him and held a hand out. "Well, now that I know you're only happy when I'm around, I guess I'm just going to have to go everywhere you go."

Logan took his hand and led him through to their bedroom, saying over his shoulder, "You won't hear any complaints from me on that. But this time around it would make me *extra* happy if you lost the shirt."

As they stepped into the bathroom and Tate's shirt hit the floor, Logan wasn't sure he could think of anything right then that could possibly make the grin on his face any bigger.

Chapter Twelve

"YOUR NINE O'CLOCK is here," Sherry said as Logan looked up from his computer the following morning. He'd been in a particularly *happy* mood when he arrived, and was just catching up on the last-minute notes Sherry had sent him regarding Robbie's cousin.

"Ahh yes, good. All three of them?"

Sherry nodded and glanced at her notepad before smiling. "Yes. I have a Mr. Bianchi, Miss Bianchi, and Mrs. Bianchi."

Logan rolled his eyes. "Thank you, Sherry."

"You're welcome. I'll send them in and hold your calls. Cole also said to remind you that Mr. Priestley will be here at eleven."

"Got it," Logan said as he stood and buttoned his grey pinstripe jacket. "Sherry?"

Sherry paused with her hand on the doorframe and looked over at him. "Yes, Logan?"

Then, quite unexpectedly, he heard himself asking her, "Are you happy here?"

Her eyes widened behind her glasses and then her lips curved. "Well, you're a pretty horrible boss—"

"Sherry," Logan said, coming around his desk and walking over to her, "I'm serious."

She laughed and laid a reassuring hand on his arm. "Yes. I'm very happy here. You're a terrific boss, and you and your brother are wonderful owners. Hard taskmasters, but fair and honest. I love working at Mitchell & Madison. Why?"

Logan patted her hand with his and thought, *Because I'm going to give you a beautiful office and a raise in the foreseeable future. That's why.* "No reason. Just an employee spot check."

She smiled and then turned on her heels to head back to her desk, and Logan pushed open his door to see Robbie heading down the hall with a young lady trailing behind him, and behind *her* was an older woman who Logan presumed was their nonna.

When Robbie reached him, Logan noted the all-black shoes, slacks, and shirt getup, but was unreasonably pleased to see a bright yellow tie today. That hint of flare, that was the old Robbie, and it gave Logan hope that he was still in there under the *Robert* who was apparently mourning his brighter, unique half.

"Mr. Bianchi, it's good to see you again," Logan said, holding his hand out, and there was no hesitation this morning as Robbie shook it. Logan did note, however, that Robbie only briefly met his eyes before glancing over his shoulder.

"You too," he said. "This is Vanessa, my cousin, and my nonna."

Logan looked past Robbie to where the women stood side by side. Vanessa was a petite woman with nondescript brown hair pulled back into a ponytail, and had a grim expression on her face, whereas Nonna was sporting a no-nonsense one, and her hair was styled in a bob, black with hints of silver through it.

"Hello. I'm Logan Mitchell, one of the partners here at Mitchell & Madison. I'd say it's a pleasure to meet you, but I'm guessing you'd rather be anywhere else, am I right?"

When Vanessa gave him a tight smile, Logan stepped back and pushed his door open. "Why don't you come into my office and we can have a chat about what's going on and what options you have, Vanessa."

She nodded, and as they walked by, Logan watched them go until Robbie went to enter and Logan reached out to touch his arm. There was no way he was going to head in there without checking in on Robbie first. And there was also no way he was letting him leave today without finding out why he was acting the way he was acting.

Tate had suggested Logan use the biggest weapon in his arsenal to draw Robbie out—himself. He'd never been able to pass up an opportunity to flirt shamelessly. Robbie's incorrigible nature had always made him such a handful. But that was back then; the man who'd just stopped and looked at Logan still had the dark circles under his eyes and a frown twisting his mouth in place of what had once been a cheeky grin.

"Sorry I didn't come to the bar last week," Robbie quickly said, as though he were about to be yelled at. "I was just tired, and..." He looked away, and Logan wanted to shake him and demand to know what the hell was going on. "And I just fell asleep instead."

"That's okay," Logan said. "You don't owe me anything. And it was probably better you weren't there anyway."

Robbie flinched at that, and Logan realized what he'd said and how it must've sounded. "Oh, I didn't mean that. It's just I got into a bit of a fight on Friday night." Robbie's eyes widened, and when Logan caught his lips twitch, he decided to just keep right on talking. "Yep. Punched someone right in the face, I did."

And that did it. Robbie's lips pulled into a grin and he laughed. "*You* punched someone?"

"Shhh," Logan said, looking across the office to where Robbie's nonna sat with his cousin. "I don't want them to think I'm a thug."

Robbie scoffed. "Fat chance of that ever happening. You look like a—"

When he cut himself off, Logan smirked. *Oh yeah...there he is.* Then he tapped a finger to Robbie's yellow tie. "We're going to finish this conversation. But it's nice to see you again, Robbie."

"It's—" Robbie stopped in his correction when Logan pinned him with a challenging look and said, "It's *Robbie*. Now come and sit down, and when we're done you and I are going to have a little talk. Got it?"

The stunned look that flashed across Robbie's face was followed by him taking in a shaky breath. Then he brought a hand up to his chest as he let it out and said, "Okay, that was super hot."

Logan schooled his expression to serious and glanced over at the two waiting for them. "You better get over there. We've got a lot to discuss."

The keen way Robbie nodded told Logan exactly what he needed to know. His tone had done what he'd intended it to, and hopefully after he was done helping the Bianchis as a whole, he could go ahead and help the one Bianchi he feared didn't even realize he needed helping.

* * *

TATE CLICKED OPEN the seventh response to his ad the following morning, and read over the person's name, past experience, and references, and then clicked it shut with a sigh.

Who am I kidding? It was going to be impossible to replace Amelia. He'd known that as soon as she'd told him she was handing in her resignation. Sitting back in the corner booth, he stared at the four other applications waiting for him and knew he had to call at least a handful and check them out. The problem was that no one was going to work with him as well as Amelia did. He'd known her ever since their days at After Hours. She knew Logan. She knew *them*. And the idea of not only having to train someone but also tread around social niceties, as he tried to ascertain if someone had an issue with his lifestyle choices, was enough to give him a fucking headache.

Really, it shouldn't even be an issue. But if Friday night, and the fight, had been good for anything, it was as a wake-up call that there were still a bunch of bigoted assholes out there that had no problem spewing their garbage to whoever would listen, and there was no way he would put up with anyone feeling uncomfortable in his place of business. No matter who they were.

He was about to go ahead and open the next application when his cell phone started buzzing on the table. Tate picked it up, and when he saw it was his dad he smiled, hit accept, and brought the cell to his ear.

"Hey there, old man."

"Tate?" his father said. "I'm sorry to bother you at work. I thought I'd get your voicemail."

"No. No bother. I'm not open or anything, just going through some job applications."

"Oh, hiring, huh? Business must be good."

"Business is great. But my manager is actually leaving. So..."

"Gotcha. Gotcha. Well, listen, I was just wondering if you boys would like to come over here this weekend for dinner."

Tate was about to accept, but then he remembered they were looking after Thomas and Lila. "Actually, we're busy Saturday looking after the kids for Cole and Rachel. But we're free Sunday, after they get picked up. We're skipping dinner at their house until the week after."

"Sure. That sounds good. Sunday works. I know you both have to work Monday, so do you want to come for lunch?"

Tate remembered a time when it was just a given he'd be showing up at his childhood home on Sunday to go to church and then have lunch. But that was a long time ago, and the family that had once lived in that home no longer existed. Now he called before he drove over there. Just in case.

"Lunch sounds good. I'll double-check with Logan, but as long as the kiddos are picked up, we'll head that way."

"Perfect. And tell Logan I've got a bottle of Widow Jane with his name on it."

"In other words, I'm going to be driving us home."

"I'll let you two work that out, but both of you need to try this. I know how Logan likes the pricey stuff."

"As opposed to me, who likes it cheap? Thanks. And just so you know, Logan will swallow any of the boys, Jack or Jim. His words, not mine."

"That sounds like him," Tate's dad said, and let out a rumbling laugh.

Tate chuckled; having actually tried Widow Jane before, he knew it was an exceptional bourbon, one that Logan would love. "Where'd you get that from?"

"Won it at a game of golf."

"Oh, wow. Congratulations, then. And I'll let him know. And we'll see you on Sunday."

"See you then, son," his dad said, and ended the call.

Tate smiled as he stared at the computer and clicked open the next job application, thinking that if his father could come around and accept him and Logan, and even come to love and respect the man his son had chosen to live with and share his life, then why the hell should he be worried about interviewing some random strangers? If they had a problem, then they could show themselves out the door. It had been his motto thus far and worked out just fine, and there was no reason to change it now.

* * *

"SO, WHAT YOU'RE saying is you won't take the case?" Nonna Bianchi—whose name was actually Cheryl—said.

Logan steepled his fingers over the notepad sitting on his desk and looked over the points he'd jotted down about the case. It didn't look good for Vanessa. No matter which way he played this out in his mind, the girl was going to do time. The only question was how much.

"No, that's not what I'm saying," Logan said, raising his eyes to meet Cheryl's. Robbie and Vanessa's nonna was a tough lady. That was one of the first things Logan had noted about her as she'd drilled him for facts about the case, himself, and his success rate. She was a pull-no-punches, straight-to-the-point kind of woman, which meant he needed to give this to her straight up. No bullshit. Even though he knew it was going to be tough to hear.

"What I'm saying is it doesn't look good." Logan glanced at Vanessa, who was twisting her hands in her lap as she stared at him with guileless eyes. Sitting there in her floral print dress and Mary Janes, he couldn't actually believe that this girl—*because that's what she is, nothing but a girl*—was up on charges of possession with intent to distribute. "The prosecutor is going to come after you to serve time for this. So you aren't going to get off without some jail time."

"Jail?" Vanessa said, and her eyes flew to Cheryl. Robbie reached over to take one of his cousin's hands. "I can't go to jail."

Logan rubbed his chin as he looked between the two women. "I'm going to be brutally honest with you. That okay?"

"Please," Cheryl said, and placed a hand over Robbie and Vanessa's.

"The fact that they found you with the drugs in hand—"

"They weren't mine," Vanessa said, and Logan nodded.

"I believe you. But the cops, they go by what they saw. And they saw you holding the drugs."

Vanessa's eyes welled and she brought her hands up to her face, shaking it from side to side. "This isn't fair. I was just trying to hide it so Nonna wouldn't get in trouble for something Jared did."

"Oh baby," Cheryl said, and wrapped an arm around Vanessa's shoulders.

Logan got up from behind his desk and his eyes met Robbie, who looked terrified, and with good reason—his cousin was looking at a tough road ahead. Logan then came around to where the three of them sat and crouched in front of Vanessa. "I'm not going to lie to you. You're in a lot of trouble here. And while I know Robbie brought your case to me, I actually think you would have a much better chance in one of my colleague's hands."

"What do you mean?" Vanessa said. "You won't be doing it? Oh my God, you think I did it."

"No," Logan said, and reached for her hands. "I actually don't. Which is *why* I want you to meet with this other lawyer."

"Logan?" Robbie said, and Logan looked over at him. "Is it the money? Because I'm sure I could—"

Logan shook his head adamantly. "Not at all. As much as it pains me to say this, my colleague is much more qualified at cases such as this, and he's going to be the one who gives you the best chance at a minimal sentence."

Vanessa sucked in a breath and clamped a hand over her mouth.

"How long are we talking here, Mr. Mitchell?" Cheryl asked.

"It's hard to tell in situations like this. It helps that Vanessa has no priors. But she's seventeen, which means if she doesn't take whatever offer the prosecutor gives—"

"You mean say that I'm guilty?" Vanessa whispered.

"Yes."

"But I'm not," she said, and Logan tightened his hands over hers.

"I know. I believe you. But if you say that and this goes to court and the jury *doesn't* believe you, you're looking at a mandatory sentence here."

"And what's that?" Cheryl asked.

"For fourteen grams? Anywhere from four to fifteen years."

"Oh my God," Robbie said in a voice rife with disbelief.

Logan swallowed and got to his feet. This was a lot to take in, he knew that, and he wanted to give them the time they needed. But before he even got two steps away, he heard Cheryl ask, "What would you do?"

Logan leaned back on the desk and looked at all three of them. "I'd plead guilty. You'll likely be offered a deal of about a year, but get out in nine months for good behavior."

"A year?" Vanessa said. "In *jail?*"

"It's better than the alternative," Logan said.

"But I didn't do it."

"Which is why risking this and not taking a deal would be a huge gamble."

"Mr. Mitchell," Cheryl said, and Logan looked over at her. "This colleague of yours. Is he good?"

Logan thought of the man who was due to meet with him and Cole at eleven, and nodded. "Yes. He's the best in his area of expertise. In fact, I'm about to meet with him today and would like to present your case to him. If you say yes, that is."

"So you wouldn't be involved at all?" Robbie asked.

"I'd follow closely and be there if any of you have any questions."

The three of them looked at one another, and Logan headed back behind his desk to give them a moment of privacy. Once he was seated and looked back at them, Cheryl nodded.

"Okay. Robbie trusts you, and it sounds like you know what you're talking about. Do you think he'll meet with us? This colleague of yours?"

Logan offered up his most encouraging smile. "I do.

Let me talk with him today and then we'll set something up as soon as possible."

The three of them got to their feet, and Logan did also so he could shake Cheryl's hand.

"It was lovely to meet you, even under the circumstances," she said, and Logan agreed. Robbie had a wonderful family who were obviously supportive of one another. It was such a shame they were caught up in a horrible mess of unfortunate circumstances.

"It was a pleasure to meet you too. I'll have Sherry call you by this afternoon with more information."

"Thank you," Vanessa said, even as tears rolled down her cheeks. She looked terrified, and Logan couldn't blame her. What she was facing, it was life changing—and not in a good way.

"Robbie, are you coming home with us?" Cheryl asked, and when Logan looked in his direction, Robbie glanced over at the older woman and shook his head.

"No. I'm…I'm going to catch up with Logan for a minute, and then I'm meeting someone for lunch."

"Oh, okay," Cheryl said, and put a hand to Vanessa's back. "Thank you again, Mr. Mitchell. We'll wait to hear from you."

"It's my pleasure. And please don't hesitate to call if you have any questions."

"We won't," she said, and a few minutes later they were out the door and Logan found himself staring across his desk at Robbie, who'd retaken his seat and was looking everywhere but at him.

Right, time to get to the bottom of this little mystery, he thought, as he came around his desk to Robbie and the seat that had been vacated by his cousin. When he stopped there, Robbie looked up at him, and Logan narrowed his eyes before slowly unbuttoning his jacket and taking a seat. He saw the way Robbie took in a breath and slowly exhaled, and again thought of how astute Tate had been on this particular topic.

"The next time you see him, sit him down, and make *him listen to you. I guarantee the second your attention is focused on him and* you're *asking him questions, he will tell you anything you want to know."*

Well, it was time to treat Robert the way *Robbie* was used to being treated. Not with caution and curiosity.

"So, do you have any questions about what I said in here today?" Logan asked, making sure he had Robbie's attention before he moved on to topics unrelated to his cousin.

Robbie looked over at him, and Logan angled himself in his seat so he was facing Robbie and crossed one of his legs over the other, and yeah, Robbie's eyes lowered to follow the move.

"Robbie?" Logan said in the most assertive voice he could muster. Robbie's eyes flew up to his face, and Logan made sure to keep his expression neutral. "Any questions about your cousin?"

Robbie shook his head. "No. I mean, I'm worried about her. But I trust you."

"Do you?" Logan asked, knowing this would be the perfect segue into what he wanted to discuss.

"Yes. Of course. That's why I came to you."

"Okay. Then how about you tell me what's going on with you?"

Robbie turned his head away, and before Logan thought about it, he leaned over and took Robbie's chin, bringing his face back around. Robbie's breath hitched and Logan asked again, "What's going on with you?"

Robbie licked his lips, about to say something, but before he could, Logan said, "Don't lie to me."

"You're being bossy all of a sudden," Robbie said, a frown creasing his forehead.

Logan released his chin and sat back. "There isn't anything sudden about that. You of all people should remember how...bossy I can be."

Robbie's eyebrow winged up, haughty and indignant, and right then Logan saw him—the old Robbie.

"Don't tell me you've forgotten. I'll be most disappointed," Logan said, urging Robbie to respond in any form other than skittish and reserved—and then it happened.

Robbie ran his eyes down over him and bit down on his lip as though he were having a most delicious thought or memory. "No one that's spent the night with you would ever forget it. Unless they had a lobotomy, and even then, I'm pretty sure Logan Mitchell *naked* would still be imprinted in their brain forever."

Logan's lips quirked and he ran a hand down over his tie. "Welcome back."

Robbie cocked his head to the side. "Excuse me?"

"I said, welcome back. *That's* the Robbie I remember. The one full of sass. The one blatantly undressing me with his eyes."

"Hey, you're the one who brought it up."

Logan glanced down to Robbie's lap and chuckled. "So I did."

Robbie's mouth parted as though he were in shock, and then...then he started laughing and the sound was, well, wonderful.

Once Robbie calmed down, Logan put a hand on his arm and said, "Hey, talk to me, would you? I'm worried about you."

"*You're* worried about me? Why?" Robbie asked.

"I don't know. You're acting different. You look worried. Tired—"

"Gee, thanks. What every man wants to hear from someone like you."

"Robbie..."

Robbie took in a deep breath and then sighed, letting it out on a rush. "Okay. Okay. I've just had a rough month.

That's all."

Logan contemplated him and said, "Rough how?"

"Just a lot of things happening at once," Robbie said. "Things I can't control."

"Such as…"

Robbie got to his feet, and Logan decided to stay put as he started to pace back and forth.

"My boyfriend broke up with me—"

Oh great, Logan thought. If this was all over some dumbass breaking Robbie's heart, he was so out. He was not the one to counsel someone on things like that.

"Then I lost my job because, of course, he was my boss." Robbie gave a self-deprecating laugh and shook his head. "And because I had no money coming in, I got behind in rent and got kicked out of my apartment and had to move in with my nonna. My life is a fucking joke, and now I don't even recognize myself when I look in the mirror."

"Wait a second," Logan said, getting to his feet and slipping his hands into his pockets. "You were sleeping with your boss? Robbie, Robbie. You don't do that because then shit like this happens when it ends."

"Yeah? Well, he didn't seem to have a problem with it until everyone found out."

"What do you mean?" Logan said.

"What I mean is, Nathan was fine screwing me at night as long as no one knew he was getting blown by the out-and-proud, over-the-top Robbie Bianchi who ran his restaurant during the day."

As Logan stared at Robbie, an uneasy feeling started to settle in his gut. If there was one thing Logan hated, it was closeted assholes who thought it was okay to disparage those brave enough to be who they were and live their lives. And it appeared that whatever happened with this Nathan had left an indelible impression on this once vibrant young man.

"Robbie..."

"I know. It was stupid of me to get involved with my boss. I get it. But he didn't seem to care about the way I dressed or acted at first."

"But then it started to change?" Logan asked as he looked over the all-black getup—minus the bright tie. "Did he ask you to maybe tone it down a little?"

"Yeah," Robbie said, sounding so defeated it made Logan want to find Nathan and— "So I thought maybe if I went with the natural hair color and less flashy clothes that maybe he'd take me back. But I guess he didn't like this look either."

"Then that's his fucking loss," Logan said. "No matter how you looked. This way or the old way. The Robbie I remember was fun and outgoing." When Robbie shrugged, Logan added, "He was also a master at giving head."

Robbie's eyebrow arched at that compliment, and then that cheeky smile of his snuck right back through. "A master, huh? Better than Tate?"

"Nice try," Logan said. "But no one I've met has *ever* given me better head than Tate. And now he's had years, and endless opportunities, to perfect his craft."

"I can't believe you're with the same guy after all this time. You're obviously infatuated," Robbie said, and rolled his eyes.

And it was so like the Robbie he remembered that Logan couldn't stop himself from laughing. "One hundred percent."

"Huh," Robbie said, sizing him up. "I'd almost be jealous if I hadn't sworn off the whole love notion."

"Have you sworn off sex, then?"

"What? No way."

"Then you should be jealous of that too. He's fucking great at it."

Robbie crossed his arms over his chest and pouted. "It's not very nice to gloat."

"You know me, I'm never nice."

"I do remember that. But that's when you're at your best."

"Damn right," Logan said, and then tapped a finger to his chin. "You know what, before you leave, I have an idea. One second."

Logan headed around his desk and picked up his cell phone, and then, hitting the last dialed number, he brought it to his ear and gestured with a tilt of his chin that Robbie should take a seat. Two seconds later, his call was answered. "Good morning, Mr. Morrison."

Robbie's eyes widened; he was obviously cluing in to who Logan had just called. But Logan merely smiled at Robbie and took his own seat, rocking back behind the desk as he listened to Tate's reply.

"Hmm. You're right. I'm sorry," Logan said, though he was anything but. "Remind me again tonight, and we'll see if I can make it up to you. But before you continue to distract me, I called for a reason. I have a question for you." There was a pause, and Robbie frowned, but Logan just continued to aim a knowing smile his way.

Two things had become crystal clear in the last five minutes. The first being that Robbie had clearly been affected by whatever that asshole had said to him during the breakup, judging by his radically altered outward appearance. And the second was that Logan just might have a solution to at least two of Robbie's problems. "Are you still interviewing for that position of yours?"

Chapter Thirteen

IT HAD JUST turned eleven when the door to The Popped Cherry opened and Tate looked over his shoulder from where he sat at the bar. He didn't usually unlock the front doors until opening time, but Logan had told him he was sending someone his way for an interview. However, the man in all black who'd just stepped inside the front door didn't look as though he knew he was expected. In fact, he looked as though he thought he was in the wrong place.

"Can I help you?" Tate said, sliding off his stool, and as he walked around several tables to get closer, the face he was staring at came into sharper focus and he knew immediately who was standing in front of him. *I'm going to kill Logan.* "Robbie."

The guy with the brown hair and face devoid of any kohl or makeup barely resembled the barista Tate remembered, and the fidgety way he twisted his hands had Tate reining in his impulse to call Logan and kick his ass.

Logan had been right. Robbie not only looked different, his entire demeanor was...off.

"Tate," Robbie said, taking a tentative step forward, so Tate took the three steps up to the entryway and held his hand out in greeting.

"I knew Logan had a meeting with you this morning, but didn't realize you were who he was sending over here."

Robbie took his hand, and Tate shook it firmly, unable to stop staring at the stranger opposite him. *Okay, he really does look* totally *different.*

"Yeah," Robbie said, and then gave an awkward laugh as he shoved his hands back into the pockets of his skintight pants. "Surprise."

Tate crossed his arms and smirked. "Surprise is right. It's been—"

"Years?"

"Yeah, it has been," Tate said with a nod, and then turned to head down into the main bar area. As Robbie followed, Tate glanced over his shoulder and said, "I think the last time we saw you I'd just gotten out of the hospital, right?"

Robbie grimaced and looked at Tate's arm. "Yeah, that's right. You broke your arm."

"Collarbone," Tate said as he directed them over to his favored booth. "That was a long time ago."

"Sure was," Robbie said as he looked around the place. "Wow, I can't believe you own this place. Well, you and Logan. I can't believe that either. I've actually been in here a couple of times. It's a great bar."

"Uhh, thanks. We like it," Tate said, as he slid into one side of the black leather booth and Robbie did the same on the opposite side.

As they settled in, Tate took a second to really study Robbie, and just like Logan, he could barely connect him with the little shit he'd met when he first started dating Logan. He seemed tense, a little nervous, and, except for the flashy tie, quite somber. It was a radical transformation.

Tate waited until Robbie had finished checking out the place, and when his eyes landed back on Tate, he gave a half-smile and said, "You haven't changed at all."

"Really?" Tate said, and chuckled. "I was just thinking the opposite of you."

"Yeah, Logan said the same thing. Just a little subtler these days."

"You? Subtle?" That really had Tate laughing. "Yeah, right. Maybe your appearance is a little less...out there. But I find it hard to believe the Robbie I used to know isn't still in there somewhere."

"And who's the Robbie you *used* to know?"

Tate rested an arm on the table and contemplated him carefully. "A man who flat out asked me if I topped or bottomed when I was just learning what the hell that even meant."

Finally, a mischievous grin hit Robbie's lips and his eyes lit up. "And now that you know?"

"You will still *never* find out."

"Fine, fine. Keep your secrets," Robbie said, and Tate had to admit that he much preferred this Robbie to the stranger who'd entered the bar.

This Robbie was a little more familiar. This Robbie he could handle. And he was determined to try and keep him talking. "So, Logan tells me you're looking for a job."

"Yeah, umm, kind of."

"Kind of?" Tate said.

"No. What I mean is, yes, I am. I just didn't go to him expecting this. But he was all, you know, Mr. Sophistication in his big, shiny office, and basically demanded to know what was wrong with me, and before I knew it, I was telling him about the horrible month I had and he was ordering me down here to apply for a job. If you think I'm qualified, that is."

Tate's lips twitched at the accurate description of Logan. He knew how it felt to be intimidated by the man's looks, money, and wit, and for that he almost felt sorry for Robbie—almost.

The thing was, he was the one who'd told Logan to go all alpha on Robbie, and apparently it had worked, because the guy currently seemed to be lost in his own thoughts. No doubt remembering how Logan had looked in that "shiny office" of his. *Potent bastard. Even miles away, Logan is still in the room with us.*

"Well, how about you tell me a little bit about yourself," Tate said. "What have you been doing these past few years? What jobs? And are you even interested in a managerial position at a bar?"

Robbie's eyes widened and he sat up in the chair as though he'd been goosed in the ass. "Managerial?"

"Yes," Tate said. "That's the position. I need a full-time manager. Someone who can run the bar when I'm not here. Someone who's willing to close during the week and every other weekend."

Robbie looked around again, and then back at Tate. "I'd manage The Popped Cherry? And work with you?"

"And sometimes Logan," Tate said, throwing out what he knew would be the biggest draw for Robbie. "If you get the job."

Robbie nodded, a determined smile now stretching across his lips. "Okay," he said, placing his hands on the table and clasping them together. "Ask me anything you want to know, and I'll tell you."

* * *

"I'M HERE TO give my confession," Logan said as he pushed open the door to Cole's office and walked inside.

As his brother looked up at him, the other occupant in the room, a man with rich auburn hair who was seated across from Cole's desk, said, "I'm only here for a week this time round, Mitchell. Your confession would take a hell of a lot longer than that."

Logan strode into the office, as Joel Priestley, a.k.a. Priest, got to his feet and extended a hand. Logan took it, shaking it firmly as he clapped the other man on the back. "And here I thought I was going to be free and absolved of everything I did last night."

Priest scoffed. "As I said, I only have a week."

"How've you been?" Logan asked as he moved to sit in the free seat.

"Good. No complaints. The flight was smooth, the bourbon they served not so much."

Cole chuckled. "You flew out here at the crack of dawn. Long night?"

"You don't even want to know," Priest said. "I can't remember the last time I lay down in an actual bed."

"And you think my confession would take time," Logan said, as a knock sounded on the door.

"Ahh, Jane," Cole said as he smiled at his PA. "If you could please bring us some coffee? Black, I think is what's needed."

"Of course, Mr. Madison. Anything else?"

"Only the usual, Jane," Cole said, referring to her use of his first name. But as always, she merely smiled and said, "Never, Mr. Madison. I'll be right back."

As the door shut behind her, Cole sat back in his chair and twirled his pen around his fingers as he sized Priest up. Logan was doing much the same.

They'd been in talks with the Los Angeles-based criminal defense lawyer for a few months now. He currently worked for a very reputable firm and had one of the best track records of acquittals in the country this year. That was quite the accomplishment for someone so young, and the fact that Mitchell & Madison had worked closely with him for some time made them a great option for him to...spread his wings, so to say. Not to mention it would also be a strong *get* for them. Having Priest on board would be a prudent call.

"As you know from our previous conversations," Logan said, "Cole and I are looking to expand the firm."

Priest looked between them with his shrewd grey eyes, and then nodded. "That was my understanding, yes."

"With the Berivax win," Cole went on, "we're in a position to do so now with less chance of—"

"Failure?" Priest suggested.

"Such an optimist," Logan said, clasping his hands over his stomach.

"A realist," Priest said in a cool, factual tone. "Most law firms can't handle a large expansion in this economy. But I've been researching you two and your firm, and I agree. You're in a prime position to do this. It's a smart move for you. *I'm* a smart move for you. But I won't uproot my whole life for anything less than partner."

No one could ever accuse Joel Priestley of lacking confidence, that was for sure. But that was one of the things that Logan and Cole admired about the guy. He was younger than they were by a few years. But that was what they wanted. Someone who was fresh. Someone who was confident. And someone who knew the law inside out. They wanted a lawyer who was hungry for it. And Joel? He was starving.

Logan narrowed his eyes on Priest's profile, trying to gauge whether he'd break under both his and Cole's scrutiny, but he didn't flinch. He didn't look away from Cole once, and Cole had one of the best poker faces around.

Joel Priestley was like a pillar of fucking granite.

"You say you're a smart move for us. How so?" Logan asked.

Priest looked over at him, his grey eyes hard as the stone he resembled, and the tight smile he gave was smug. "You and your brother aren't stupid."

"Thank you," Logan said with an equally conceited smile.

"You would have done your research, your vetting. Ninety percent of my clients will stay with me even long distance. That means I'll bring to your firm quite a bit of business. Not to mention I've got an incredible record—"

"And are clearly modest," Cole interjected, and Priest looked at him.

"You don't want modest. You want a sure thing. I am that sure thing."

Logan slowly nodded as he glanced over at Cole, whose expression was inscrutable. They already knew what they wanted the outcome of this week with Priestley to be. But they'd also agreed they wanted to see him in action, so that was what had to happen next.

"Okay," Logan said, and waited until he had Priest's attention again. "I have a case for you while you're here. It might take a little longer than a week, though. Would that be a problem?"

"No. I'll call the office and tell them I'm taking some of the leave owed me."

"Very good," Logan said. "Like I said, I'd like you to take this case on, and I'll be there if you need anything. If you're a sure thing, then this should be a walk in the park."

At least I hope so, Logan thought, as he remembered Vanessa's tear-streaked face.

"Then let's walk," Priest said with a clipped nod. "Show me the files, give me an office, and I'll get to work."

As Logan got to his feet, Cole and Priest followed suit. They each shook hands, and then Logan said, "I hope for your sake you're right. Because this girl refuses to plead guilty and she's innocent. I can feel it in my bones. And she's looking at years."

Priest didn't flinch. Didn't show one iota of concern. Actually, not even an ounce of emotion. "Where can I get to work?"

And without any more conversation, Logan led him out of Cole's office and down to the conference room.

* * *

IT WAS CLOSE to midnight when Tate unlocked the front door and headed inside the condo. All of the lights inside were off save for the lamp in the bedroom, and after he tossed his jacket over the couch, he headed straight for the low-lit room and the man he knew he'd find in it.

As he got to the door, he looked inside and expected to find Logan asleep. But instead he was leaning back against the headboard, glasses on, the sheet draped across his waist, a book in hand.

Tate rested his shoulder against the doorjamb as he ran his eyes over the scene that greeted him. "My little book nerd."

Logan looked up and lowered the hardback to rest on his lap. "Little?"

Tate crossed his arms and continued to look Logan over. "Okay, how about my *sexy* book nerd?"

Logan picked up his book, shut it, then set it on the nightstand. "Much better," he said, and whipped the sheet aside, exposing his very naked body. "Now why don't you get undressed and get into bed?"

Unable to ignore such an enticing invitation, Tate pushed off the doorjamb and unbuttoned his vest as Logan's eyes followed his path, and when he was finally over on the left side of the room, Logan began to slowly stroke himself.

Yes…he's definitely sexy. So very, very fucking sexy.

Tate dropped his clothes to the floor as quickly as possible, and once he was between the sheets, he scooted over to Logan's side and replaced his hand with his own. As he leisurely stroked him to full mast, Logan wrapped his arm around Tate's shoulders and pulled him to his side. Tate gently kissed his way up to Logan's ear and asked, "How was your day?"

"Productive," Logan said. "How was yours?"

Tate paused in what he was doing. "Interesting. You made a good call today."

Logan turned his head on the pillow, and Tate grinned over the fact he still wore his glasses. "If this conversation is about to involve the person I think it is, can it happen when your hand is not— *Ahh, fuck.*"

"When it's not what?" Tate whispered against Logan's lips.

"Tate…"

"Hmm?" he said, and then reached for Logan's glasses. He slipped them free of Logan's face and then put them on, pushing them up his nose. "You were saying?"

"Can we talk about *him* when your hand's not wrapped around my cock?"

Tate tightened his grip and kissed him, and when he pulled back, Logan flipped one of his curls away from the thick black rims framing his eyes. "These look good on you."

"Not as good as they look on you. But tonight, I thought they'd help me see better when I get up close and personal with you."

"Then by all means, you should keep them on."

Tate grinned as he worked his way down Logan's body and kissed every inch of skin he could reach. When he finally settled between Logan's legs, he scraped his teeth over his inner thigh and said, "Oh, and don't worry, I don't plan to do any more talking tonight. It's too hard to carry on a conversation when my mouth's full. We'll just leave it at 'I hired him.' And come back to that later."

Logan's head snapped up off the pillow and his eyes widened as he looked down at Tate, but no words came from his mouth. The only sound that emerged was a satisfied groan as Tate sucked his cock between his lips, and then proceeded to get up close and personal with his very sexy book nerd.

Part Two

Family: A group of people related to one another by blood or marriage.

Scratch that...

Family: is love. Family is acceptance.
Family is who you choose to surround yourself with.
And those you can't live without.

Chapter Fourteen

"UNCLE LOGAN? CAN we get ice cream? Can we? Pleeease?"

Logan followed along behind Thomas, who was tugging his hand as he led them up the frozen food aisle and stopped in front of the rows of colorful cartons of ice cream.

Tate was trailing behind with Lila strapped in the shopping cart as they wove their way through the aisles of Mariano's. They'd picked the kids up around forty minutes earlier and decided on the way home they'd brave the grocery store to grab some dinner supplies for the night.

"Hmm…" Logan said, as Thomas let go of his hand and put his palms on the glass door. "What flavor do you like best?"

Thomas glanced back at him with wide eyes and a huge grin. "*All* of them."

Logan chuckled and ruffled his hair. "A man after my own heart. But if you had to pick just one?"

Thomas scrunched his nose up and looked back at the selection in front of him. "I like chocolate."

"That's a good choice," Logan said.

"But I also like strawberry," Thomas said. "Also

when Dad gets vanilla and pours caramel all over it. *That's yummy*."

"Sundaes," Tate said as he brought the cart to a stop behind the two of them. "I love sundaes. We should do that."

Logan looked back to where Lila was happily chewing on the blueberry puffs Rachel had said were a lifesaver—and so far, she'd been right—then his eyes rose to lock with Tate's, whose were alight with mischief. "Sundaes, huh?"

"Yep," Tate said with a grin. "A tub of vanilla ice cream and every topping you can think of."

"Yesss," Thomas said, and nodded enthusiastically. "Let's do that."

Logan turned back to the fridge and opened the door so Thomas could pick out the ice cream of his choice, and when he picked out the tub with the blue bunny on it, no one was surprised.

With the ice cream in the cart, they headed off down the aisle, Thomas holding the side this time as Logan stepped up beside Tate and lowered his voice. "I'll make sure we circle back around for the nuts. I know they're your favorite part of dessert."

Tate's lips curved into a delicious grin, and then Lila beamed at the two of them and shouted, "Nuts!"

A boisterous laugh escaped Logan before he could stop it, and he took Lila's little cheeks between his hands and smacked a kiss to her lips. "That's exactly right, little miss. Let's go get Uncle Tate some nuts to eat."

Tate rolled his eyes and shoved him in the shoulder as they started off down the aisle again, and Logan winked at him before he jogged forward to grab hold of Thomas's hand. "Okay, mister. What's next?"

"The stuff for the pizzas."

"Yes. Now, remind me what we're having again? Mushrooms?"

Thomas shook his head. "Eww...no."

Logan pursed his lips and directed the group toward the produce area. "What about olives?"

"Yuck. I don't like them either."

"No?" Logan stroked his chin. "Anchovies?"

"Nooo. Uncle Tate doesn't like anchovies."

Logan wagged his finger at him. "You're right. So...what's left?"

"Cheese," Thomas said, aiming his most convincing grin up at Logan.

"Just cheese?"

"Just cheese!"

Logan raised an eyebrow. "Nice try, buddy, but Mom made me promise there'd be something green and something colorful on tonight's pizza. That means veggies."

As they walked into the produce area, Logan headed toward the back wall where there were rows of carrots, celery, Brussels sprouts, peppers, and cucumbers. He picked up a Brussels sprout and showed Thomas. "This is green."

"No way," Thomas said, shaking his head and looking at the other choices. "Not on pizza."

"Not ever," Logan agreed, and tossed it back into the black bin.

Then Thomas picked up a package of red and green bell peppers. "These are *okay.*"

The put-out tone made Logan chuckle, as he dropped the peppers inside the cart. "Yeah, they'll do. What else?"

Thomas turned around and walked past Tate and his sister to the display of potatoes, garlic, turnips, and onions, and picked up a yellow onion. "Dad always puts this on our pizza."

"That works," Logan said as he took the onion. "But it feels like something's missing." He walked over and put the two bags in the cart, and when Thomas was beside him, Logan read off the list. "We have the pizza base, pizza sauce, the veggies, the cheese…what are we missing?"

As Thomas looked over the contents, his face took on a serious expression. "The pepperoni!"

"Right," Tate said. "You can't have pizza without pepperoni."

"Agreed," Logan said, as a blond woman wandered by them and Lila raised a hand to wave her chubby fingers at her.

"Hi," Lila said to the woman, who'd now stopped next to the four of them to wave back at the little girl.

"Hello, sweetheart," she said, and then looked at Tate. "She's just precious."

Tate tickled Lila under the chin and then flashed his heart-stopping smile at the blonde, and Logan was surprised the lady didn't melt into a puddle at his feet with the way her face softened.

"She sure is," Tate said, and Lila, using any excuse in the book she could to be kissed by Tate, plumped her lips and pointed.

"Kiss?"

The lady laughed at the demand. "She sure knows what she wants, too."

"Don't we all," Logan muttered low enough that Tate caught it and glanced his way, but the distracted lady did not.

"What's her name?" the woman asked, finally looking over at him.

"Lila," Logan said, and placed a hand on Thomas's shoulder. "And this here is her big brother, Thomas."

"Hello there, Thomas," the lady said even as Lila started tapping Tate's hand and bouncing in her seat, the blueberry puffs now gone, along with the calm.

"Hello," Thomas said shyly, as he moved into Logan's side.

"Unca Tate. Kiss," Lila demanded again, not shy at all, and pointed with both fingers to her mouth. The lady started laughing, and Tate, knowing he'd never get any peace until he complied, leaned down to kiss Lila, making her squeal.

"Well, I'll let you all get going. I just couldn't help but stop and say how cute these two are."

"We'd agree with you there," Tate said, even as he squeezed Lila's cheek, making her clap her hands. "Have a great day."

"Thank you. You too," she said as she wandered off, but before she turned down her aisle, she glanced back one last time to look at them.

"I swear," Logan said in Tate's ear, "it was bad enough when you used to just flash that smile. Add in a kid, and you're practically irresistible."

"Practically?" Tate said.

Logan scoffed. "Okay...totally."

"That's better," Tate said with a grin, then pointed to his lips. "Kiss?"

Logan leaned in and pressed a quick kiss to his mouth. "Let's go and get the rest of this stuff and head home. Okay. What's left, Mr. Madison?"

"Umm...the syrup and sprinkles for the ice cream," Thomas said, looking up at the both of them.

"Yes. You're right." Logan took Thomas's hand and grinned at him. "Lead the way. We'll follow."

And as they took off toward their next destination, Logan glanced back to make sure Tate was good to go, and he was right behind them smiling down at the little girl who was happily waving at any and all passersby.

* * *

TATE PUSHED THE shopping cart up the aisle behind
Logan and Thomas, and smiled at the picture they made. It
always gave him such a kick to see Logan in this role,
because it was so different to the man he'd met back when
they'd first gotten together.

But, Tate thought, as he looked at the way Thomas
stared up at Logan as though he had all the answers in the
world, it was a role he'd once again mastered. Actually, Tate
wasn't sure there was anything Logan wouldn't be good at if
he put his mind to it.

"Here's the caramel," Logan said, passing a bottle to
Thomas. "And the chocolate and the strawberry."

"And the sprinkles," Thomas said, reaching for a
shaker full of rainbow-colored sprinkles. "Lots and lots of
sprinkles."

"You got it," Logan said. "Why don't you go give
them to Tate? I've got to run around the corner and grab
something, and I'll be right back."

As Logan walked backward to the end of the aisle, he
mouthed *nuts* to Tate and winked, then vanished around the
corner.

Thomas dropped the sprinkles into the cart and then
looked up at Tate and asked, "What else?"

Tate inspected the contents, and as a thought entered his head, he couldn't help his smile. It was an entirely inappropriate thought. "Cherries. We're missing the cherry."

"For on top!" Thomas said.

"That's right. It's not a sundae without a cherry on the top. So, how about we go around and find Logan then track down the—"

"Tate?"

At the sound of his name being said by a woman, Tate took Thomas's hand so he could turn around without worrying he'd run off, and when he spotted who it was standing there in the grocery aisle with him, he tried to say something…anything…but nothing came out.

Jill.

If he weren't seeing her with his own eyes, he wouldn't have believed he was face to face with his sister after all these years. But there she was with her familiar brown eyes and long, wavy hair, taking a tentative step toward him, making him want to back the fuck up.

"I…I thought it was you," she said, stopping when she realized he wasn't smiling, nor was he offering her any kind of greeting. Then her eyes drifted down to Thomas, who had a tight grip on his hand, and then up to Lila, who chose that exact moment to say, "Hi!"

Tate wasn't sure how he was still on his feet when he was close to positive his heart must've just stopped. Because no matter how hard he tried, he was unable to move, and still hadn't said anything.

Jill blinked a couple of times and offered a wobbly
smile to Lila, and then brought her attention back to Tate.

"I can't believe it's really you," she said, and Tate
saw her swallow as though she were nervous, and really,
after four years of no communication, no fucking attempt to
reach out and see how he was, she had reason to be nervous.

Knowing he needed to say something, especially
since he could now feel Thomas's eyes on him, Tate looked
down at the little boy and made himself offer a smile that
was much calmer and reassuring than he felt at that
moment.

Then he looked up at the stranger—*yes, she's a total
stranger to me now*—opposite them. "It really is me." There,
that was better than nothing.

"I saw your hair," she said, halfheartedly pointing at
it, then she caught her lip behind her teeth like she used to
as a kid, and Tate had the insane, and really fucking stupid,
impulse to reach out and comfort her.

She took another step forward and twisted her hands
together. "How have you been? Are these…are these your
children?"

Tate wondered what she would've said or done if
he'd said yes. But he wasn't about to lie, so instead he shook
his head. "No. They're Logan's brother's."

Jill's mouth parted and Tate heard her mutter, "Oh,"
as she nodded. Then she smiled again at Thomas, and Lila

chose that moment to tap him on the arm. "Unca Tate." He glanced over his shoulder at her, and she held her arms up. "Lift."

Tate ran a hand over her hair and said, "In a minute, missy." Then he raised his eyes just in time to see Logan come strolling around the corner. He had a massive smile on his face, a hand in the pocket of his shorts, and he was rattling a can of nuts.

Damn, this is not going to end well.

"Found 'em," Logan said as he reached the end of the cart and tossed them inside, and when Tate didn't immediately respond, Logan frowned. "What's wrong?"

"Ran into someone," Tate said, and gestured with his head behind him.

As Logan looked around his shoulder, Tate saw his eyes narrow and the smile fall from his face, then he muttered, "Shit."

"Shit!" Lila shouted, proudly mimicking Logan. Both of them swung their heads around to the little girl, who grinned at them.

"Oh no. No, Lila," Logan said, shaking a finger in front of her. "You don't say that word."

"That's a bad word," Thomas said. "That's what Mommy says whenever Daddy uses it."

"And she's right. It's a bad, *bad* word," Logan said as he aimed his eyes at Tate. "You okay?"

When Tate nodded, Logan let his eyes wander past

his shoulder to where Jill no doubt still stood. "How about you go deal with her while I try to remove my foot from my mouth over here?"

Tate took in a deep breath and then let go of Thomas's hand before he turned around and made his way back over to where his sister stood.

When he was close enough that he could talk in a lowered voice and not be heard by the kids, Tate said, "Was there something you wanted, Jill?"

She flinched at the cool tone, but Tate wasn't going to feel guilty, not even for a second. Here was a woman who not only rushed his coming out to his mother, but then stood by while she'd disowned him and thrown him out of their home. Throwing him away as if he were nothing more than a piece of garbage.

Not once had Jill tried to reach out to him. Even when he'd been in the hospital, she'd only visited when their mother had come by, and when Tate had finally woken and kicked her from his room, Jill had been nowhere in sight.

He remembered when his father had come to him after that. When he'd shown up at Logan's condo and extended an olive branch. Somewhere in the back of his mind he'd expected to see Jill standing right there beside him. But no, not even after their father had separated from their mom had she bothered with the brother whom she'd once said "disgusted" her.

So, no, he didn't feel guilty for the anger and betrayal he felt in that moment. He felt that those emotions were pretty fucking justified. She'd had countless opportunities to make things right, to come to him, and she hadn't taken one of them.

"Well?" he said, wanting her to either speak or get the hell out of his way. He'd been having such a great day, too. *Jesus, talk about a mood spoiler.*

"I…" She stopped and took in a deep breath, raising her chin so she could face off with him. "I miss you. And when I thought I—when I *saw* you standing there, I knew I had to say something. Even if there was a chance you might ignore me or just keep walking."

He hardened his heart against the automatic softening that was taking place. "And why shouldn't I do either of those two things?"

"Because you're a better person than I am."

"No, I'm not," Tate said, crossing his arms. "If you could read my mind right now, you wouldn't be saying that to me."

Jill went to reach for his arm, but then thought better. "You have every right to hate me—"

"Yes, I do," Tate said.

"I understand."

"Do you? Do you understand why I can't even stand to look at you right now? You made your choice, Jill. You made it four years ago, and so did I. Goodbye," he said, and turned, about to head back to the family waiting for him, but he felt a hand on his upper arm.

He froze with his back to Jill and his eyes locked on Logan's worried ones, then he turned back to see his sister was holding out a card to him. Tate lowered his gaze to see it was a business card, and then looked into eyes that resembled his own.

"This is my business. It has all of my numbers on it. If you ever change your mind, I'd really like a chance to make this right."

Tate thought about just walking away, but something in her eyes had him reaching for the card. As he gripped the small piece of cardboard, she kept a stubborn hold of it, reminding him that the two of them shared that particular trait.

"You seem happy," she said.

"I am."

"I'm glad," she said, and then let go of the card. "I hope you call, Tate. It was good to see you."

Tate said nothing in response to that. He couldn't. He was numb. Instead, he just turned on his heel, forced a smile on his face, and headed back to where Logan stood with the kids.

* * *

THE STRAIN ON Tate's face as he walked back toward him

and the kids made Logan want to wrap his arms around him and tell him that everything was going to be all right. But he could tell from the way Tate was trying to play it off with a bright smile for the children that that was the last thing he wanted right then.

When he came to a stop in front of Lila and lifted her from the shopping cart to blow a raspberry on her cheek, Logan let his eyes slide to the woman still watching her brother.

Jill looked the same as she had four years ago. Maybe a little more mature from the years that had passed, but there was no major difference from the woman Logan last remembered seeing seated on her mother's couch that horrible day Tate had been kicked out of his house. And just as that thought entered his mind, Jill's eyes found his, and Logan had to admire the way she held his stare, because he knew his was full of anger and judgment as he sized her up.

What did she say to him? Logan was dying to ask. But as he finally tore his gaze from hers, he decided he would wait until later. Right now he just wanted to check in with Tate and make sure he was okay. He placed a hand on Tate's lower back and leaned in to kiss his cheek.

"You ready to go?"

When Tate looked at him, Logan could see the hurt swirling in his eyes. But Tate smiled at him and nodded. "Sure am."

"Okay," Logan said with a final glance at the woman

now walking away from the four of them. "But you and I, we'll talk more about this later. Yes?"

Tate leaned in and pressed a kiss to Logan's lips. "Yes." Then he looked down at Thomas and said, "Let's go home. We have pizzas and sundaes to make. Right?"

Thomas pumped a fist in the air and exclaimed, "Right!"

As Logan reluctantly let Tate go, he took Thomas's hand, and a look of silent understanding passed between the two of them.

He would follow Tate's lead on this and push it to the side. But when he was ready, when the reality of what had happened here today found its way through the anger, and the hurt set in, then Logan would be right there ready to catch him.

Chapter Fifteen

AFTER THE PIZZAS were made and in the oven, Logan set the kids up in front of the TV on the living room rug, where he could keep an eye on them, and then headed back into the kitchen, where Tate was cleaning off the island and stacking the dishwasher.

All through dinner preparations Tate had laughed and joked around with the kids as he always did, but he couldn't fool Logan. The light that usually sparked in his eyes was missing tonight.

"Hey there," Logan said as he picked up the sponge on the counter and came around the end of it. Tate looked over his shoulder and aimed a tight grin his way.

"Hey."

"You need some help?"

"Nah, I've got it," Tate said as he pushed the bottom rack of the dishwasher in and shut the door. Logan tossed the sponge into the sink and leaned up against the island, waiting for Tate to turn around, and when he did, Logan loved that his eyes automatically went to check on the kids, but...

"Tate," Logan said, wanting his attention, and when

he had it, he asked softly, "You doing okay?"

"Yeah. I'm fine."

"Fine, huh?" Logan said as he crossed the kitchen and placed a hand on his chest. "You don't have to pretend right now. It's just me."

Tate brought a hand up to lay it over the top of Logan's. "I'm not pretending."

"Well, I don't believe for a minute you don't feel anything."

Tate shrugged as if to say, *Sorry, can't help you there*, but Logan wasn't going to let him get away with that. He smoothed his hand up over Tate's shoulder to cup the back of his neck, and looked him dead in the eye.

"The man I know, the man I love, he feels everything. He taught me to feel things I didn't know I was *capable* of feeling. So, I'm going to ask you again. Are you doing okay?"

Tate licked his lips and then sighed. "Okay, fine. No. I'm not. But tonight's not the time to talk about it. And honestly…" Logan waited, knowing there was more coming and not wanting to interrupt. "I don't know how I feel about it yet to even be *able* to talk about it."

"That's understandable. I can't even imagine," Logan said, and when he heard a high-pitched squeal, his head snapped around to see Lila on her feet clapping and jigging up and down in an adorably uncoordinated dance. He assumed she thought it was similar to the one the purple dinosaur on the TV was doing—she was wrong.

When Tate chuckled, Logan looked back at him and said, "Kids." Then he shook his head. "I swear she gives me another grey hair each time we watch them."

Finally, Tate's eyes lit up as his lips curved and he raised his hand to run it through Logan's hair.

"Nope. I see no grey," Tate said, and bent his head to take Logan's lips in a sweet kiss. Logan melted into the touch, and when Tate raised his head, he whispered, "Thank you." Logan narrowed his eyes, and Tate said, "You're always here when I need you the most."

Logan let his hand fall away so he could take hold of Tate's, and once their fingers were entwined, he brought them to his lips, kissed them, and said, "Where else would I be? You're where my heart is. So that's where I stay."

* * *

A COUPLE OF hours later, the pizza had been eaten and the sundaes devoured and Logan had taken Thomas into the bathroom to clean up. Tate had settled in on the couch and was watching Lila as she brushed the hair of the doll she was playing with.

He'd been looking forward to this time with Logan and the kids all week, and he hated that Jill, of all people, had ruined that for him. With only a handful of words, she'd managed to turn him into a fucking basket case, and Logan knew it. He could read Tate better than anyone else, and trying to hide shit from him was just pointless. Especially when it was something as big as this.

Tate shifted on the couch, unable to get comfortable as he sat there thinking about the run-in with his sister. He went over her words in his head, trying to find the catch in them. Trying to find the lie she must've been telling. Because there was no way she could've meant what she said. Was there?

This was the woman who'd flinched away from him that first time she'd seen him with Logan. The same woman who'd spewed words of hatred his way and then showed no regard to his feelings whatsoever as she and Diana had gone and destroyed any hope he had of telling his mother about Logan. This was the woman who had so callously cut him from her life instead of trying to for one second understand what he was going through.

And now she wants me to just…call her?

It was as though all of the ugliness from back then had come crashing back in and he was once again covered in the rank stench of their disapproval. And he hated that they still had the ability to make him feel that way, even after all this time.

"You brush." Lila's voice cut into Tate's thoughts, and had him smiling down at the doll she was holding up to him. Tate took it and the small pink brush she held out, and then Lila climbed up to sit on the couch beside him.

"She's very pretty," he said as he stroked the brush through the doll's wavy black hair, then winked at Lila. "Like her mommy."

Lila grabbed hold of his bicep and pulled herself up until she was standing beside him, and then he felt her small palm stroke over his hair, mimicking the actions of a brush.

Ever since Lila had been born, he'd gravitated toward her. With her shock of black hair and big blue eyes, she was the spitting image of Rachel, and from the minute she'd been put in his arms, the love affair had begun. It worked out perfectly, really, because Thomas was all about—

"Uncle Logan, can we watch *Minions* now?"

Tate looked over to the bathroom where Thomas was bouncing on his toes beside Logan, who'd rolled the sleeves of his black shirt up his arms.

"That was the deal," Logan said, as Thomas parked it on the rug. "You helped with dinner and ate everything on your plate so, yep, that means it's *Minions* time."

Tate couldn't help his chuckle at Logan's grimace. They must've seen *Minions* at least five times now, ever since Cole had suggested it one afternoon they'd babysat—stating it was payback for all the trouble Logan had ever given him—and that was the day Thomas had declared it was his favorite.

Once Logan started the movie, he snatched up the remote and came over to the couch to sit on the other side of

Lila. "You're good at that," he said, looking at the braid Tate hadn't realized he was even doing.

Huh... seemed Jill had even managed to sneak her way into his subconscious.

"Guess that's what happens when you grow up with a sister," Tate said, and Logan's eyes immediately softened. Tate looked away to check his handiwork again before he handed the doll back to Lila. "Here you go, little miss."

"Thanks," she said, and brought the doll to her chest in a tight hug before she turned, looked at Logan, and pointed to her cheek. "Kiss?"

Logan scrunched his nose up at her and shook his head. "I don't wanna."

Lila giggled and playfully shoved his shoulder, leaning into him. "*Kiss*," she said again. This new habit of hers was one hundred percent irresistible.

But Logan looked away from her, playing hard to get. "Nope."

The doll was dropped and forgotten as Lila, determined now, climbed over Logan's leg, grabbed either side of his face, and planted a big raspberry kiss on him.

A hearty laugh came from Logan, and in a flash he swooped her up and tackled her down onto the couch by Tate's leg. He kissed both of her cheeks, and as she laughed and squealed in delight, Tate couldn't stop himself from joining in.

Wow. Who would've, or could've, ever imagined Logan

Mitchell like this? He was perfect with them. Completely and utterly perfect. And when Logan glanced up and locked smiling eyes with Tate, he couldn't stop himself from leaning down, cradling Logan's cheek, and stealing a kiss for himself.

Lila clapped when Tate raised his head, and then, as she always did, she declared, "Again!"

Tate chuckled. "She is definitely related to you."

Logan's lips quirked, and he shrugged. "Well, yeah. She's obviously a genius. Now you better hurry up and do what she says. Or things might get ugly."

Tate glanced down at the grinning Lila. "Highly doubtful," Tate said, but took hold of Logan's face and whispered against his lips, "But you're pretty hard to resist right now."

As Tate kissed him again, Logan smiled against his mouth, and when he pulled away, Logan looked down at Lila, who gave him a huge grin.

"Happy?" he asked her, and when she nodded, Logan looked back to Tate and said, "I better be just as irresistible without the aid of a two-and-a-half-year-old, because this... *This* is a temporary thing."

Logan's expression had Tate laughing so hard he kissed Logan once more for good measure, because just like always, Logan had managed to take every other worry off his mind.

* * *

AS THE *MINIONS* finally—*thank God*—came to an end, Thomas was passed out on the sleeping bag he'd spread out halfway through the movie, and Lila was snuggled in against Tate's side with her eyes shut and her thumb shoved in her mouth.

Logan was lounging on one side of the couch as he stared across the now silent space to where Tate had his arm wrapped around the little girl, and when he picked up the remote and switched off the TV, Tate glanced over at him.

"Why do I get the feeling I've been replaced tonight?" Logan asked.

Tate placed his elbow on the arm of the couch and rested his head in his palm. "Never. You're stuck with me forever."

As the lamplight played over Tate's features, Logan enjoyed the sheer pleasure of looking at him. The dark eyes, thick lashes, and kissable lips. "Forever's a long time."

"What? Worried you couldn't put up with me for that long?" Tate chuckled.

"No," Logan said, and his serious tone must've caught Tate's attention, because he sobered instantly. "I'm worried it won't be long enough."

And wasn't that the truth. Something had changed in him over the last few months. Made him realize how special the man beside him really was. It wasn't as though he could

possibly love Tate any more than he already did. *But maybe
it's a different layer? One that comes after years of being together?*
Logan thought. *Or maybe it's just because he looks perfect sitting
there staring at me like he can't imagine a day without me. Yeah,
that's probably it.*

Tate's eyes wandered over him, and then he slowly
shook his head. "It's not fair to say something like that when
I'm trapped all the way over here."

"No?" Logan said, as he got to his feet and wandered
around the back of the couch. Tate's eyes followed him as he
went, until finally his head was tipped back on the cushions
to look up. "What would you do if you weren't trapped in
place by a demanding woman?"

"Come down here, and I'll show you," Tate
whispered, and Logan placed his palms on the back of the
couch on either side of his head and leaned down to brush
his lips over Tate's.

As Logan slowly kissed and nipped at the mouth
moving under his, Tate raised an arm up to slide his fingers
through the back of his hair and hold him in place. A groan
rumbled up Logan's throat, and when it threatened to slip
free, he slid his tongue between Tate's lips and sealed their
mouths together.

Damn, he needed to stop this or he'd get zero sleep
because he wouldn't be able to relax, and then it'll be hello,
ceiling for the rest of the night.

Logan lifted his lips and sighed. "To be continued..."

he said. "Tomorrow. Now, you bring her. And I'll get him."

Logan headed around the couch to pick up Thomas, as Tate got to his feet and scooped Lila up in his arms. Luckily, their bed was massive, since the second bedroom was set up as Logan's office and, well, Tate's storage unit ever since he'd moved in.

They headed into their room and set the kids in the center of the mattress, and as Logan pulled the duvet over them, he looked up and saw Tate standing over in the bathroom doorway. He had one shoulder against the doorjamb, and his hands in the pockets of his shorts. A thoughtful look was stamped across his face as he studied the sleeping children, and once Logan had them covered, he came over to him and smiled.

"You're really good with them," Logan said, as he stepped around Tate to go to the sink. He grabbed his toothbrush and toothpaste and then handed the tube to Tate. He rested his hip against the bathroom vanity, and Logan caught his grin in the mirror. "What?" he said before he stuck the toothbrush in his mouth.

"*You're* really good with them too, you know, Uncle Logan." Logan rolled his eyes and started to brush, as Tate turned to face the mirror beside him and nodded. "You are. It's kind of shocking, when I think about it too hard. But Thomas, he absolutely adores you."

Logan removed the toothbrush and spat into the sink, rinsing the basin as he said, "Well, he's pretty adorable, so…"

"So nothing," Tate said, bumping into his side as Logan started brushing again. "Just admit it. You love being around those kids."

Logan finished, spat, then rinsed his mouth clean before he shoved his toothbrush in the holder and looked at Tate. "Of course I love being around them. I'm not a monster…"

"But…" Tate said. "I hear a but in there somewhere."

"But," Logan said, and took the step needed to close the distance between them. He placed his hands on Tate's waist and couldn't stop himself from slipping his fingers under the material to touch his warm skin. "I'm selfish. I'm sorry. Don't hate me, but it's who I am. Always has been. I go after what I want, remember? And I want you. *Just* you," Logan said, and kissed his way up Tate's jaw to his ear. "I wasn't lying when I said forever wouldn't be long enough."

"No?" Tate asked, dropping his toothbrush, forgotten, on the bathroom sink so he could grip the front of Logan's shirt.

"No," Logan said, his breath ghosting over the curl by Tate's ear. "It's not long enough, because I'm just getting started." *And wow…* Wasn't *that* a revelation?

"God, Logan," Tate said, as he squeezed his eyes shut, and Logan knew he was having the same difficulty keeping himself in check that he was. When he seemed to finally get himself under control, Tate opened his eyes and said, "I don't hate you."

"No?"

Tate shook his head. "No. Why would I hate you? Because you don't want kids? Did I ever say that I did?"

"No. But we never really—"

"Logan?"

"Yeah?" Logan said, as he wrapped his arms around Tate's waist, his fingers desperately looking for a way inside those shorts, even though there was nothing he could do about it tonight.

"I think there's something *you* need to remember about me."

"Oh? And what's that?"

Tate pulled back and picked up his toothbrush just when Logan would've slipped his hands inside the back of his pants, and then he grinned at him in the mirror and said, "I don't share."

That night when Logan climbed into bed, he didn't stare at the ceiling as he waited to fall asleep. No, instead he lay down beside his nephew and stared across the vast expanse of the California king at the man whose eyes were locked with his and knew he was right—*they* were just getting started.

Chapter Sixteen

COLE AND RACHEL showed up the following morning at eight thirty on the dot, just as they'd said they would, and Tate had to admit the two of them looked more relaxed than he'd seen them in months.

Cole was dressed for the summer day in khaki shorts and a loose hunter-green shirt, and Rachel was particularly radiant with her bright smile and purple-highlighted ponytail swinging to and fro, as she stood in a white halter-neck dress that had red—*are they poodles?*—all over it. She looked retro and stylish, except for the odd green scarf she had wrapped around her neck. That didn't match at all. Not that Tate was about to point that out.

"Cole," Logan said as he handed his brother the kids' overnight bag. "How many times have I told you? If you're going to bite your wife hard enough to leave a mark, do it where it's not so obvious."

Well, I wasn't going to mention it, Tate thought with a laugh as he handed Lila over to her mom.

"I was just doing as I was told," Cole said, which had Logan looking over at Rachel.

"Good for you, Mom."

Cole shrugged the bag up his arm to his shoulder. "Speaking of doing as you're told, I see one of my kids. Is the other one whole?"

"Yes, Dad. I didn't break any part of them," Logan said, and Cole's lips twitched. "Thomas, time to go."

"Mom! Dad!" Thomas said as he came barreling down the hall.

"Hey there," Cole said as he picked Thomas up and situated him on his shoulders. "Did you have fun?"

"It was the best," Thomas said as he used Cole's blond head to balance with. "We made sundaes."

"The best sundaes I've had in years," Tate said, giving Thomas a high-five.

"It was all the sprinkles," Thomas proclaimed, with all the certainty of a culinary expert.

"I think you might be right," Tate said, and stepped back beside Logan. "Remember that for next time."

As Cole put a hand on both of Thomas's knees, he smiled at the both of them. "Thanks again, guys."

"Anytime," Tate said, just as Logan said, "So this is a once-a-year deal, right?"

Rachel laughed as she turned around to head out the front door. "Aww, poor Logan, did you actually have to think of someone other than yourself for the night?"

"Excuse me, that is not accurate at all," Logan said as they all walked up the hallway and out into the building's corridor. "I think about Tate every night."

As Tate and Logan stood outside their door, the family of four stopped by the elevator, and Cole looked back at them and smirked.

"I'm sure you do. But thank you. We really needed this weekend, and I never doubted you for a second, brother."

As the *ding* went off and the elevator doors opened, Logan said, "Sure you didn't." But Tate knew how much Cole's trust meant to Logan.

"See you two next Sunday for lunch once you recuperate from the kiddos," Rachel said with a wave, and then the Madisons disappeared inside the elevator, leaving the two of them in the silent hall.

Tate turned to Logan, who was still looking at the empty hall, and took his hand. "What time is it?"

Logan looked at his watch. "Just turned eight forty, why?"

Tate grinned as he walked backward into their place, tugging Logan along with him.

"Oh, I like that smile," Logan said, following eagerly. "Do you?"

"Mhmm," Logan said, as he kicked the door shut and leaned back on it, pulling Tate into his body. "Want to tell me what you're thinking?"

Tate chuckled, knowing what was on his mind *definitely* wasn't what was on Logan's.

He's going to kill me, he thought, as Logan's hands

trailed over the denim covering his ass, so he could grab a cheek in each hand. Tate sighed as he placed a hand on either side of the wood by Logan's head and stared at the handsome face only inches from his own.

Okay, you need to ask him, he told himself. *Just open your mouth and ask him.*

Last night, his father had left a voicemail asking if they'd want to attend today's church service, since they'd be over that way today. It wasn't that odd a request. It was something he had done regularly until four years ago. And after everything that had happened yesterday, he'd gotten to thinking it might be nice to sit in a church again, especially one he hadn't grown up in. To absolve himself of all the guilt and thoughts that had been running through his head about his mother and sister—*yeah, I'd like that.* But he wanted Logan to come with him, and he knew convincing him was not going to be easy. In fact, it would likely involve bribes, and possibly chains, to drag him there. Logan didn't *do* church. *But...*Logan hadn't done relationships before him, either. So maybe? Maybe he'd do it this once. Just for him.

"Well..." Tate started, as Logan kissed the side of his neck. "I was thinking."

"Yes," Logan said, as he began a slow grind of his hips. "That's your first mistake. You should stop."

Tate let his head fall to the side as Logan gnawed along his jawline to his ear, and then one of Logan's hands was slipping between them to palm him through his jeans. A groan left his throat as Logan massaged his throbbing erection and said, "I want to feel you in my hand."

Fuck yes, I want that too, Tate thought. But when Logan's fingers went to the button of his jeans, he finally kicked his ass in gear, lowered his hands from the door, and placed them over Logan's, stilling them.

When Logan frowned, he swallowed, and then before he even knew he was going to, Tate said, "I want to take you to church."

* * *

LOGAN FROZE WITH his hands under Tate's, and tried to discern whether Tate was messing with him. But the earnest expression in Tate's eyes told Logan all he needed to know—he was serious.

He wants me to go to...church?

Logan opened his mouth, and then paused, then tried again to speak, and Tate started to laugh.

"Don't tell me I've rendered you speechless." Tate laced their fingers together and brought Logan's hands up to either side of his head against the door, caging him in.

"I...uhh." Logan let his words drift off as Tate kissed the spot right below his ear, and when his cock reacted as though it'd been sucked, he gave Tate a gentle shove back. "Let me make sure I'm understanding this. You want to take me to *church*."

Tate's grin was infectious as it curved his lips into a full-on mischievous smile. "That's right."

Logan couldn't stop the sound of disbelief that slipped free. "And just so I'm clear, we're not talking about you on your knees worshiping me until I shout, 'Oh my God.' Are we?"

One of Tate's eyebrows rose as he glanced down Logan's body to where, *yeah, fuck me, I'm totally goddamn hard.*

"Well," Tate said, moving in against him until one of his legs was wedged between Logan's. "No. But if you come to my church today, then I'd be more than happy to *come* with you tonight, at yours."

The gorgeous fucker. He has me right where he wants me, Logan thought, as he turned his head to the side and Tate's teeth nipped at his ear and his thigh moved higher between Logan's legs, massaging his hard-on.

"Please," Tate said. "I really want to go. And I'd like you there with me."

Shit. How can I say no to that? The answer was that he couldn't. *And* wouldn't. Not if Tate asked him. Not if he needed him. Logan was willing to do anything when it came to Tate—he'd proven that from the minute they'd met and he'd agreed to Tate's "relationship" policy. And yeah, that'd turned out pretty well in the end. *But...church?*

Logan brought his face back around so he was looking into Tate's eyes. "Is this how you ask everyone to

Sunday mass?"

Tate's eyes widened a fraction. "You even know what it's called. I'm impressed."

Logan swiped his tongue along his lower lip and then looked to either side of the door, where his hands were still pinned in place. "Believe it or not, I'm not completely ignorant when it comes to matters of religion."

"Been to Sunday mass often, have you?"

"Not even once," Logan said quickly, making Tate laugh. "But Tate?"

"Hmm?"

"If you plan for that to change this morning, you need to let me go so I can go and console myself in the shower before we leave."

When Tate released his wrists, Logan lowered his arms and pushed off the door to step around him, and as he went, he heard Tate say, "Make it count. That way you won't be bored during confession."

Logan stopped in his tracks, looked back at Tate, and said, "You didn't say anything about confession."

"I'm just messing with you."

"Oh, well, I wasn't too worried. I haven't been to church once in thirty-seven years. Do you really think I'd be lacking in things to atone for?"

"Definitely *not*," Tate said. "In the last week alone I can think of enough points to mention that you'd be in there for hours. But…I figured if you only focused on your most recent transgression, maybe we'd get out of there by the time *evening* mass started."

Logan narrowed his eyes and pointed at him. "Laugh it up, Morrison. You'll eventually pay for this."

Tate threw his head back and laughed as Logan headed into their bedroom, and just as he stepped into the bathroom, he heard Tate call out, "I can't wait."

And for those three words right there, Logan figured the least he could do was wash up and go and thank God.

Chapter Seventeen

THIRTY MINUTES LATER, Logan was pushing open the glass doors of their building's lobby, where Tate had said he'd meet him with the car. He straightened his tie for at least the twentieth time and tugged on his shirt sleeves, feeling uncomfortable for the first time ever in his outfit.

Am I really going to do this? Logan thought, as he slipped his sunglasses on. It was a warm day today, but not as hot as last week, otherwise he'd be sweating in his pants and dress shirt before they even got to Elmhurst.

The throaty rumble of Tate's car had Logan's head turning to see the black '68 Shelby Mustang GT500 coming down the street toward him, and he wandered down to the curbside to enjoy the view.

There'd been a time where he couldn't imagine anything sexier than seeing Tate straddling the motorbike he used to ride, but that was before the accident he'd had that almost cost him his life. It was also before he bought the vehicle he was currently sitting in.

As Tate pulled to a stop beside him with his window down and his elbow resting casually on the door, Logan shoved his hands into his pockets and slowly shook his

head. Today was going to be an exercise in
restraint...because *holy shit*, Tate sitting behind the steering
wheel of this beast of a car in a black V-neck tee, dark blue
jeans, windswept hair, and Aviators was tempting as all hell.

"You're wearing *that* to church?" Logan said, and
Tate offered him a slow smile and pulled his sunglasses
partway down his nose.

"What's wrong with what I'm wearing?"

*Other than the fact it's going to be impossible to be close to
you and not be hard as a fucking rock?* "Aren't you supposed to
dress"—Logan pulled a hand from his pocket and gestured
to himself—"like this?"

Tate chuckled and shrugged. "Pretty sure God
doesn't care either way. But you look very smart this
morning, if that's any consolation."

Logan reached up and whipped his sunglasses off to
glare at Tate. "Are you having fun?"

"A little," Tate said with a grin, then pushed his
glasses back in place. "You better get in if we're going to get
there on time."

Logan walked around the front of the car, suddenly
feeling as though he were dressed more fittingly for a
funeral, which was apt, considering where he was going,
and made sure the road was clear before he climbed in the
passenger seat and looked over at his driver for the day.
"Please remind me again why I'm doing this?"

"Because you're a good guy?"

"No," Logan said, shaking his head. "That's definitely *not* it."

"Then it must be because you love me," Tate said as he lowered a hand to place it on Logan's thigh. But there was no way Logan could keep himself decent if Tate was in one of his teasing moods, which clearly he was, judging by the crook of his lips when Logan caught hold of his wrist, halting him.

"Something the matter?" Tate asked.

"No," Logan said as he directed Tate's hand to the chrome gear stick with the polished head. "But if you could please keep your hands on the steering wheel and stick shift, I'd feel..."

"Yes?" Tate said, and Logan pinned him with a fierce stare.

"Less inclined to fuck you in the back seat before church."

Tate let out a bark of laughter and leaned over to kiss him quickly on the lips. "In that case, I'll be sure to keep my hand on you when we head home."

Logan rubbed his forehead. "Tate?"

"Yeah?"

"Drive. Now."

And with a chuckle and a flick of his wrist, Tate turned the radio on blast and hit the gas.

* * *

SEVERAL HOURS LATER, with his hands full, Tate pushed through the screen door at the back of his father's house. He had a glass tumbler in one and an ice-cold Coke in the other. It was just a little past three, and after they'd gotten home from church, his father had handed Logan a glass of *much-needed* bourbon and directed him to the outdoor patio, and then they'd fired up the grill.

He'd cooked them all some spicy shrimp skewers, served with a wild rice pilaf, and after they'd finished eating, Tate had told Logan to sit and relax while he helped clean up. With the food covered and the kitchen counters wiped down, Tate's father had sent him outside while he stacked the dishwasher and finished up.

As the door slapped shut behind him, Logan turned his head in Tate's direction and offered a lazy smile. He'd removed his tie once they'd gotten home and unbuttoned the top two buttons of his shirt, but as always, his lawyer looked handsome.

"Dad thought you could do with another one of these," Tate said as he slid a second glass of Widow Jane across the glass tabletop and took a seat in the white wicker cushioned chair beside Logan. "He's impressed you made it through the entire service without bolting."

"Well, the two of you boxed me in. Where was I going to go?"

Tate grinned at the memory of Logan shifting

uncomfortably in the pew between him and his father at Cathedral of the Sacred Heart and then winked. "That was his suggestion, not mine."

"Your dad knows me well."

Tate raised the Coke to his lips and took a gulp, before lowering it to the table. "Who ever would've thought *that* would be the case."

Logan saluted him with the tumbler. "Not me. But…"

"But?" Tate said, when Logan's words drifted off and he looked out at the backyard.

"But I like it," Logan said, staring at the big tree in the back corner where Tate had built his first treehouse. "Every time we come here, I feel like I learn a little more about you."

Tate rested an arm along the back of the chair, and when his fingers grazed Logan's shoulder, Logan turned his head and aimed those perceptive eyes toward Tate.

"And what did you learn today?"

The side of Logan's lips quirked up. "That you have your father's smartass tendencies. Did you know he called me a heathen, right in the middle of the service? Told me to relax because no one knew I was a total heathen. As if that was going to help." Tate grinned, and Logan took hold of his chin and brushed a quick kiss over his lips. "But I also learned that this part of you, the Sunday family lunches and church? This tradition was important to you." Tate was going to answer, but Logan placed a finger against his lips. "Don't deny it."

Tate shook his head and threaded his fingers through the hair at the nape of Logan's neck. "I wasn't going to. I was going to say that the tradition you're talking about no longer exists."

"That's not true. We just did it with your dad. We could alternate if you wanted to? Since it's something you grew up with."

He leaned in and kissed Logan gently. "That's really sweet. But not necessary." When Logan's eyes narrowed, Tate laughed and sat back. "I don't want you to start attending church on Sundays, Logan. That's not what this is about. I don't need to be in a church to believe in God. I pray every night just fine without it."

The look that crossed Logan's face then was a mix between disbelief and incredulity. Which only made Tate's amusement escalate.

"I didn't know that."

"Good to know I can still surprise you," Tate said, and took another sip of his drink. "All I'm saying is that if a tradition can't bend, if it can't be flexible over the generations, then it won't survive. And this one didn't survive. How could it when there were stipulations involved like the one my mother placed on it about you?"

"Tate..."

"No. You need to hear this," Tate said. "You're right

in one sense. This tradition was important to me. *Family* always was. And if you asked me four years ago if I ever thought I'd be sitting in this house and that it would be empty because of a choice *I* made? Then I would've told you there was no way. That this family was stronger than that."

Logan clenched his jaw and looked away, and Tate hated the fear he saw flash into Logan's eyes. This topic was always such a difficult one between them. For him, it was the pain and loss of his mother and sister over the person he fell in love with. For Logan, it was the guilt of *being* that person. And seeing Jill had brought all of those feelings rushing back to the surface—for the both of them.

He reached out and brought Logan's face back around. "My tradition was always about family, and *you*, Logan, are my family. So if we want to go to Cole and Rachel's or visit with my father or, hell," he said, and nipped at Logan's lower lip, "if we want to stay in bed naked all day on a Sunday, I don't care. As long as you're there. That's *my* new tradition and the one that's most important to me."

Logan's eyes darkened at the declaration, and Tate had to remind himself that his father was just inside, otherwise he was liable to kiss Logan. And God knew once that happened, he'd have a difficult time stopping.

"You really pray each night?" Logan said, pulling Tate's thoughts from the idea he was currently having.

"Mhmm," Tate said, and reached for his Coke again.

"When? I don't ever see you."

Tate chuckled. "Yes, you do, you just don't know it."
When Logan just stared at him, Tate knew he was waiting
for him to continue. "Usually right after you kiss me
goodnight. You wrap your arm around me, and it's peaceful.
That's when."

He wasn't sure what he expected from Logan after he
said that—maybe some smartass comment about him being
able to *really* show him heaven. But instead, Logan's eyes
glistened and Tate was momentarily stunned by the wave of
emotion that seemed to have overtaken the man staring at
him.

"Are you okay?" he asked, touching Logan's arm.

"Yes. I was just thinking about what you said."

"What about it?"

"About where you find peace," Logan said. "I
thought that was why you went to church today."

"It was. But it was also for answers. To quiet all the
questions and doubts in my head so I could think more
clearly about Jill. Does that make sense?"

Logan took his hand and kissed his knuckles. "Yes, it
makes total sense. Sitting there next to you today in church, I
too found my own brand of peace. And while it wasn't due
to the man everyone else was there to see, I still found the
experience an enlightening one, because it was with you. So
thank you for that."

Wow. Tate had not expected that at all, and as he sat
there staring at Logan, there were no words to tell him just

how much love he felt.

Then the back door swung open and his father came out with the bottle of Widow Jane in his hand.

The two of them looked over to see him raise it and then point to Logan's glass, effectively ending the moment. "Drink up. There's more where that came from."

* * *

LOGAN COULDN'T SAY he was unhappy about Will Morrison's timely arrival. Things had been getting intense on Tate's father's porch. But damn, everything Tate had just said? It was like he'd somehow crawled into his brain, found all of the demons he worried about, and slayed them in one fell swoop.

"How are you two doing out here?" Will said, as he pulled up the seat opposite them.

Tate left his hand where it was resting along Logan's back, and used the other to raise the Coke can to his lips. After taking a long drink of it, he lowered it and nodded. "Good. We're good, Dad. Lunch was great."

Logan cleared his throat. "Really, the shrimp was amazing. We need to find out what you put in that marinade."

"Remind me before you leave and I'll write it down."

Logan brought the tumbler up to his lips and took a sip before sliding his glass over to Tate's father with a wink.

"Your bourbon's not bad either."

Will gave a hearty laugh as he tipped the bottle up, refilling the glass. "I knew you'd appreciate it."

Woo, I'm gonna be feeling that in the next few minutes.

"Do you like scotch?" Logan asked, thinking of the Macallan that Cole had given him last week.

"I do."

"Ever had a glass of Macallan? My brother finally cracked open his twenty-five-year-old single malt the other day, and damn," Logan said, remembering the smoothness of it. "That was some potent stuff."

Tate started laughing. "Potent, meaning he had three glasses and fell asleep at the office. Wonder if you're gonna pass out after this one."

"Excuse me," Logan said, aiming a pointed look Tate's way. "I had had a busy few weeks. Months, really."

"That's right," Will said, pushing the glass back Logan's way. "Your big case was this week. How'd it go?"

Fucking brilliant, was Logan's initial thought, but he managed to catch himself. "It went well. We won."

"Congratulations," Will said, and Tate chuckled before saying, "What he's *not* telling you is the case settled at thirty-five million dollars. It's almost unheard of to win against the big pharmaceutical companies."

Tate's father's eyes almost bugged out of his head as he looked from his son to Logan, then back to Tate.

"Did you say thirty-five *million* dollars?"

"I sure did," Tate said. "He kicked their ass."

Damn, Logan thought as he looked over at Tate, who was smiling broadly at him. The pride that was evident on his face... *That makes me feel like the king of the fucking world.*

"That's impressive, son," Will said, regaining Logan's attention. "Really impressive. And what about you, Tate? You said you were hiring on a manager, right?"

"That's right," Tate said. "And I just found one."

"God help us all," Logan muttered, and Tate reached under the table to pat his thigh.

"What's wrong with who you hired?" Will asked, and Logan just shook his head and raised his glass to his mouth, letting Tate try to explain Robbie.

"Nothing," Tate said. "It's just someone we knew when we first started dating, that's all." When Will stared at the two of them, waiting for more of an explanation, Tate said, "He's got a ridiculous crush on Logan, always has. When I told him he sometimes worked at the bar, he practically offered a blood sample to be hired."

Logan coughed and almost choked on his drink before he lowered his glass and glared at Tate.

"What? It's true," Tate said with a shit-eating grin, and Logan looked over at Tate's father, wondering if he'd be concerned at all by what he'd just heard.

"I almost feel sorry for the guy," Will said, aiming a knowing smile at his son. "Logan barely notices anyone else is *in* the room when you're around. Does this guy know that?"

That answers that, Logan thought as he aimed daggers at Tate, who just continued to grin. "Oh, he knows."

"*Any*way," Logan said, desperately wanting to change the topic. "That's enough about us. What's new with you, Will? What ever happened to that Anne lady? You still seeing her?"

"Nah," Will said, brushing his hand through the air. "Found out we didn't really have much in common."

"Sorry to hear that, Dad," Tate said.

"Don't be," Will said with a pearly-white grin that matched his son's. "I have another date set up this week."

Logan sat forward at this new piece of information, his drink forgotten. "Really? Do tell us more. What's her name?" When Will laughed but didn't say anything, Logan added, "Or his. I'm not one to judge."

Tate snorted. "As if he doesn't already know that."

"I do," Will said. "But I think it's safe to say that this Morrison male isn't going to switch teams this late in the game."

Logan's mouth fell open, and he whipped his head around to look at Tate, and saw him looking as gobsmacked as he was. Then Logan busted up laughing, because hot damn, who would've ever thought Tate's father would be joking with them about that...*ever.*

When Logan finally got himself under control, he said, "Okay. So, what's *her* name?"

"Jackie," Will said, and then took a sip of his bourbon. "I met her at church."

Ahh, Logan thought. *Church. Making people come together. Possibly in more ways than one.*

"What's she do, Dad?"

"She owns the local nursery. In Bloom."

"That's perfect," Tate said. "You've always loved your garden. Something in common."

"Exactly. I've been in there a few times now. She's really very lovely. I think you'd both like her."

"So when's the big day?" Logan asked.

"Friday. We're going out to dinner."

Logan slapped the table and sat back. "Well, I can't wait to hear how it goes."

"Me neither," Tate said, slinging his arm back around Logan's shoulders. "That's exciting."

"First dates always are," Logan said, and Tate laughed.

"How would you know? You never had a first date until *me.*"

Logan looked at him and grinned. "And it was very exciting. Wasn't it?"

As Tate slowly smiled, Logan wondered which part of their first date he was recalling. Dinner and the blow job shot? Or after, when Tate had fucked him for the first time? He sure as hell knew which part he was thinking of.

"It was *very* exciting," Tate finally said.

"Exactly," Logan said, and turned back to face Will. "Well, we should probably think about leaving soon if we're going to get home before the Cubs are done and the city becomes a madhouse."

"True," Tate said, getting to his feet.

Will followed suit, and Logan finished his drink and stood also. As they headed inside and down the hallway, Logan excused himself to use the bathroom, and when he came back, he found Will standing in the kitchen and Tate nowhere in sight.

"Thanks again for lunch and the poor Widow Jane," Logan said, shaking Will's hand.

"No problem. You know you're welcome anytime. Tate just headed upstairs, said he had to grab something, but I think he might've gotten lost."

Logan looked over to the staircase. "Guess I should go hunt him down, then."

"Yeah, you should. But, uhh, before you do..."

Uh oh, Logan thought, as Tate's father ran a hand through his hair in a gesture just like his son. With Tate, that usually meant he was nervous or concerned. But right then, Logan had no idea which was the case with Will.

"I wanted to ask you something."

Without Tate around? Yeah, okay, this did not sound good. Sure, Logan and Will had a great relationship these days and had ever since that afternoon Tate had brought him home after their trip to New York. But that didn't mean the guy might not have a problem with something he had said or done.

"Sure," Logan said, hoping he didn't sound as nervous as he felt. "Shoot."

"I'll make it quick. It's just…it's been a long time since Tate's come to church, and I know that had a lot to do with his mother attending the old one. But even when I switched, he never really showed much interest. I'm not going to lie—it was a bit of a shock when he said yes today."

No shit, Logan thought. *Was a hell of a shock to me too.* But he wasn't about to say that, so he stood silently and waited for Will to continue.

"Earlier when we were cleaning up, he finally told me about running into his sister and, well, it started to make sense."

Oh no. No. No. Please don't ask me what I think you're about to ask me. But he knew he was out of luck when Will eyed him in that direct way Tate did.

"He says he doesn't want to see her. But Logan, I don't think that's true."

"I…uhh," Logan started, and then shook his head. "I don't know, Will. It's not really my—"

"Business? Place?" Will said. "Of course it is. Look, just talk to him, please. He listens to you, and I think he'd really regret it if he didn't at least meet with her."

"I don't know that he's ready for that. He's pretty angry right now. He's hurt."

"And rightfully so. I'm not saying he should forgive her. But I know my boy, and Tate doesn't *volunteer* to go to church. He was looking for answers today. Looking for peace of mind. And I know it's because of Jill."

Logan sighed, knowing those words to be true. He'd thought the same thing even before Tate had confirmed it, which was the only reason he'd said yes to attending in the first place. But that still didn't mean he was going to urge Tate to do something he didn't want to do. The choice was his, and his alone, in the end. "Okay. I'll talk to him. But I'm not making any promises."

"Of course," Will said, as he clapped Logan on the shoulder. "Just talk, that's all I ask. He loves you. He'll open up to you."

Logan wasn't so sure he had anything good to say when it came to Jill. But his father was right about one thing: Tate had come in search of answers today, and maybe, if they talked, they could find some.

Chapter Eighteen

TATE STOOD IN the doorway of his sister's bedroom and stared at the room. He hadn't gone up there with the intention of taking a walk down memory lane, but after the last couple of days he'd had, that was what he found himself doing.

He pushed the door to her room all the way open and scanned the interior. Not much had changed. Hers was the room situated in the middle of the second-floor landing, and Tate always remembered her complaining it was the smallest. His parents had the master at one end of the floor, and his was all the way at the other end.

As he stepped inside, he noted her walls were still plastered with the movie stars and boyband members she'd had crushes on. She had her desk pushed up against the window that overlooked the backyard, and her bed was flush against the opposite wall.

He walked to the computer that was still set up there, and spotted a photo on her desk beside a pink and purple notepad. The frame was a bulky silver one with the word *family* across the top, and inside it was a photo of the four of them, as they had once been.

He picked it up to take a closer look and recognized it as having been taken at Jill's high school graduation. Diana had taken that photo. He remembered the way she had followed them around that day, flirting shamelessly with him. He was young there, too—*shit…twenty, maybe?* Tate had his arm slung around his baby sister as they stood between their parents and all smiled for the camera.

God, that seemed like forever ago. He'd purposely avoided coming into her room whenever he visited his father, and now he knew why. This was too much. It was too fucking sad to see. And it made him furious that somehow this happy family unit had become fractured and destroyed because he'd fallen in love with someone that half of them didn't approve of. Someone wonderful they'd deprived themselves of knowing.

Tate put the photo back on the desk and shook his head. *What am I doing?* But, deep down, he knew. After seeing Jill this weekend, he'd had this sudden need to remind himself of the girl he'd once known. The one who was kind. The one who was always there to help a friend or stand up for one. The girl he used to adore.

And while this room offered a glimpse of who she had once been, the only way he'd be able to know if she still existed somewhere inside the hateful woman he'd once seen would be to meet with her. To call her.

He sighed as he ran a hand through his hair and turned, about to head down to his room where he'd originally been going to grab a couple of things he thought Thomas might like. That was when he saw Logan lounging against the doorjamb with his arms and legs crossed, watching him.

He had a thoughtful look on his face, and Tate wondered just how long he'd been standing there.

"Hello," Logan said, a curious expression now crossing that striking face of his.

Tate slipped his hands into his jeans as he wandered over. "Hi."

"What are you doing up here?"

"Was just coming to get a few G.I. Joes for Thomas. I thought I'd take them over next Sunday."

Logan's gaze drifted past his shoulder to Jill's room, and then a frown appeared on his brow. "Your sister was into G.I. Joe?"

Tate rolled his eyes. "Funny."

"That's me, hilarious," Logan said, and shoved off the door to brush by Tate and walk over to the desk in Jill's room. Tate turned to see him pick up the photo he'd just been looking at, and when Logan glanced over at him, he grinned. "How old are you here?"

"Twenty."

"Hmm," Logan said, and when he looked back at the photo he ran a finger over it, and Tate felt his cock twitch. "Wearing your favored ripped jeans, I see."

"I don't think I owned any back then that *weren't*

ripped."

"Well, that hasn't changed."

"True," Tate said, and shrugged. "That was a long time ago."

Logan fingered the edge of the frame as he watched him for a few seconds, and Tate made sure to hold his gaze. One thing about Logan that was always such a surprise was his ability to wait people out. It was surprising because Logan was notoriously impatient when it came to getting what he wanted. But when it involved finding out pertinent facts, when he was determined to know what someone was hiding, he was a master at getting to the bottom of things. It was what made him so good at his job. That persistence. Whether it be in your face or subtle and silent. He always ended up with the answers he was looking for, and right now, Tate knew Logan was looking for signs that he was about to freak out or have a breakdown of some sort.

When neither occurred, though, Logan finally said, "Do you want to talk about it?"

"My jeans?" Tate said, trying the avoidance route and failing.

"Your *sister*."

Tate shook his head. That was the one thing he *didn't* want to talk about right now. In fact, he just wanted to forget about it for the moment. He'd already made a decision, and he'd deal with it tomorrow. "No. I already made my mind up about her."

"You did, huh?"

"Yeah, just a few seconds ago, actually. But I don't want to talk about it right now. I want to enjoy my afternoon with you."

"Fair enough. But we *will* talk." Logan narrowed his eyes, waiting for a response, and when Tate nodded, he let it go and glanced back at the photo in his hands. "You look really fucking hot in this photo."

The comment was so unexpected that it made Tate laugh as Logan continued to study the image. "I'm glad you think so."

"I definitely think so. Where were you again when I was in college?" Logan said.

"In high school."

"Mhmm, that's right." Logan absently placed the photo down and strolled back over to Tate. "I think I would've liked to have tempted you back then."

Tate grinned, his earlier worries leaving him for now as Logan's magnetic presence surrounded him.

God, he hasn't done anything other than look at me and I want to touch him. That's some kind of power right there.

"You tempted me just fine when we met," Tate said, as he took Logan's hand, leading him out into the hall and down to his room. As he shoved open his bedroom door and they walked inside, he glanced back to see Logan standing with his hands in those pressed navy slacks of his, and said, "You're tempting me right now."

Logan chuckled and shook his head. "Don't blame me for whatever inappropriate thought is running through your mind, Mr. Morrison. I'm slightly inebriated, and will not do anything in your father's house. I think we've had this conversation before."

Tate tapped his index finger to his lips, and when Logan's eyes immediately fell to them, he grinned. "Then you shouldn't have looked at me like you did a minute ago."

"And how did I look at you?" Logan asked, his mouth curving into an arrogant smirk, and shit, he was all sex in that moment. There was no way Tate wasn't going to go and taste him. *Not in this fucking lifetime.*

He walked back to where Logan was and reached around him to shove the door shut, and when it clicked into place, Logan cocked his head, as if to say, *Now what?*

Tate crowded in on him until Logan's back was up against the door, and then he placed one hand on it and snaked the other down to massage it over the zipper of Logan's pants. As Logan's breath caught, Tate placed his lips at his temple and said, "You looked at me like you want me to unzip your pants and take you to church."

A raspy laugh left Logan as he gripped the front of Tate's shirt. "If you're not referring to *my* kind of church right now, I'm going to kick your ass."

"If you mean by the end of the next five minutes you're going to be trying not to shout, 'Oh my God,' then my ass is safe."

"For now," Logan said, his eyes promising all kinds of decadent things to come. "You're really going to do this? Here. And you think I'm a bad influence."

Tate nipped at Logan's ear and hummed in the back of his throat. "No. I think you're the best fucking thing that ever happened to me. And right now, I want to show you."

"Your timing is— *Oh shit*." Logan's words got caught on a groan when Tate squeezed his fingers around him. "Damn, Tate."

"Perfect? I think I'm right in time to take care of this." Tate unbuckled Logan's belt, then unbuttoned and unzipped him.

"Tate," Logan said, "remember your father's downstairs."

Tate dipped his hand into Logan's black boxers, and when he found the stiff erection waiting for him, he licked his top lip and said, "I don't care."

Logan's head fell back against the door with a thump, and he curled his hands into the material he was holding as his hips bucked forward so he could fuck the fist now surrounding him.

"Hmm," Tate said. "That's it. I love how insatiable you are. You can't help yourself from taking what you want, even when you know you shouldn't. Like when you take me. I love how you hold me down and go fucking wild. Greedy to the very end."

"Jesus," Logan said on a ragged breath, as Tate

lowered his head and nuzzled into his neck.

One thing that the years had definitely enhanced between the two of them was the intensity of their physical relationship. When they'd first gotten together it was all about learning one another, and for Tate especially, learning not only what he liked but what Logan liked.

But now...*now* the two of them were in perfect sync. And while they enjoyed the quiet, gentle moments in bed tangled between their sheets, when it came to their sex—for the most part—they liked it dirty, rough, and raw, and that was exactly what Tate was about to give the man he had pinned to his childhood bedroom door.

"Give me your mouth, Logan."

In an instant, Logan's hands were in Tate's hair, holding him in place while he connected their lips. Tate closed his eyes and sucked on Logan's tongue as he stroked the throbbing cock he held in his hand. Relaxing the arm he had braced against the door, Tate angled his body so he could grind his aching shaft against Logan, and when a muffled grunt came, Tate did it again.

Logan tore his mouth free, and with their faces this close, their noses brushed and their breath mingled.

"*Ahh...* So good, Tate," Logan said as he jacked his hips forward, his dick sliding through Tate's fist.

"You're so sexy," Tate whispered. "The way you move. The way you sound. The way you say my name like it's a prayer."

Logan growled, his arousal now at a fever pitch, judging by the flushed cheeks and tightly bunched jaw, and then Tate bit down on his lower lip and said, "Say it again like that as you come down my throat."

* * *

AS THE ALCOHOL swirled around his brain, Logan reminded himself that he needed to keep his voice down as Tate lowered to his knees in front of him. He was also trying to work out how in the world he'd gone from tracking Tate down so they could leave, to standing in his childhood bedroom with his pants unzipped and his cock about to be sucked. *Because fuck me, the man at my feet doesn't seem interested in going anywhere at all.*

As Tate pushed the ends of his shirt out of the way, Logan shut his eyes, trying to focus on anything other than coming, and when nothing more happened, he looked down to see Tate siting back on his heels, watching him with an expression that Logan wanted to memorize.

It was a mix of adoration and lust. Lust being at the forefront when Tate slicked his tongue over his lips.

"Why'd you stop?" Logan asked, his chest heaving as he stared into those scorching brown eyes.

Tate's shiny lips parted as he blew a warm breath of air over the cock he'd just been holding, making a shiver race up Logan's spine. "I was waiting until I had your attention."

Logan clenched his teeth together as Tate smirked and rose on his knees so he could tug Logan's pants a little further down. Logan was about to accuse Tate of delighting in his frustration when he took hold of him and flicked his tongue over the head of his cock.

Holy fucking shit, Logan thought, as Tate began a slow, torturous stroke up and down. *Up and fucking down.*

If Sunday was supposed to be about giving thanks and worshiping the Almighty, then Logan was pretty sure he was close to doing so real loud, because the man who'd taken him to church this morning was now hellbent on making him see heaven.

* * *

TATE GLANCED UP Logan's body and curled his fingers into the edge of his pants to pull them aside so he had even better access to the thick shaft. A low grunt came from above, and as Logan pumped his hips forward in an effort to get closer to his mouth, Tate used his tongue to tease the sensitive underside of his cock.

"Tate," Logan said, in a hoarse tone. "Now's not the time to fuck around." Logan then cursed as if his patience was nonexistent, and Tate loved that. He wanted Logan to lose it—wanted him to fuck his mouth hard and erase any thoughts from the past week. He'd wanted that since he'd turned around in his sister's bedroom and seen Logan lounging against the door.

Raising his head, he caught Logan's fierce look and told him, "Then you better hurry up. Don't want Dad knocking on the door."

"Motherfucker," Logan said. "This is not a good idea— *Ahh shit.*" Tate rooted his nose against Logan's pelvic bone and kissed his way down to the underside of his cock until Logan growled and pulled his head up by his hair.

"Well," Tate said with a raised eyebrow. "You want me to stop?"

* * *

LOGAN WASN'T SURE what he wanted. His dick was so damn hard he could feel every pulse in it, and it was distracting as hell when trying to make a rational decision. So when Tate licked and nuzzled in against him again and his hair teased over his bared length, Logan reached down to take a handful of it.

He twisted his fingers through the silky curls tormenting him, and when Tate ran his tongue from root to tip, Logan squeezed his eyes shut, knowing that if he continued to watch what Tate was about to do then he would likely shoot his load all over his face before he was even in that talented mouth.

Not that he was opposed to that idea or sight. But not

here, that was for damn sure. Plus, he wanted to get between Tate's very fuckable lips—that was where he'd invited him, and *that* was the place Logan intended to come.

He felt Tate's hands on his hips as he angled his body toward his eager mouth, and Logan bit back a harsh cry when a warm tongue swiped across his sensitive tip and then dipped inside the slit.

Are you fucking kidding me, Logan thought, as he gritted his teeth and said, "If you don't hurry up and suck my dick—"

"What? You gonna walk out of here?"

Logan narrowed his eyes on Tate's juicy mouth, and thought, *You sexy fucking cock tease.*

"I didn't think so," Tate said, and the gravelly tone of his voice grated over all of Logan's aroused nerves. "But you're right. Enough is enough." Then his lips surrounded the head of Logan's shaft, and he couldn't help but watch in awe as Tate braced a hand on his thigh, used his other to angle his cock so he could get a nice, deep swallow, and then aimed his eyes up at him, clearly giving him the go sign.

* * *

TATE THRILLED AT the carnal sound that came from Logan as his hips thrust forward off the door. With his thick erection now in Tate's mouth and his hands in his hair, Logan was directing the pace of this face fuck, and Tate was getting off on it just as much.

"Yes, yes…oh *shit*, Tate," he heard, and he flicked his gaze up Logan's body to see his teeth bared, his jaw locked, and the cords of his neck strain as he tried to hold back his shouts. He was a goddamn feast for the eyes, and when Logan let go of his hair and brought his balled fist to his mouth to bite down on it, Tate knew he had him.

Tate closed his eyes and listened to the blood ringing in his ears, as Logan's labored breathing filled his otherwise silent bedroom. Then Logan's body tensed, his fingers snagged in the hair he still had hold of, and the warm, salty taste of his climax hit Tate's tongue.

Tate swallowed the evidence of Logan's enjoyment, and when he raised his head and sat back on his heels, he palmed himself through his jeans and swiped his thumb over his lips to make sure they were clean.

"Fucking hell," Logan said, his breathing heavy, his eyes blurred from the alcohol and arousal swirling together—and Tate couldn't get enough of him.

"I love seeing you like this," Tate said, and then chuckled.

"What, with zero brain function and an inability to remember how to move?" Logan asked, as he reached down and started to right his clothing, tucking his now satisfied cock away for the time being.

Tate got to his feet and, without saying a word, crushed their mouths together as he ground his erection

against Logan's thigh. As Logan raised his hands to take
hold of his face, he licked his way into Tate's mouth and
tangled their tongues, no doubt greedily tasting himself, and
once he was done, he nipped at Tate's lips and said, "Such a
bad boy. It's probably good you weren't around while I was
in college."

"You think so?"

Logan nodded and copped a quick feel of the hard-
on Tate was willing to subside—at least until they got in the
car and, like, five minutes away from home.

"I never would've left your bed, your dorm, or *you*,
for that matter," Logan said as he zipped his pants. "So, yes,
my education thanks you." Tate laughed at that as Logan
buckled his belt and said, "Don't think you've distracted me
from why I came up here."

"I know. I know."

"Good. Because I haven't forgotten," Logan said as
Tate opened his closet to grab the box of toys he'd originally
come up there for. "I came up here because we need to talk."

"And we will. After a good night's sleep." Tate shut
the closet door and checked his clothes to make sure he was
presentable, and then shrugged. "Let's end tonight on a
good note. We can come back to all of that other stuff
tomorrow."

"Okay," Logan said, nodding in agreement, and then
he pointed at the small tub. "G.I. Joe?"

"Mhmm. And if Dad asks, we'll just say you had to

help me find them because they were hiding deep in the closet."

Logan started laughing as he ran a hand down Tate's cheek. "Well, I have been known to lend a helping hand in that particular circumstance. But there was never any hiding from you. Not even in the beginning."

"Nope," Tate said, and kissed him gently. "Once I knew what I wanted, I took it. I tend to do that." He winked at Logan, who just shook his head as he walked by, and all Tate heard as they left his room was Logan's chuckle and "Touché, Mr. Morrison. Touché."

Chapter Nineteen

TATE STOOD OUT on the balcony the following morning in his grey sweatpants cradling a cup of coffee. He could see the appeal this time of the day held for Logan—it was relatively quiet as the streets began to fill and the Windy City woke up—but he was still more inclined to sleep in if given the choice.

However, this morning, his brain had been too busy to offer up much of a decision, so he'd left Logan showering when he got out of bed, and figured he'd start the coffee for when Logan finally came out hunting around for it.

When they'd gotten home last night they'd spoken briefly about the Jill situation, but really, Tate had already made up his mind. It was just the when and where and what the end result would be that was now weighing on him.

He raised his mug, needing another hit of caffeine, and took a sip as the glass door slid open behind him and he saw Logan walking his way, dressed and ready for work.

"Good morning," Logan said, trailing his fingers up Tate's naked back.

"Mornin'. There's coffee inside if you want it."

"Thanks, I'll grab some on my way out. I have to head to court this morning, so that's perfect." Logan leaned in for a kiss and absently fingered one of the curls by Tate's ear. "Hey?"

"Yeah," Tate said, as he leaned in to the familiar touch.

"This business with your sister. You sure you're good with it? I can come with you, if you like."

Tate considered Logan's offer but shook his head. "No, I'm fine. Really. I'm just going to call her up and see if she wants to meet. She'll either say yes or no."

"She'll say yes, otherwise she wouldn't have given you her card." Logan looked out at the surrounding buildings, then rested his forearms on the rail and sighed.

"Would you rather I not go?" Tate asked, studying the pensive man beside him.

"No," Logan said. "Look, I told your dad I wasn't going to influence you either way on this, and I'm not going to. This is your decision. You're the one she hurt. And it has to be your choice in the end if you want to see her. Not mine. And not his."

A headache threatened at the base of Tate's skull as he turned to look at the city below. "I don't know," he said. "My brain is telling me that I'm insane to even think about calling her after what she did. That she doesn't deserve it and I—*we*—shouldn't have to go through all of this again with her. But Logan...she's my sister."

Logan took a step forward until his shirt and tie were grazing Tate's arm, and then he kissed his bare shoulder and said, "Call her." Tate looked directly at him, and Logan said, "You should call her. Your heart won't be happy until you can deal with this. It's who you are."

Logan was right—he just had to do it and get it over with. "Yeah, okay. I think I'm going to. It's what I keep coming back to."

"Then it's what you should do," Logan said.

"And you're sure that *you're* okay with that?"

"Me?" Logan asked.

"Yes. You."

"Why should it matter? She's your sister, Tate, and if you want to sit down with her and ask her where the fuck she's been for the past four years, I'm not going to stop you."

Tate grinned and took a sip of his coffee. "Eloquent as ever. I always wonder how you curb your tongue when you're in court."

Logan shook his finger as he headed back to the sliding door, and just as he stepped through it, he said, "Don't you know by now I can do just about anything with my tongue, Mr. Morrison? I'll see you tonight at the bar around eight. Call me if you need me."

"I'll see you tonight, Logan. Have a good day."

"Count on it," Logan said with a wink, and then he disappeared inside to head off to work.

* * *

AFTER SPENDING THE morning in court, Logan quickly grabbed some lunch on his way back to the office, knowing he was already running late for the sit-down that Priest had set up with Robbie, his cousin, and his nonna.

Shit, he'd really wanted to be there when things got underway, but he couldn't help that the morning's case had run over. So there he was making a mad dash for it.

With a glance at his watch, he cursed as the elevator hit Mitchell & Madison's floor, and then he rushed through the lobby, barely stopping to give Tiffany a wave.

When he got to Sherry, he looked at her expectantly, wanting the lowdown on how things were going in the meeting she had set up. But when she grimaced and pointed toward the conference room, Logan stopped and said, "What does that face mean? Because it doesn't look good."

When one of her perfectly shaped eyebrows winged up, Logan replayed his words in his head and corrected himself. "I meant it doesn't look good for what is going on in *there*. Not that your face doesn't look good."

"Stop talking, Logan," Sherry said with a roll of her eyes.

"Okay. Good idea. So, what *do* you mean?"

Sherry got to her feet and leaned a little over her desk. "That young man who originally set all of this up—"

"Robbie?"

"Yes, Mr. Bianchi. Well, he doesn't seem very happy with Mr. Priestley."

"Really?" Logan said, and glanced over his shoulder at the shut door. He knew Priest could be a hardass, but he was intelligent and fantastic at his job, and Robbie should've been smart enough to be able to see that. So what was the problem?

Looking back to his PA, Logan said, "How do you know?"

"Well, he came out here and said: 'I'm not happy with this Priestley guy.'"

Logan's lips twitched as Sherry stared at him, unamused. "Did he say anything *else*, Sherry?"

"He asked where you were, and said something about men who wore suits thinking they were all God's gift to earth."

Logan was more than a little amused by that last comment, because if he didn't know better, that sounded like the old—

"Well, it's about time you got here."

Robbie.

As Logan turned around, he saw Robbie standing just outside the conference room in skinny black pants and a bright red fitted shirt. His patent leather shoes were the same color as his top, and as he marched over, Logan grinned.

"Where have you been?" Robbie said, and Logan blinked once to make sure he wasn't imagining what he was seeing. "Logan?"

"Court," he said, finally letting his eyes wander down the man opposite him. "Is there a problem?"

"No," Robbie said, crossing his arms. "But that new lawyer you got us? He's an ass."

Logan glanced over Robbie's shoulder to the open conference room door. "How about you let me put my stuff down and I can come in there and see what's going on."

As he headed into his office, Robbie followed closely behind, and Logan said over his shoulder, "Congratulations on the new job, by the way. Tate said you'll be coming in to get a feel for the place tonight."

"Thanks," Robbie said as Logan put his briefcase down. "And yeah. He said to get there at six."

"Well, he's the boss," Logan said as he gathered up a notepad and pen and turned back. "Is that the reason you dressed up?"

"Dressed up?" Robbie said.

"Yes. You're…" Logan gestured with his pen. "You seem a little more like yourself today."

"Oh," Robbie said, and looked down at his clothes. "I guess so. He just said to wear what makes me feel comfortable."

Logan smiled, because that sounded exactly like something Tate would say. "I think you're going to like working for him."

"I do too. Plus, he's not exactly hard to look at."

"You just concentrate on your *job*, Robbie.
Remember, that's what got you into trouble at your last job,"
Logan said, shaking his head, and Robbie just shrugged.

"Oh please, you know it's true. Tate's hot. But he's
always been a little moodier than you. Testier."

"Uh huh," Logan said, gesturing for Robbie to turn
around. "Okay, time to head back to the meeting. Not sit
here and gossip about Tate."

"Actually..."

Logan looked up to see Joel Priestley standing in his
office doorway. He had on a pristine grey suit and a black
dress shirt, which made his auburn hair stand out in a way
that commanded one's attention.

"I think it would be better if he sat out of the
meeting."

Oh shit. What the hell did I miss here? Logan thought,
as his phone buzzed in his pocket and he tore his gaze away
from the two men facing off with one another to see who it
was.

* * *

TATE STARED AT the card in his hand as the phone rang
by his ear. After the twentieth pep talk to himself, he'd taken
a seat in the living room and dialed Jill's number, and was

now waiting anxiously for her to pick up.

How did it come to this? That I'm scared to talk to my own sister?

But he knew. The reason was right where he'd pushed it to the back of his mind. It was that look on her face from four years ago. That disgust. The discrimination he'd seen that day in Logan's office. And that thought alone was enough to piss him off and make him want to hang up.

Just when he thought that was the perfect idea, the phone connected and he heard Jill saying, "Hello."

Tate's heart was pounding so hard he was surprised she couldn't hear it through the phone as he sat there in the otherwise silent condo, trying to remember how to speak.

"Hello?" Jill said again. "Tate?"

I can still hang up, he told himself as he shut his eyes and rested his head back on the couch. *I can hit end and it will be like this never happened. Logan won't think less of me—in fact, he'd probably be happy about it.*

"Tate? Is that you?"

Deciding it was now or fucking never, he finally grew a set of balls and said, "Yes, it is."

Silence greeted him for several heartbeats before she said, "One second." Then he heard some muffled talk, as though she'd covered the mouthpiece, and then she was back. "I'm so happy you called."

He tried to ignore the fact that she did actually sound happy to hear from him. "Would you rather I call back? Is this a bad time?"

"What? No. I was just leaving the hairdresser, actually. This is perfect."

He wasn't so sure about that, but he was in it now, and he wasn't going to back down or pussy out. He needed to say what he'd called to say and then hang up. "Right, well...I was just calling to see if maybe—"

"Yes," she said before he could even finish, and Tate shook his head.

"You don't even know what I was going to say."

"I know," she said. "It's just...I didn't think you'd call at all. I mean, I hoped you would, but I really didn't *think* you would. If that makes sense."

"It does," he said as he stared at the photograph sitting on the side table by the remote. He picked it up and smiled at the image staring back at him. It was one of his favorites. It was of him and Logan at the cabin last Christmas. They'd snapped a selfie out in the snow with him in his beanie and Logan with snowflakes all over his jet-black hair and eyelashes as he kissed Tate's cheek. "I wasn't going to," he told her as he continued to look at the two grinning fools in that photo.

"No?" she said softly. "What changed your mind?"

"I don't know. But Jill?"

"Yes, Tate?"

He put the photo back on the table and sat forward, thinking about his next words carefully. She needed to know one way or another before this reconciliation or intervention—*yeah, that thought has definitely crossed my mind*—that he and Logan were non-negotiable. They were a package deal. And if she didn't get that, then he didn't need her in his life.

"If you want to meet just to try and convince me that what I'm doing with my life is wrong and that it's a sin or some shit—"

"Tate?"

"What?" he snapped, not even caring that he sounded pissed. He *was* pissed, and maybe it would do Jill some good to know that this wasn't all going to be fixed with a few nice words. If that was what she was hoping for.

"I don't want that at all."

"Then what do you want? Because I have to say I'm a little bit fucking confused by your sudden need to see me. Don't you still talk to Dad? He's had my number all these years, Jill."

He gripped the back of his neck, frustrated. *God, why does this have to be so hard?*

"Can I meet with you?" Jill asked, her voice soft and low, just the way he remembered it, and Tate shut his eyes and sighed.

"When?"

"Are you free today?"

"Today?" he asked, his eyes snapping open so he could look at the clock on the wall.

"Sure. If you can. If not, you tell me when."

He knew she was trying to do this while he was in a lenient mood, and he guessed he couldn't blame her for that. But did he really want to do this today? Right now? *Ugh, what the hell. Might as well rip the Band-Aid off.*

"Okay. How about coffee at the Daily Grind on La Salle? Do you know it?"

"I'll find it," she answered. "What time?"

"About an hour. Can you do that?"

"Yes, I'll be there. Oh, and Tate?"

"Yeah?"

"Thank you."

Don't thank me yet, he thought, wondering how this meetup would end. "I'm not promising anything here, Jill. But I'll see you in an hour."

"Okay, I'll see you then."

"See you," Tate said, and ended the call. Then he took in a deep breath and let it out. *See, you did it,* he told himself, and when he got to his feet to head through to the bathroom and get ready, he sent a quick text to Logan: **Meeting Jill in an hour. Wish me luck.**

Logan: You sure you don't want me to come? If you say yes, you might actually save my life.

He frowned at the message. **Why's that?** Then he shoved his sweats to his ankles and stepped out of them as a video message came through.

Hitting the play button, he immediately recognized

Robbie, but the man he was standing opposite wasn't anyone Tate was familiar with. He was a tall guy in a grey suit with a fulminating look on his face as he glared at Robbie, who had his hands on his hips and was saying, "You have the personality of a tree stump." Then the video cut off and a text came through.

Logan: Apparently, Robbie doesn't like priests.

Ahh, so that's Priestley. **Well, I'm naked and about to get wet. So I'm going to leave you with your priest problems (which seem to be following you lately—maybe it's a sign) while I go and sin for a bit.**

Logan: Fuck you.

Tate laughed. **Maybe tonight. Right now you need to rescue my newest employee. He's the one who will enable you to do what you just wrote above—more often.**

When all he received back were several ellipses, Tate chuckled and got under the warm water.

He'd go and see Jill, get that over and done with, and tonight he'd hang out with Logan and maybe give Robbie a bit of tit for tat. After all, it was about time he got his revenge on that particular man. And anyone that had Robbie that riled up had to be worth ribbing the guy over for a night or two.

* * *

LOGAN STUDIED THE two men in his office as he slipped

his phone into his pocket and tried to push the visual of Tate naked in the shower out of his mind. He had other issues to deal with right now that he'd rather do without an erection. Namely making sure Robbie didn't claw Priest's face in the next two seconds. Which had Logan coming back to his original question. What the hell had he missed in that meeting?

"Okay, you two," Logan said, walking over to where Robbie and Priest stood glaring at one another. "What's going on here?"

"What's going *on*," Robbie said, turning to aim his annoyance directly at Logan, "is he is an ass."

"I'm sorry," Priest said, his tone ice cold. "I wasn't aware I was here to make friends with you."

"See?" Robbie said, pointing a finger at Priest. Holding up his legal pad between them, Logan made sure to keep his amusement at the situation to himself.

"Wind it back a bit," Logan said, looking to Priest, who'd shoved his hands in his pockets, probably to make sure he didn't strangle Robbie—Logan knew that feeling. "What happened?"

Priest let out an irritated sigh and looked at Logan. "I was going over the case with Mr. Bianchi and his family, and he didn't like what I had to say."

"Because you delivered it with all the emotion of a dead fish," Robbie said, and then crossed his arms. "That's my cousin's life you're talking about in there."

Priest aimed his eyes at Robbie, and Logan didn't envy Robbie being at the end of that formidable glare. "And I'm the one who's saddled with the responsibility of making sure she still *has* one at the end of this. I don't have the luxury of getting emotional, and you interrupting me every five seconds because you don't like my tone or feel as though I'm not holding your hand through the process is not going to win this case."

Robbie's face turned the same shade as a beet, and Logan wouldn't have been surprised to see steam coming out of his ears as Robbie took a step forward and jabbed a finger in Priest's direction. "You are an *ass*."

"I might be. But I'm the ass who is going to save hers. So you need to back off and let me do my job, sweetheart." Priest looked at Logan and said, "If we're quite done here, I'll see you in there." And then he turned on his heel and left the office, leaving a dumbfounded Robbie in his wake.

Several seconds passed by, and then Robbie whirled around and aimed his furious eyes up at Logan's. "You have to fire him."

Logan chuckled and shook his head. "No way. This is too entertaining."

"Did you just see the way he talked to me?"

Logan stepped around Robbie, held his hand out with the notepad, and nodded toward the conference room. "I did. And he's right."

"What? You can't be serious."

"I'm dead serious," Logan said. "Joel Priestley's one of the top defense attorneys in the U.S. right now, and he didn't get that way because he's nice. He would go to his grave to keep a client's secrets." Robbie's mouth fell open, but Logan just kept on talking. "That *ass* is your cousin's best bet of not spending years in jail when all the evidence says that she should. So, how about you and I go back in there and you try to keep your mouth shut? And if you're a good boy, I might even buy you a drink later tonight."

Robbie made an indignant noise and rolled his eyes, and as he walked by Logan, he said, "Fine. But I still want it on record somewhere that *that* man is an ass."

Chapter Twenty

WHEN TATE GOT to the Daily Grind and stepped inside, he scanned the interior of the familiar coffee shop to see if Jill had arrived. When he didn't spot her, he went ahead and ordered his drink and a chocolate muffin, then headed for one of the booths down the side wall so he could sit and watch the passersby while he waited.

He looked around at the other people with their friends or family or just sitting by themselves talking on the phone, and remembered a time when he'd been so self-conscious in this shop with Logan that he'd inspected everyone who looked his way, just in case they knew him.

Funny, he thought, taking a sip of his drink. That this was the place he'd told Jill to meet him at. Almost like it was familiar and neutral territory for him. *And how coincidental is it that this is where I first met Robbie, when I'm about to train him tonight at work.* It was weird sometimes, how life worked out.

Like with Robbie, for example. The man Tate remembered in this shop had been lively, over the top, and totally out there. He hadn't cared one way or another what anyone thought of him, and his lack of filter had been right up there with Logan's.

Robbie had been the first person to really make Tate wake up to himself and admit that Logan was who he wanted. Yeah, it'd been because the damn flirt used to constantly put the moves on Logan. But he'd spurred Tate on and made him really accept who he was. And on that last day when he'd seen Robbie here at the Grind and had been brave enough to tell him that Logan was off the market...*that* had been a great fucking day.

However, time had changed Robbie, and Tate still wasn't quite sure why. He supposed that was one of the reasons he'd offered him the position at The Popped Cherry when he found out Robbie was qualified.

He had a lot to thank that kid for, and if he could help him out in some way, then this was his way of doing that—not that he'd *ever* tell Robbie that.

"Tate?"

Tate glanced over his shoulder, and when he saw Jill standing there, he slid out of the booth and got to his feet. He towered over her—always had, even as kids—and as they both stood there not knowing what to do, Tate shoved his hands into the pockets of his jeans and said, "Hey."

"Hello," she said, and offered a timid smile. Then she glanced around the coffee shop, and he took a moment to really look at her.

She hadn't changed at all, from what he could see. She wore a red dress and pointy black slip-on shoes for the summer day, and her hair was around her shoulders in loose waves.

"This place is nice," she said, and when her eyes finally came back to meet his, Tate just nodded. Then she glanced at the table, spotting his food and drink. "I'm just going to go order real quick, and I'll be right back."

"Okay."

As she headed off toward the registers, Tate retook his seat and pulled his phone out for something to do. He scrolled through several emails, a few old texts, and when nothing caught his eye, he shook his head. *Put your phone away, dumbass. You came here to talk. So talk.*

As he shoved his phone into his pocket, Jill came back, slid into the seat opposite him, and took a sip of her coffee. A chocolate muffin was on the plate in front of her, just like him, and when she lowered her cup, she hummed and said, "They make a delicious hazelnut latte."

Yep, same as me too. Some things never change.

"Yeah, the coffee and food here are pretty good," he said as he settled into his seat, trying to get comfortable.

"How'd you find this place? It's kind of out of the way from your old apartment, isn't it?"

Tate nodded and looked around. "I guess so," he said, and then thought, *Okay, Jill, moment of truth.* "It's one of the first places Logan brought me on a date. We used to come here a lot. It's close to his—well, *our* place and where he works."

Jill didn't so much as flinch as she peeled the wax paper off the bottom of the massive muffin in front of her and cut it into quarters. "Oh, that's right. His law firm is in the building down the street. I remember."

So do I, Tate thought. *I remember you looking at me like some kind of disgrace to humanity up in those offices.*

"Yes," he said, and congratulated himself on not saying anything more.

"You used to work in the same building, right? At that bar? After Hours?"

Tate reached for his own muffin and removed the paper for something to do with his hands. He didn't think he'd actually be able to stomach any food right then, but hell, he couldn't just sit there. "That's right. That's where I met him."

Jill sat back in her seat and regarded him in the same bold way he and his father had about them. *A Morrison family trait, through and through.* "Logan Mitchell of Mitchell & Madison. That's him, isn't it?"

Tate narrowed his eyes on her and his spine stiffened. The question was innocent enough, but at the same time she could've asked him what the weather was outside and he would've been on edge.

"Tate?"

"Yeah, that's him. He owns the law firm with his brother, Cole Madison."

Jill picked up a piece of her cut muffin and popped it

into her mouth, and once she'd finished it, she said, "I looked him up online a couple of years ago. And recently they were in the news with a case they were working on. Umm, Berivax, wasn't it? The big drug company."

"That's right," Tate said in a clipped tone, wondering where she was going with this. Then she said something that would've floored him, had he not already been sitting on his ass.

"He's extremely handsome. Logan, that is."

Tate knew his eyes had to be as round as the plates on the table, because Jill's hand paused on the way to her mouth and she said, "I'm sorry. I shouldn't have said that. It's just..." She lowered the uneaten piece of muffin to her plate. "You're not talking, and I—"

"What do you want me to say, Jill?" he finally said, sitting forward in the seat and resting his forearms on the table. "I'm still trying to work out what you want. We haven't seen each other in years, and you made it abundantly clear why. So, I guess I'm trying to wrap my head around your motives. Why are you here? I find it hard to believe it's to tell me that my boyfriend's hot." Tate paused for a moment and then added, "Even though he is."

When a tiny smile tipped the corner of her lips, Tate relaxed a little despite himself. Jill swallowed and sat back, looking as though she were thinking over her next words.

"I'm sorry, Tate."

He was sure he'd misheard or, *shit*, was in some kind

of alternate reality, because surely she hadn't just said—

"I'm sorry for everything. I'm so appalled by my own behavior toward you. I hardly even recognize it as myself."

The self-recrimination in her voice managed to cut through Tate's incredulity as he sat thoroughly stupefied by what he was hearing.

"I can't tell you how long I've wanted to tell you that. And before you say it, I know Dad has your number. But my relationship with him..." She shook her head. "It hasn't been the same since your accident."

Tate let out a breath he hadn't even realized he'd been holding, and brought a hand up to scrub it over his face. This was...it was unbelievable.

"Tate," she said, sitting forward and reaching across the table. When her fingers grazed his, Tate slowly withdrew his hand. She didn't sit back, however. She stayed as she was, her eyes imploring him to listen. To give her the chance she'd never given him. And as he stared at her, he fought every instinct he had to get up and leave her sitting there by herself, the same way she had done when he needed her. "I...I don't even know how to put this into words—"

"Try," he finally said, his voice barely audible.

When her eyes found his, they were glassy, and Tate steeled himself against the urge to reach over, take her hand, and tell her it would be all right. That wasn't his job anymore. She'd thrown her big brother away years ago when she'd banished him from her life. So if she wanted that back, if she wanted to mend what she had broken, then she needed to be the one to do the reaching.

"Right," she said, and drew her hands back across the table to place them in her lap, her food forgotten. "I suppose the best place to start is at the beginning." She took in a shaky breath and let it out. "I'm sorry for the way I acted, or reacted, that first day in Logan's office."

Tate didn't move. Didn't speak. The only reason he even knew he was breathing was that he hadn't passed out from lack of oxygen. But he thought it might be a real possibility soon.

"I have no excuse," she continued, and chewed on her lower lip as though she were trying to hold her emotions in check. "I was in shock, but that doesn't excuse the awful things I said to you. The way I treated you…" she said, her words fading as a tear escaped her eye and rolled down her cheek. "I'm so ashamed of myself."

Tate had to look away from her then, because no matter what she'd done to him over the last few years, seeing her sitting there in pain was harder than he'd ever expected it to be.

She brought a hand up, brushed the tear from her cheek, and sniffed. "Then that Sunday came around, and you and Logan came to the house."

"I remember," he said, the ugly memory of that day

forever ingrained in his brain as one of the most awful experiences he'd had in his life. But it was also the day Logan had told him that he loved him for the first time, and even though it hadn't been perfect, the memory of *that* allowed Tate to shove the rest of that day to the very depths of his soul. Somewhere in the cracks and shadows, where he didn't have to look at it. He just knew it was there.

"That day was horrible," Jill said.

"I agree."

"Mom was—she was so hateful that day."

Tate blinked, but braced himself against the mention of the woman he no longer allowed himself to think about.

"She said things I never imagined she would say to either of us. And it was such a shock that I think we all just blindly followed. Me and Dad."

Yeah, but Dad came and found me years ago, he thought. *Where the fuck were you?* He ground his back molars together and told himself to hear her out, not fly off the handle. She was getting there. She was explaining. Or at least trying to.

"That day you left with Logan," she said so quietly he almost missed it. "It was as though you died."

Tate flinched, and when more tears rolled down her face, she gulped back a big breath of air, the pain evident in her expression as she struggled with her words.

"He said something before he left the house that day—"

"Who did?" Tate asked, his eyes zeroing in on her.

Does she mean Dad?

"Logan. You'd left, and he was standing there in the middle of a room of people who hated him, but he didn't care. I'll never forget it. He fought for you. Stood up for you. Told Mom that he hoped when she looked at the empty chair at her dinner table that afternoon that she realized what she'd done and would come to her senses."

Wow... How did I not know that? Then Tate remembered how he'd told Logan he needed space later that same day, and hell, he wanted to kick his own ass right then for that.

"I'd never seen Dad as mad as he got that day. When Logan finally left, he told Diana to get out, and then he just...lost it. Told Mom she was way out of line and how dare she kick you out of their home just because they didn't understand the choice you'd made. He went postal, and she shut down."

Tate didn't know what to say, so he reached for his coffee and brought it to his lips. When he took a sip and it was lukewarm, he grimaced and put it back on the table.

"It was ugly after that. Sad and depressing to see them. It really was like a death in the family. Mom blamed Logan, Dad blamed Mom, and I blamed everyone. Eventually, it seemed like it was easier for everyone to stop talking. So we did."

Tate knew that part. He remembered all too well how he'd tried to contact them and all of their phones had been disconnected. What he hadn't realized was not only had they stopped talking to him, they'd stopped talking to each other.

"Then we got the call from Diana," Jill said, her voice now sounding like a distant echo of itself. Tate looked off over her shoulder, unable to meet her eyes while discussing this topic, because he knew exactly what call she was referring to. It was the call that Logan should've gotten. The call that he'd been lying in a hospital bed. Dying. But instead, they'd called the family who had decided life would be easier for them if he wasn't in it. To this day, it still infuriated him.

"Mom was beside herself," Jill said, cutting into his thoughts. "Convinced this was God's way of bringing you back to her. Bringing us all back together. We were there every day."

Tate's hands clenched where they were on the table, this conversation now making him want to punch something. "Logan was there every day too. Something that none of you seemed to give a shit about until Dad's guilt made him track him down. Where was your shame then, Jill? Where was your compassion when he was stuck in a waiting room wondering if I was dead or alive?" He shook his head. "I expected better from you, out of all them."

"I know," Jill said, and had the good grace to lower her eyes. "I can't begin to imagine how you must feel. How he felt—"

"No. You can't. Because that would require you actually caring about me. *Loving* me."

Jill's eyes flew up and she worried her top lip with her teeth. "That's not fair."

"Fuck fair," Tate said, his hurt and fury finally coming to a boiling point. "How has any of this been fair? So I fell in love with someone you didn't approve of. How is that worse than standing by and letting your own brother be disowned without saying a word?"

Jill shrank back in her seat and said softly, "It's not."

"No, it's not. At least I was brave enough to say how I felt. To love who I wanted to love regardless of the opinions of closed-minded, bigoted people. It's just disappointing to know those people are your family. I'm sorry, *were* my family."

Tate slid out of the booth and got to his feet, too irate to sit any longer. But before he could go anywhere, Jill reached out and took hold of his wrist. When he stopped and looked down at her, she said, "Please don't go."

Tate steeled himself against the regret and sadness he saw in her eyes and said, "Why should I stay?"

Jill's chin quivered, and as tears began to spill down her cheeks, she said, "Because I need to tell you that I'm sorry. I'm sorry I broke your heart. I'm sorry I wasn't brave like you." She brought a hand over her mouth and whispered, "God, Tate. I'm so sorry."

As he stood there, staring down at Jill, he thought of

Logan that morning urging him to call his sister and the belief he had in Tate that he would always be the bigger person. The better person.

So, not wanting to disappoint himself or Logan, Tate reached out and swiped his thumb over his sister's cheek, brushing away a tear, and then he said, "Okay. I'll stay."

* * *

LATER THAT AFTERNOON, Logan was sitting in his office with the door shut, enjoying the peace and quiet he'd managed to find in the last half-hour. After calming Robbie down enough that he was able to sit in on the rest of the meeting with Priest in silence, Logan was exhausted.

Jesus, the two of them were like oil and water, and while it was amusing, there was no way Logan wanted Priest scared off because Robbie was acting like…well, Robbie. And to top it all off, the Bianchis had left the meeting without budging from their original position: Vanessa was adamant that she was innocent.

It was frustrating and a little terrifying to have someone so set in their ways that they couldn't see the upside to telling a white lie to save their own ass. But she didn't want to lie. *I guess I can't fault her on her morals*, Logan thought, and sighed as he leaned back in his chair. But it sure as hell put them in a difficult position.

As he twirled the pen through his fingers, he thought

about Tate and wondered how his morning had gone. All day he'd been on Logan's mind. What he was doing and *whom* he was meeting. And he'd had to put the phone away several times, fighting back the urge to call and make sure he was okay.

He was about to shut his eyes for five minutes when his cell phone started to vibrate on the desk. And as if he'd known Logan had been thinking about him, Tate's name appeared on his caller ID.

Logan tossed his pen down, smiled, and then hit accept. "Good afternoon. I was just thinking about you."

Aren't I always, Logan thought as he turned his chair around so he was facing the large windows that flanked the back wall of his office. *I definitely need to make sure my new office has a view like this—or better.*

"Is that right?" Tate said. "You mustn't be very busy if you have the time to sit around and think about me."

"There's nothing more worthy of my time than thoughts revolving around you. Unless, of course, they're *inappropriate* thoughts about you."

Tate laughed, and Logan smiled. It was a nice sound to hear. He'd be lying if he said he hadn't been worried about how this meeting with Jill would affect Tate. But from what he was hearing, he seemed…okay?

"Now that, I'll never complain about," Tate said, and Logan could picture the smile he could hear in his voice.

"You at work already?" Logan asked, as he shut his

eyes and let Tate's voice wash over him.

"Yeah, I, uhh, just got here a few minutes ago."

Logan's eyes opened at that piece of information, and he glanced at his watch. "Really?"

"Yeah, I spent a few hours talking with Jill."

Logan wasn't sure why that made his pulse race. But whenever Tate's estranged family was the topic of conversation, his anxiety level went off the fucking charts. The fact that Tate had spent *hours* talking to Jill instead of the thirty minutes he would guess it would take to tell someone to fuck off bothered Logan.

What if she'd tried to convince him that their relationship was wrong? What if she'd told him that family was more important than he was? Would Tate believe her? It wasn't like there was anything *tying* Tate to him. And it wasn't like they hadn't tried to come between them before.

And yeah, Logan was aware that he was being overly paranoid and probably a whole lot of crazy, but *fuck*. It wasn't like he didn't have just cause. Taking in a breath, he told himself to be cool about this. "And how'd that go?"

"Umm, it was difficult," Tate said.

Okay...

"She apologized."

Come on, Tate, Logan thought, as he got to his feet and headed to the window. As he stared out at the traffic below, Logan rested his forehead on the glass, willing Tate to say more. Hoping he'd give him some kind of indication that he was okay. That they were. Or that he wasn't. Either way. Just give him something.

"Logan?"

"Yeah?" he said, his breath catching as he held it.

"Why didn't you ever tell me what you said to my parents when my mom threw us out of their house?"

Logan thought back to that day, one of the worst in his life, and racked his brain trying to recall exactly what he'd said. He was pretty sure it involved some curse words over how stupid he thought they'd acted. But he couldn't quite pinpoint the exact phrase. "I don't know. I was pretty angry. I'm sure it wasn't anything nice." There was silence as he waited for some kind of response, and when Tate said nothing, Logan added, "They'd just kicked you out of your home. I wanted to shake them up. Remind them that they were hurting the greatest man I'd ever met. If I said something I shouldn't have, I'm—"

"Logan," Tate said.

"Yeah?"

"I love you."

Logan turned to rest his shoulders up against the window and let out a sigh of relief, not having realized that was exactly what he needed to hear right then. "I love you too."

"And I'm sorry that after you did that for me, I pushed you away the very same day."

Logan shut his eyes, imagining Tate's face in perfect

clarity. God, he wished he was there with him so he could touch him. "You have nothing to be sorry about. That was a long time ago."

"It was. But it doesn't mean I can't feel regret over the way I acted back then."

"Well, you shouldn't. There was a lot going on in your life, and if that's the only thing you have to apologize for, then you're doing just fine, Mr. Morrison."

Tate chuckled, and after a few seconds he asked, "Do you think we could go up to the cabin this weekend?"

Logan opened his eyes and walked back to his desk to check his calendar. When he saw nothing he couldn't reschedule, he said, "Sure. What were you thinking? Friday through Sunday?"

"Yeah. I only have Amelia this last weekend and then I'll have to work the first few with Robbie, so I might as well take advantage of it. Plus, I want to talk to you more about Jill and some of the stuff she said, and I think I'd like to go up there and unwind."

Logan could appreciate that. It was quiet out at their cabin, and this time of the year was perfect. The beach and lake were great if you wanted a swim, or they could just hang out. Either way, if Tate wanted to get away, then there was no way Logan wasn't about to pack up the car and go.

"Sounds good to me. We can leave Friday morning, if you like."

"That's perfect. You're still coming down to the bar

tonight, right?"

"Of course," Logan said. "You don't think I'd miss Robbie's first night, do you? I plan to test his skills."

"Logan..."

"Please, as if you aren't thinking the same thing. That guy has it coming."

"Mhmm," Tate said, and Logan could hear the grin there. "How'd it go with him and Priestley after the little argument this morning?"

Logan thought back to the meeting and felt a sly smile stretching his mouth. "I think I'll let you ask Robbie that."

"That bad?"

"Well, all I'll say is..."

"Yeah?"

"Please wait for me to get there before you ask him." When Tate's loud laugh came through the phone, Logan said, "Promise me."

"I promise."

"Good. Then I'll see you at eight."

"See you then."

When Tate ended the call, Logan dropped his head back on his seat, realizing the weight of his worry over Tate's meeting must've been what was making him feel so tired, because suddenly he was wide awake and couldn't wait for the clock to hit eight so he could head down to The Popped Cherry and have a drink with his bartender.

Chapter Twenty-One

"WHO'S THE DEER in the headlights tonight, Morrison?"

Tate glanced up from the three shot glasses he'd just put on the counter in front of Robbie, and spotted Hoyt taking his regular seat on the stool at the end of the bar. It was about two hours into basic show-and-tell with Robbie, and with happy hour now underway, The Popped Cherry was starting to fill.

He flashed a grin in Hoyt's direction as he stepped around Robbie, grabbed a glass, and pulled a pint of Guinness for the middle-aged construction manager of one of the building renovations down the street. He slid the dark stout across to Hoyt and said, "He's going to be replacing Amelia soon. Name's Robbie. Tonight's his first night."

Hoyt grabbed a handful of peanuts and popped them in his mouth before he raised his glass to Robbie. "Good luck to ya. At least you're starting him off on a slow night."

"This is slow?" Robbie said as he pushed three shots of Patrón to a man who was handing over cash. Once he'd given him the change, Robbie turned to face Tate, who was leaning against the counter. "It's close to full in here."

"Of course," Hoyt said. "It's happy hour. But this is nothing compared to the weekends."

As Robbie's eyes widened, Tate chuckled, because Hoyt was right. This was relatively slow for them, which was why he'd asked Robbie in. To have a test run of sorts.

"You're going to do fine," Tate said as he strolled over to Robbie and handed him a small black bar towel with The Popped Cherry logo on it. "Hold on to this, though—you're going to need it. I'm going to work with you tonight while Amelia runs everything else. We'll concentrate on getting you up to speed with the specials on the menu, since you're already familiar with most of the basics."

"Of course he's familiar with those. Any self-respecting bartender knows the names of the men they're willing to put in their mouth. Right, Tate?" As Logan's voice found him, Tate looked up to see him coming through the side access door that led to their loft.

It had just turned eight and Logan was right on time, and *damn* he looked fucking unreal.

He'd obviously arrived a little earlier, because he'd changed out of the suit he'd worn to the office and was now wearing distressed jeans that outlined his legs perfectly—and the denim lovingly cupped what was between those thighs in a way that was close to indecent. But that wasn't all he had going for him—with Logan, it never was. He'd paired the jeans with a grey Henley, and had left the top buttons undone. And Tate could see a glimpse of the hair that smattered the broad chest filling out the material.

With his glasses gone and contacts in, Logan's eyes were an arresting blue, and the thing that topped off the entire look and made Tate go from having a twitching dick to a full hard-on was the leather jacket Logan wore—it was Tate's. And it made his possessive side real happy to know that Logan was wrapped up in something that smelled like him.

When Logan caught his bold perusal, he swiped his tongue along his lower lip, and Tate was, as always, amazed at how effortlessly sexy the man was.

"That's right," Tate said as he strolled down to where Logan had stopped, needing to get closer.

"Hey there, Logan," Hoyt said as he slid the bowl of nuts his way.

"Oh no, you go ahead. I'll eat some later tonight." When Logan looked over at him and winked, Tate reached across the bar, took the back of Logan's neck, and pulled him in to greet him.

As their mouths connected, a groan left Logan's throat and his fingers came up to hold Tate's chin as he returned the greeting. When the choice to either stop or let things get out of hand became a real concern, Tate made himself put a halt to things. They would have this coming weekend to explore that.

"Evening," he said against Logan's lips, and just like that, he knew his night would be infinitely better than his day.

"Evening. I see your victim is here, awaiting his trial."

Tate grinned as he released Logan, and they both glanced over to where Robbie stood staring at the two of them like his brain had just exploded from what he'd witnessed—which was far more than he'd ever seen them do before. Logan chuckled, and the low sound of it in his ear had Tate turning back to face him.

"Why don't you come and order a drink from our newest employee, Mr. Mitchell?" Tate straightened behind the bar as Logan regarded Robbie, who suddenly started to fiddle with the towel in his hands. Tate couldn't help his laughter at that, because Logan sure had a way of making a guy nervous. He could attest to that.

As Logan strolled down to Robbie, he gestured to the other end of the bar farthest away from the crowd then headed over there to take a seat. The smile Logan aimed at the dazed Robbie was full of devilry as he picked up a tiny black straw from one of the glasses on the counter and bit down. "Hello, Robbie. I think it's time for a little payback. Don't you?"

* * *

LOGAN WAS LUCKY he could still form a coherent sentence after that stamp of ownership Tate had just laid on him when he'd first arrived. But he figured sitting his ass on a barstool and messing with Robbie for a bit was probably a good plan to get his brain back in working order.

"Payback?" Robbie said, as he looked at Tate, who was now walking over to them.

"Yes," Logan said, pulling the straw from between his lips, and when Robbie's eyes dropped to the move, Logan chuckled. "Payback. For all the shit you used to give Tate when we first met."

"I...I didn't give him that much shit."

Logan arched a brow. "Really? I must be mistaking the invite to a threesome, then."

"On more than one occasion," Tate added with a smirk.

When Robbie's mouth fell open, he looked as though he wasn't quite sure what to say next. But then the sides of his lips slowly curved and the flirt Logan remembered snuck through. "Well, could you blame me? I was just being friendly."

"Is that what you call it?" Tate said. "If my memory serves me correctly, you were willing to be *very* friendly."

Robbie looked between the two of them and gave an innocent shrug. "Have you seen you two? I'm still willing *and* friendly."

"Why am I not surprised? But forget it," Tate said, and rolled his eyes.

Logan continued to watch the two of them and

grinned. "Aww, this is so nice. The two of you coming together for the greater good."

Robbie snorted, and when Tate looked at him, he shrugged. "Sorry. Whenever he talks, my brain automatically goes, *Well, there.* Does he even realize the way he looks? Or the way people take his words? It's all—"

"Sex? Trust me," Tate said, looking in Logan's direction. "He's aware of everything that comes in and out of his mouth."

"You would know," Logan said, trailing his eyes down Tate's vest to settle on the zipper of his pants.

"Yes, I would," Tate said, catching Logan's attention with the arrogance in his voice. "That's what makes him the perfect person for you to work around tonight." Tate glanced over to Amelia, who was down the other end of the bar laughing with a couple who'd just sat down. "He's going to be your guinea pig."

"Wait up," Logan said with a frown. "I didn't agree to *that.*"

"He needs to learn a few of the staples. Even you know those," Tate said. "He also needs to learn how to concentrate on more than one person, and *you* are the biggest distraction I can think of to place in the path of anyone."

Logan raised an eyebrow at Tate's smug face, and then he looked at Robbie, who appeared stuck somewhere between nervous and excited. "I'm going to take that as a compliment."

"It was meant as one," Tate said as a customer came up to the bar. "I'll be back, you two. *Try* to behave."

As Tate moved down to the man and greeted him, Logan looked across to Robbie and gestured with his straw. "The uniform looks good."

Robbie looked down at the black vest, red shirt, and black pants. "Yeah, I like it. Tate said I could get away with the red tonight, but I need to get a burgundy shirt by next week."

"Such a hardass, that boss of yours."

When Robbie's eyes landed on his, Logan raised his eyebrows, acting the innocent. But Robbie was right: most of his thoughts were less than innocent, and, well, Tate really did have a hard—

"He seems nice enough," Robbie said, interrupting Logan's train of thought.

"Tate?"

"Yeah. I wasn't so sure he liked me. But he's been really cool."

Logan let his eyes travel up to Robbie's hair and noticed for the first time he'd cut the sides shorter, so the longer strands on top now formed a perfectly styled faux-hawk. It was still the natural color he seemed to now favor, but with the new cut, there were definite hints that Robbie might be thinking of re-embracing that side of himself.

"Tate's a good guy. The best I've ever met. He's fair

and honest, and if you ever fuck him over, you'll have me to answer to."

Robbie arched an eyebrow and held his hands up in mock surrender. "Message received. Down, boy."

"Just making sure shit is crystal clear. That man over there has one of the biggest hearts I know. So if you take this job, you better be ready to give him one hundred percent."

"Is this how you two always interview people?" Robbie asked, bracing his hands on the bar.

"How's that?"

"By double-teaming them?"

Logan scoffed. "You wish."

Robbie sighed. "I mean…he's the welcoming committee who makes you *want* to work here. Then you come in and lay down the law."

Logan's lips curled slowly, and Robbie visibly swallowed. "What can I say? We each have our strengths."

Robbie nodded and then blinked a couple of times, as though trying to remember his name. "Uhh…okay, so, if you're going to bust my balls all night, we might as well start, right?"

Logan narrowed his eyes and nodded. "Sure. How about we begin with my staple, since it's important to please the management."

"And what might that be?" Robbie asked.

Logan was just about to answer when a tumbler slid in front of him with a slice of lime in it. "A gin and tonic is his drink of choice," Tate said with a wink. "Amelia said she'd handle things for a bit, so how about we run through a few drinks and get Logan good and...relaxed?"

Relaxed my ass, Logan thought, when Tate aimed a heated look in his direction.

That look didn't make his body feel relaxed. *Fuck no.* Those smoldering eyes and that crooked *I know you want me* smile had Logan about two seconds away from reaching between his legs to palm the erection now throbbing there. Add in alcohol, and God only knew how this would end up, because it seemed that Tate was hellbent on playing with him tonight in front of Robbie.

Fine by me. Game on, Logan thought, and then raised his glass to take a sip.

"Come on, then, do your worst, boys—*relax* me."

* * *

TWO HOURS LATER, the bar was full of the usual after-workers along with the hump day crowd. Tate had Amelia and one of his other bartenders working the counter while he, Robbie, and Logan occupied the far corner of the bar.

Throughout the night, he'd had Robbie taking orders and making the basics for customers while he'd been beside him filling the orders from the customized menu. During the in-between moments, he'd had Robbie mixing some of their most requested drinks and then passing them off to Logan for a taste test, because nothing was more fun, or distracting, than a tanked Logan.

So far, Logan had finished his gin and tonic, downed a Throat Tickler, complained the entire way through a Cherry Banger and just now licked up the remnants of one of his favorite shots—The Ivy League.

When he finished and slammed the shot glass down on the counter, he slid it over to Tate and wiped his thumb over his lower lip.

"How was that?" Robbie asked, a frown marring his forehead. "I have the Tongue Twister up next for you."

Tate had to give Robbie credit: he was a quick study and was meticulous in the measurements he poured and mixed, which resulted in a really great-tasting drink. Thank God, considering he'd already hired him.

"It was strong, but good," Logan answered, and the lazy way his eyes shifted between them told Tate he was definitely feeling the effects of the alcohol. "I think I might need a bit of a time-out, though."

Tate chuckled. "Feeling *relaxed*, are we?"

"Oh, I'm feeling something, all right," Logan said as he focused on Tate, and when he bit down on his full bottom lip, Tate had to fight every instinct he had not to grab him and head upstairs for a quick fuck. Shit, he doubted they would even make it up the stairs.

"Damn, okay," Robbie muttered from beside him, and when Tate looked over, Robbie's eyes were fixated on

Logan. "How do you ever say no to him?"

"He doesn't," Logan said, arrogant as ever.

But hell if he's not wrong, Tate thought. He couldn't actually remember a time he'd ever said no to Logan. And when he was like this? Forget it. "You having trouble keeping up there, counselor?"

Logan ran his eyes all over him, and Tate shook his head. *Jesus,* he was hot. Adding a couple of drinks to the mix didn't take away from that one little bit. It just guaranteed Logan's sex appeal was even stronger. Something the dumbfounded Robbie seemed to be having trouble dealing with.

"Definitely not having trouble keeping it *up,*" Logan said, and pushed forward on his stool to lean over and crook a finger at Tate. Tate laughed and moved forward so Logan's lips could brush over his cheek, and then he said, "Want to come around here and see for yourself?" He took Logan's chin between his fingers and kissed him quickly before moving away and pointing at him. "Sit and behave. We're training a new employee."

Logan grinned shamelessly, and then his dark eyes found Robbie. "Isn't sexual harassment in the training manual? Come around here, and I'll show him what he's *not* allowed to do to you."

Robbie looked as though he liked the idea of that, but Tate knew if he got close to Logan without the barrier of the bar, there'd be no telling what would happen. "I don't think so. But I think that's enough alcohol for you."

"Perhaps," Logan said, a serious expression crossing his face. "I have to go to work with Priestley tomorrow, and I don't want him riding my ass."

"I'm so glad to hear that," Tate said with a laugh, and that was when he realized Robbie had stiffened beside him and a fierce scowl had crossed his face.

He wasn't the only one who'd noticed the change, either, because Logan started chuckling and said, "I bet Robbie wouldn't mind that, though."

"Mind what?" Robbie said, and the demand was pitched a little higher than his usual tone.

"Priestley, riding your ass," Logan said, subtle as a sledgehammer.

Robbie's mouth fell open and his eyes became so round they came close to encompassing his entire face. "You're joking, right?" When Logan winked at Tate, Robbie shook his head adamantly. "You've had way too much to drink if you think I would ever let that...that arrogant asshole anywhere near me."

"Methinks thou protests too much," Logan said, twirling one of the black straws between his thumb and forefinger.

"And I think you've lost your fucking mind," Robbie said.

Tate crossed his arms as Logan tsked at Robbie and pointed the straw at him. "Is that any way to talk to one of your new bosses?"

"You just said I wanted one of *your* coworkers to ride my ass. Is that any way for you to talk to your *new* employee?"

"Now that you mention it, you're probably right. But..." Logan said, his eyes alight with mischief. *Fucking troublemaker.* "What do you think, Tate? He's a little bit *touchy* about this subject, isn't he?"

At the reminder of Robbie's words to him all those years ago, Tate nodded and tapped a finger to his chin. "He does seem a little bit uptight about this."

Robbie narrowed his eyes on them both and fumed. "You two suck."

"Hmm, and often, too," Logan said. "But the real question here is, do you think Priestley does? I bet he's an arrogant fucker in the bedroom. He sure didn't take any of your shit today. What do you think, Robbie?"

Robbie sputtered a couple of times and looked at Tate as though he might save him. But Tate was too busy trying not to laugh his ass off. *Ahh, payback can be such a fun little bitch.*

"I don't care what he is in the bedroom," Robbie finally said.

"Sure you don't," Logan said, and started to laugh as Tate finally lost it.

Poor Robbie. His face was bright red, either from embarrassment or arousal.

"I *don't*," Robbie said.

Logan nodded as he bit down on the straw and flashed an unrepentant grin. "Then why are you strangling that poor bar towel?"

Robbie's hands stilled immediately, then he threw the towel on the bar top and turned on Tate. "I'm due a break, aren't I?"

Tate bit the inside of his cheek, trying to get himself under control, and nodded.

"Then I'd like to take it."

"To call Priestley?" Logan asked. "I have his number if you want it."

Robbie's head snapped around, and the *fuck you* look he gave Logan was full-on old barista Robbie. It was dripping with haughty indignation, and the tilt to his chin told Tate that no matter how much Robbie was protesting, there was definitely something about this Priestley guy that had gotten under his skin.

Robbie stepped around Tate and marched off down the bar to the door that led out the back, and Logan started to laugh so hard he ended up wiping tears from his eyes.

"You enjoyed that way too much," Tate said, as he bent over to rest his arms on the counter so he was eye level with Logan.

"Maybe a little. But come on, he's had that coming for a long time. Plus, you saw his reaction."

"I did."

"And," Logan asked, as he reached out to link their fingers together. "What did you think?"

Well, if anyone understood the denial of one's sexual attraction to another person, it was Tate. He'd been a master of doing that when he first met Logan, and right now, Robbie was reacting the same way he had, even though the interest was there in his flushed cheeks and curious eyes.

"I think you're spot-on," Tate said. "He protested a little too hard and a little too loud."

"Hmm, reminds me of someone else I used to know. By the way," Logan said, and then lowered his voice, "that sounded dirty."

"I could recite the alphabet to you right now and you'd take it as a come-on."

"Probably. Want to try? Start with F and we can end with U."

Tate pushed forward on his toes until he could kiss Logan hard. "Or you could head upstairs, shower, and get in bed and wait for me."

Logan's lips curved. "I could. Couldn't I?"

"Mhmm. And when I come up there, I'll make you protest hard *and* loud."

Logan chuckled. "Oh yeah?"

"Yeah. But if you don't get the hell out of my bar in the next five minutes, I'm not going to be held responsible for fucking you in the stairwell."

When Logan's eyes lit, Tate shook his head and

straightened, and then he pointed to the door. "Go. Your presence here has been much appreciated, but hell if you aren't also *my* biggest distraction."

Logan winked and bit down on the straw a final time as he sauntered out of the bar, leaving Tate hard as hell and, as always, so damn glad that man was his.

Chapter Twenty-Two

IT WAS THE end of the week, and a beautiful Friday morning, as Tate floored his Mustang up I-90 and the two of them relaxed into the drive that would take them to their cabin for the weekend.

The sun was out, the sky was clear, and Logan couldn't think of another place in the world he'd rather be than sitting beside Tate with his window rolled down and the Killers blasting from the stereo.

They'd stopped for a quick bite and coffee, but neither wanted to linger before hitting the road, both eager to get to their home away from the city.

Logan looked across to see Tate with one of his arms resting on the open window and the other hand casually holding the steering wheel. In his ripped jeans, he looked so cool and relaxed that Logan wanted to tell him to pull over so he could shove him in the back seat and unzip those jeans. As the thought entered his mind, Logan placed his hand on Tate's thigh, and when he automatically put his over the top and shifted it up his leg to rest between his thighs, Logan thought, *Fuck it.*

He angled his body so he could lean over and kiss

Tate's cheek, and then he inhaled, and the scent of their shampoo and soap wafted around, making Logan want to nuzzle his nose behind Tate's ear. "You smell fucking amazing."

Tate added pressure to the top of Logan's hand as he spread his legs a little wider. "Considering we showered together, I'd say I smell exactly the same as you."

"Mhmm, I remember," Logan said. "But you still smell amazing. I think it's just you. Your skin. The way the soap reacts to it."

"Maybe it's pheromones. Maybe my body's reacting to you being so close."

"I'm not sure there is such a thing. But," Logan said, and squeezed his hand around the cock he could feel swelling behind the denim, causing Tate to groan in the back of his throat, "your body is definitely reacting to me."

"I think you need to go back to your side of the car," Tate said, just as Logan nipped at his earlobe and tightened his grip. "Like...*shit*, Logan. Now."

Logan chuckled but relented. If there was one thing he was overly cautious about when it came to Tate, it was driving. Ever since his accident, any time they were in a vehicle that was moving, Logan wanted all attention on the task at hand. *Even if that does mean I'm now sitting here with a serious case of blue balls.*

Deciding to distract himself, Logan reached for the volume and turned the music down. Talking was a good idea. If they talked, he wouldn't just sit there and stare at Tate for the next forty or fifty minutes thinking of all the ways he was going to enjoy that strong body as soon as they reached their destination.

Tate must've been of the same mindset, because he glanced over for a second, blew out a sigh, and then pressed the heel of his hand against his obvious arousal. "So," he said. "You never did tell me what happened yesterday with Priestley and the prosecutor."

"And you want me to tell you *now*?"

Tate laughed at his put-out tone. "Don't worry. The second we're out of the car and inside the cabin, you can do whatever you want to me. But for now, this seems like a safe enough topic."

Well, when he puts it like that... Logan rubbed a hand over his chin as he thought about yesterday. "They offered eleven months. They won't budge off that, though."

"Eleven months in jail?"

"Yeah. Since there's no time served, it would be the full eleven months, too."

Tate nodded. "Okay. And what did Robbie's cousin— Sorry, I can't think of her name."

"Vanessa."

"Right. What did Vanessa say to that?"

Logan shook his head, remembering Priestley's frustration, not to mention his own. "She said the same thing she's been saying from the get-go."

"That she's innocent?" Tate said.

"Yep." Logan sighed and looked out the window. This case troubled him on all levels. There was the Robbie factor. The Nonna factor. And then Vanessa herself. She was a sweet kid. She didn't deserve this. And the really shitty part of it all was both Logan and Priestley believed she was one hundred percent innocent. "I understand her position, believe me. And there's no way I'm advocating she lie. But in this instance, telling the truth is going to ruin her life."

When Tate's hand found his leg, Logan turned to see him looking at him for several heartbeats, then he was back facing the road.

"You're doing everything you can for her. Taking her case pro bono. You have Priestley, who you say is the best, first-chairing it. Logan, there's nothing else you can do now other than counsel her. You've told her the options; now she has to make her own choice. That burden doesn't fall on you."

"It does if we lose. If she says no to this deal, which it looks like she will, then this immediately goes to trial. And with what the police have as evidence, it'd be a miracle if she walked out of there free."

Tate ran a hand through his hair. "When will you know what she wants?"

"The deal's off the table in forty-eight hours. That means Priest will know sometime tomorrow if he has to prepare for court on Monday."

"Shit."

"Yeah," Logan said. "You know, this is why I didn't go into criminal law."

"Why's that?"

"Because of cases like this," Logan said. "People think it's hard to get up and defend someone who is without a doubt a deplorable human being. But you know what's worse?" When Tate looked his way, Logan shrugged and said, "Defending the innocent." He shook his head and then rested it back on the seat. "When you know someone is innocent deep inside your bones and she's as young as Vanessa? Nothing puts more pressure, or is harder, on a lawyer than walking into that courtroom with the deck stacked against him, hoping that somehow he's going to pull a wild card and come out the winner. That's the worst position to be in, and if she comes back and tells Priest she doesn't want to take that deal, then that's what he's going to be walking into."

* * *

TATE WISHED THEY were already at the cabin as Logan's words came to a close. He wanted to touch him in that moment, tell him it would all work out. But really, he didn't know that. He *hoped* this Priest guy was as good as Logan said, but what if he wasn't? What if Robbie's cousin ended up going to jail for fifteen or more years? That was a heavy

burden to carry. And he could understand exactly what
Logan was saying. "How does Priestley feel about it?"

"I don't know. The guy's a vault," Logan said, and
then turned his head on the headrest and removed his
sunglasses. "But if it was me up there on trial, I'd want him
sitting first chair."

Tate took in Logan's serious expression and wanted
to ease him if he could. So he gave him a crooked smile and
said, "That's good to know, considering how much trouble
you like to get into." Logan arched an eyebrow, and Tate
reached over and ran a finger down the line of his jaw.
"She's lucky to have you two. But are you sure you should
be here with me this weekend?"

Logan grabbed his hand and nodded. "Of course.
This is Priest's case now. Plus, there's nowhere else I should
ever be if you need time away with me. And that's what you
asked for this weekend."

Sweet. It was something Logan claimed he wasn't.
But when he said things like that, there was no denying it.
As Logan absently kissed the back of his hand, Tate smiled
and said, "I can't wait to get up there. The weather is meant
to be perfect for the next three days."

"I saw that this morning. High seventies, mid
eighties. I'm loving this weather."

"Maybe I'll work on my tan," Tate said, and a slow,
sensual smile crossed Logan's lips.

"You should definitely work on it. And be sure to do

so in a way that won't leave any lines on this gorgeous skin of yours."

Tate scoffed. "In other words, stay naked all weekend?"

"I'm not seeing a problem with that."

Neither am I, Tate thought, as Logan's eyes traveled a fiery path down his t-shirt and blue jeans.

"In fact, I think you should start as soon as we arrive," Logan said. "You won't want to miss an opportunity in case the clouds roll in."

Tate looked out the windshield at the cloudless sky, then back to the man sitting across from him. "Yeah, I can see that'll be a real worry."

Logan shrugged and said, "You never know."

Tate laughed and relaxed back into his seat as he pushed his foot a little harder on the gas, suddenly wanting to get to the cabin as soon as possible.

AS TATE TOOK the turn onto their street, lush greenery flanked either side of them as he slowed the Mustang to a crawl and they wove their way through the quiet neighborhood.

What he loved most about coming up there was the feeling of solitude it afforded the both of them. It'd been years since Logan had first brought him there after he'd asked for some "space," and in all that time Tate had never been so aware of how much he must've hurt Logan that day.

Never had he looked back at it after they'd worked things out and he'd apologized. *Until today,* Tate thought.

It seemed as though memories from when they'd first gotten together were flooding back into their lives from all sides lately. But that was to be expected, he supposed, after meeting up with Jill and seeing Robbie again for the first time in years.

When he turned the car onto the narrow dirt drive, it took them into the dense foliage of the property, and Tate took the small fork in the road that led them around the first and largest pond, to where the barn stood. He pulled the car to a stop and Logan got out to open the wide double doors, and as Tate pulled the car in and parked it beside Logan's truck, he finally let out a sigh.

Now I can relax, he thought, as he shoved open the car door and climbed out to see Logan at the trunk getting out their bags. Once the car doors were locked, he came around the end to grab his black duffel, and kissed Logan hard and long until he groaned, then Tate pulled away.

"What was that for?" Logan said.

Tate slung the bag over his shoulder and took Logan's hand. "You were there and I wanted to."

As the two of them strolled outside, Logan licked his lips and said, "I'm *still* here if you want to again."

Tate chuckled and kept walking along the path that wound around the man-made pond that sat directly behind the cabin. It was beautiful with the way the sun was reflecting off the water, and before they headed inside, he wanted to go down and enjoy it for a minute.

Dropping his bag on the grassy bank, he tugged on Logan's hand, heading for the small pier that jutted out to the middle of the water. As they strolled out to the spot where they'd spent many afternoons eating lunch and enjoying the surrounding view, Tate smiled to himself.

Yes, this is exactly what I need this weekend. Logan, peace, and quiet.

When they got to the end of the wooden planks, Logan stepped in behind him to wrap his arms around his waist, and Tate closed his eyes as warm lips found his neck.

"I don't see you losing your clothes, Mr. Morrison."

Tate sighed as he leaned back into Logan's hold.

"Well, it's hard to strip when you're all over me."

"Complaining?" Logan asked by his ear, as he slipped his fingers under the hem of Tate's t-shirt.

"Not ever."

"Hmm, good. I'd be real disappointed if you were."

Tate turned his head, found Logan's eyes, and said, "Then you'll never be disappointed."

Logan's lips met his then for a kiss that straddled the line of being a sweet tease and a turbulent taking. Logan's tongue went from gently tracing Tate's lower lip to sinking inside his mouth for a thorough taste. And as Logan sucked on his tongue, he stepped around in front of Tate so he could slide a hand into the back of his hair.

Tate let out a throaty groan as their lower bodies met, and when Logan smoothed a hand around his waist and down to his ass to pull him closer, he took hold of Logan's cheeks and savored the intoxicating taste of him.

Logan grunted, and Tate pulled back enough that he could bite down on his lower lip, causing him to curse.

"God," Logan said, his eyes blazing as he ran them all over his face. "I can't wait to get my hands and mouth all over you."

Tate wanted that exact same thing, but before that, he wanted to tease the man currently kneading his ass. Have a little fun with him. After all, that was why they were up there. To relax, zone out, and enjoy one another. "Oh yeah?"

"Count on it. I plan to be in every part of you in the next hour—"

"That's mighty presumptuous."

"Damn right it is," Logan said, and kissed his jaw. "My tongue," he said, and scraped his teeth over the stubble of Tate's cheek. "My fingers," he said, as he thrust his erection against him. Then Logan brushed his lips over Tate's ear and whispered, "And then my cock. All inside that tight little hole of yours in the next sixty minutes. Time it, Tate. It's going to happen."

He put his palms on the white t-shirt covering Logan's chest and dug his fingers into the firm pecs below. It was a deep V-neck that went with Logan's black jeans in a way that made him look like he should be on a magazine cover, not standing on a pier delivering promises hot enough to make Tate want to melt at his feet.

But that was where they were, and Tate shoved him back a little way, smirked at the cocksure man staring at him, and said, "I don't know about that. You seem a little hot and bothered. Maybe you need to cool down before I take my clothes off. I'd hate you to lose it before you got your tongue, fingers, *and* cock inside of me."

"Tate…" Logan said, looking over his own shoulder, clueing in to what Tate was up to. "Don't you dare." But Tate winked at him and gave a nice, hard shove, laughing his ass off as Logan fell off the pier into the cool, clear water under the warmth of the late summer sun.

Chapter Twenty-Three

HE IS SO going to pay for that, Logan thought, as he righted himself in the water and caught sight of Tate's back as he jogged off the pier toward the bank. When he reached the grass, the cocky shit wandered to the edge of the water and called out through his cupped hands, "Feeling a little cooler there, Logan?"

Logan narrowed his eyes and shot him the finger, which only made Tate laugh harder. *Oh, yeah, laugh it up*, Logan thought, as he imagined all the ways he was going to exact his revenge. Because while he supposed the little cool-off should've dampened his arousal, the victorious grin on Tate's face just made Logan's desire kick up a gear. That sneaky fucker was going to get what was coming to him, and Logan was going to enjoy the hell out of giving it to him.

He swam a little way in, and when he finally got to his feet and stood, he took immense satisfaction in the way Tate's expression morphed from triumphant to turned on.

Logan knew he must have looked like a fucking disaster, but he was also aware his white shirt was now plastered to every inch of his body, and his jeans? His jeans were uncomfortable with how snug they were as he stood in the thigh-lapping water, dripping wet. Yet, even as unkempt as he felt, Tate had caught his lower lip behind his teeth in a telltale sign that he loved what he was looking at. That was when Logan knew exactly where to start with *this* particular revenge.

Reaching for the edge of his shirt, Logan peeled the wet fabric over his head, and then ran a hand through his slick hair. Tate took one of his hands out of his pockets and started to palm himself through his jeans.

Yeah, there you go, look at me, Logan thought, as he stood there wet, half-naked, eating Tate up with his eyes. "You know, if I were you, I'd be running. Because when I get my hands on you…"

Tate's lips crooked up on one side. "You'll what?"

Logan started to walk forward, the water sluicing around his legs as droplets ran in rivulets down his naked chest. "When I get my hands on you, I'm going to make you pay for that little stunt."

As he got closer, the water now at his knees, Tate started walking backward, never once taking his eyes off Logan.

"Hey, it's not my fault you got yourself so worked up you needed a cool-down."

Logan's feet finally hit the grass of the bank, and he cocked his head to the side, regarding Tate closely. "You think that cooled me down?"

Tate licked his top lip. "Didn't it?"

Logan shook his head, threw the wet t-shirt on the ground, and said, "No. It fucking didn't. And Tate?"

"Yeah?"

"You better start running."

* * *

AS LOGAN'S WARNING hit his ears, Tate's cock throbbed and his heart raced. The look in Logan's eyes was downright predatory—had been since he'd emerged from the water like some kind of god Tate wanted to worship.

Soaked to his skin, Logan shouldn't have looked as good as he did, but he looked sexier in wet clothes than he did the dry ones. How the hell that was humanly possible, Tate had no idea. But when Logan tossed his shirt on the grass and started in his direction, he knew he only had minutes, if that, to get to wherever the hell he wanted to be for what was about to happen next.

And what was about to happen was going to be torture.

Pure. Sexual. Torture.

The kind of torture that would have his eyes rolling to the back of his head, his cock begging to be sucked, and his ass wanting to be taken. And the man stalking him as he backed away toward the barn looked ready and willing to be the one inflicting the punishment.

"Where's it going to be, Tate?" Logan asked, a hand going to the silver button of his jeans, and when Tate stumbled, he didn't miss the way Logan's eyes sparked in reaction.

He liked that he had him running. Liked the chase.

Of course he does, goddamn deviant.

"Inside or out here with Mother Nature?" Logan asked, looking at the branches of the huge maple hanging over his head.

When Tate got back on the path that led to either the barn or the house, he decided it was time to take this little game up a notch, and reached over his shoulder to gather his shirt in his hand. As he tore it over his head, he noticed Logan was closer than he had been before, and he was looking at Tate as though he wanted to consume him.

Tate balled his shirt up and threw it at him, and when Logan caught it, he brought it up to smell and said, "There are those pheromones you were talking about." Then he tossed it on the ground, and Tate knew it was on.

He turned and made a run for the barn and the doors Logan had left open, and could hear the gravel crunching under the feet of Logan, closing in behind him. He should've known better when it came to trying to outrun Logan though. He'd never win. Logan had been running since college. But that didn't mean Tate wasn't going to make him work for it. He got to the barn just before Logan did, and headed over toward the truck, figuring he could use it as a buffer.

What he didn't realize was the truck was parked so close to the other end of the space that there was no way for him to get around it, so now, when he turned back to Logan, he found himself trapped.

He knew it, and when Logan came around the front of the truck, the smug look on his face told him that Logan did too.

* * *

"UH OH. This doesn't look so good for you..." Logan said as he sauntered forward and Tate continued to back up toward the bed of the truck. "You've got nowhere to go, Mr. Morrison."

Tate didn't look worried in the slightest as he continued walking backward. In fact, one of his hands was massaging the obvious erection behind his jeans, even as Logan stalked him.

"Yeah, looks that way," Tate said with a shrug, and when his back hit the corrugated wall of the barn, Logan kept coming for him, his fingers now unzipping his wet jeans and spreading the material apart.

When they were toe to toe, Logan reached out and took Tate's chin between his thumb and forefinger, and as Tate's lips parted and his breath caught, Logan swiped his thumb over his bottom lip and said, "You are so fucked."

Tate's eyes darkened with lust as he flicked his tongue over Logan's thumb and said, "I can't wait."

You fucking flirt, Logan thought, as he dipped his thumb between Tate's lips, and when he sucked on it, Logan growled. Tate shifted then, and Logan glanced down to see that he was undoing his own jeans to shove a hand inside so he could grab hold of his dick and stroke it.

"Damn. You're just begging for it today, aren't you?"

Tate's cheeks flushed at the words, and his sex-hazed eyes were heavy as he slowly blinked and Logan withdrew his thumb, dragging it down over his lip.

"Yes," Tate said, and arched his head back as he gave himself a nice, slow pull. "I want to feel you in me."

Logan gnashed his teeth at the provocative words. Tate was seducing him with that mouth as well as his actions as he stood there masturbating for him. But there was no *way* Logan was about to let him off the hook that easy or be denied the pleasure of being the one to get him there.

As Tate's mouth parted on a sigh, Logan placed one hand by his head on the wall, then drew his other fingers down the center of Tate's chest and abs, where he stopped and swirled his fingertips around Tate's navel. "Get these jeans out of my way, Tate."

Tate worried his tongue over his lip, and then he was moving. He kicked his shoes off and shoved his thumbs into the sides of his jeans and boxers, and Logan moved aside so he could bend over and push them both to his ankles. Once they were gone, the socks removed also, Tate straightened and was naked as the day he was born.

Logan placed his hand back where it had been by his head, and then lowered his other to take hold of Tate's stiff cock. When Tate cursed and squeezed his eyes shut, Logan flicked his tongue over his earlobe and said, "You know you deserve a whole lot of payback for what you pulled out there. Don't you?"

Tate turned his head, and the sunlight slipping through the wood-paneled walls of the barn bathed his face, making his eyes the color of copper. He was gorgeous, and frustrated, as his jaw bunched and ticked. It was obvious he wanted Logan to move his hand, but Logan wanted him to make him beg.

"I ahh..." Tate started, until Logan tightened his grip. "*Fuck*, Logan."

"Yes," Logan said, ghosting his lips over Tate's. "We already established *that's* going to happen. And very soon, but first," he said, giving Tate a final squeeze, "*first* I'm going to hold true to my word and get my fingers and tongue inside you. Because with how I'm feeling, you're going to need to be good and stretched to handle me."

* * *

TATE SHUT HIS eyes to try and get himself under some

kind of control, because he knew if he didn't rein it in here and now, he'd come the second Logan's tongue touched any part of him. *And fuck, I want to enjoy that dirty-talking tongue.* When he opened his eyes back up, it was to see Logan now naked, kicking his stiff, wet jeans away from him, and Tate couldn't help the smirk it brought to his lips. As Logan walked back the couple of steps needed so he was standing close enough that their cocks were grazing, he speared his fingers through Tate's hair and pulled him forward from the wall.

"Laugh it up, because you won't be for long," Logan said, and then he crushed his lips down over the top of Tate's.

Tate's hands went to his hips in an instant, as Logan wrapped his other arm around his waist and flattened his palm on his lower back. Tate slid his tongue inside Logan's mouth to rub it up against the one tangling with his, and when he felt Logan's index finger slide down between his cheeks, Tate bucked his hips forward, wanting more.

Logan twisted the fingers he had in his hair and tugged his head back so he could press kisses up Tate's jaw to his ear. When Tate grunted, Logan shifted them both, pivoting to the left so he could back him up until his ass was against the bed of the truck, and then he started to grind his erection against Tate's.

Tate ran his hands down to grab a firm ass cheek in each hand and pull Logan as close as he could physically get him as Logan brought their lips back together in a kiss that bordered on brutal. Tongues dueled, lips were bitten, and when Logan finally tore his mouth free, it was swollen and red, and made Tate want to either suck it or fuck it. Either way would be fine with him.

Logan took a step back, and the both of them reached down to fist their dicks as they sized each other up. Naked and fully aroused, they were both clearly ready to go, and Tate couldn't stop himself from spitting in his palm and starting to *really* jerk himself off.

"You dirty fucker," Logan said as his eyes greedily took in all that he was seeing, and Tate could tell by the way Logan had to clamp a fist around the base of his cock that he loved what he was looking at.

Him, leaning bare-assed up against the side of the truck with his legs spread and his fist rapidly stroking his aching length.

"I'm going to let you keep doing that. But don't you dare come until my cock's inside you. Got it?"

Tate nodded, but said nothing as Logan took the couple of steps needed to stop in front of him again, and then he reached around to the back of the truck.

Logan bit the shoulder closest to him, and when he straightened with an old blanket that had been left in there from the last time they'd visited and taken the truck to the beach, he folded it over once and then dropped it on the ground at his feet. And Tate knew whatever was about to follow was going to test every ounce of control he possessed.

Chapter Twenty-Four

LOGAN WAS ABOUT to tell Tate to brace himself or something along those lines, he was sure. But before he got the words out, Tate brought his left hand up again to spit in his palm. It was filthy, obscene, and made his erection ache like a motherfucker.

With a groan, Logan decided to hell with talking, and went down to his knees in front of Tate before the guy got himself off and Logan didn't get a chance to do all the things he wanted to do to him. *And there's a whole fucking list of them.*

When he was exactly where he wanted to be, Logan looked up at Tate and smiled. Not a sweet *I love you* kind of smile. No, Logan knew the smile he'd just sent Tate's way said, *I love you, but there isn't going to be anything* sweet *about what's going to happen next.*

Logan moved up to his knees, braced his palms on Tate's muscled thighs, and squeezed, then lowered his head to drag his tongue from the base of Tate's cock up to the tip. As he did, he heard Tate curse, so he did it again, and this time when he reached the flushed head, Logan flicked his tongue over it to clean up the pre-cum that had gathered at the slit.

"Shit," Tate said, and Logan peered up at him to see his eyes locked on him.

"Everything okay up there?"

When Tate quickly nodded, Logan looked back at the veiny length only inches from his face. Tate's left hand was clamped around the root, and Logan said, "Hook your arms inside the bed of the truck."

As the request made it to his ears, Tate took in a shuddering breath and released his hold to hook his arms over the sides of the truck. The position put Tate's body on complete display for Logan. His arms were out of the way so his chest and abs were visible, and so was the erection jutting proudly out toward Logan's face.

"Fucking hell. Yes. That's *perfect*," Logan said, and then sat back on his heels for a second to take a look at the view this new position gave him. "Jesus, Tate, you look so damn fuckable. Spread your legs a little wider for me."

When Tate complied, moving his bare feet farther apart, Logan groaned and licked his lips.

"Do you have any idea what I want to do to you right now?"

Tate's eyes fell down to the hand Logan was using on himself, and he said in a voice that had gone a little hoarse, "I think I have some."

"Oh yeah?" Logan said, moving up so he could circle Tate's cock and hold it up to swipe a wet path over his balls and the underside of his length. "What do you think I'm going to do to you?"

Tate's fiery eyes found Logan's, and his face looked strained as he said, "Everything your depraved brain can think of until I can't fucking stand it anymore. Or you can't. Either way."

Logan flashed him his most immoral smile and said, "Have I mentioned how much I love the fact you know me so well?"

Tate thrust his hips forward, and when his cock brushed Logan's cheek, he said, "Not today, you haven't."

Logan directed Tate's cock exactly where he wanted it, teased the underside of it with the tip of his tongue, and then said, "Then how about I just show you instead?"

Then he swallowed Tate between his lips, to the back of his throat.

* * *

TATE'S ARMS FLEXED, and he flattened his palms on the inside of the truck as Logan took his entire length down his throat, making a shout rip out of him.

Holy shit, he's a master at that. He always had been from the first time to right now. Logan could render Tate useless in one second flat when he pulled that move, and as he did it over and over again, Tate squeezed his eyes shut and bit so hard into his bottom lip that he was surprised he didn't draw blood.

His pulse was jackhammering with every suck of
Logan's mouth, every flick of his insatiable tongue, as he
knelt at Tate's feet in their barn with the doors wide open. It
wasn't lost on Tate how on display he was, either. Logan's
naked ass and back were on show to anyone who might
happen to stroll onto their property—even though that
would be a first. And he was naked, standing stretched out
with his arms behind him over a truck's side to give Logan
better access to himself, and his legs were braced wide apart
so he could—

"Ahh...*fuck.*"

Logan's lips had him fully surrounded, and
somewhere in there—*likely when my damn eyes were shut*—the
deviant at his feet had wet his fingers and was now slipping
them back behind Tate's balls to stroke one of them over his
hole.

Tate's eyes flew open, and he looked down at the
dark head going to town on him. Logan's nose was
burrowed into his short, dark curls as he sucked him and
fingered his back entrance, and when he finally drew his lips
off, Logan aimed those blazing eyes up at Tate and tapped
his right ankle.

Tate frowned, and Logan said, "Put it over my
shoulder."

The request made a shiver race up Tate's spine,
knowing how exposed that would leave him. It was just like

that night after Spiagga, but this time he was standing, and nothing on the planet was going to stop him from following that order.

With his arms locked tight, Tate raised his leg, and then Logan put it exactly where he wanted it. Draped over his left shoulder, leaving Tate wide open and definitely all up in Logan's face.

Tate panted as he looked at the scene the two of them made, because *Christ* it was hot, and then Logan turned the heat up even more. Slowly, so fucking slowly Tate thought he might die, Logan sucked his fingers into his mouth and then brought one between his spread legs to massage it over Tate's hole.

Tate jerked forward, unable to help himself, and Logan used his other hand to guide Tate's cock back into his mouth.

"Fuck...fuck," he chanted, as Logan eased his finger in and out, breaching the tight muscle and starting to stretch him. Tate brought one hand around from where he was hanging on like his life depended on it and grabbed a fistful of Logan's wet hair to hold him steady so he could fuck that hot, willing mouth.

Logan groaned around him as he continued to work him with his lips and finger, and when he rubbed against his prostate, Tate froze and yanked Logan's mouth off him. "Jesus. You're going to make me come."

Logan gave him a smile that would rival the devil's.

"Turn around then and let me finish getting you ready. 'Cause I really need to get inside you."

* * *

AS LOGAN GENTLY removed Tate's leg from his shoulder, he sat back and waited for him to turn. He could taste the evidence of Tate's arousal on his tongue, and it was all he could do not to just end it like that, because *damn*, he tasted good... But no, he was going to get *in* his man before they left this barn. Just as he'd threatened to do back when he'd first brought Tate here, all those years ago.

When Tate's feet were both on the ground, he went to get up, and just when Logan thought he'd turn, Tate grabbed a fistful of his hair, pulled his head back, and fastened his mouth on top of his. His tongue delved inside and swept the interior of Logan's mouth, and when Tate started to suck on his tongue, Logan had to clamp a fist around his dick and say a prayer that he wouldn't come from a fucking kiss.

It wasn't just a kiss, though. He knew what Tate was doing. He was indulging all of his senses by taking a kiss that tasted of himself. Tate growled and kept a firm hand in Logan's hair and the other at his chin holding him steady so he could take what he wanted, and Logan didn't have one goddamn problem with that.

When Logan's lips were finally freed, Tate's eyes

were wild as he took a step away, turned as requested, and braced his hands on the side of the truck. And this time, Logan didn't even have to request he spread his legs, he just did.

And hell if that isn't the best fucking sight I've seen today, Logan thought, as he placed a palm on either side of Tate's ass. He squeezed and spread him, teasing him, and when Tate was apparently done with being patient, he aimed a glare over his shoulder, and Logan drew the flat of his thumb over his hole, pushing it in *just* a little. When he removed it, Tate muttered a profanity and Logan chuckled.

"You want something, Tate?"

Logan saw him reach down and start stroking himself, and leaned forward to kiss and bite Tate's right ass cheek. When Tate grunted and shoved back at him, Logan finally took pity on him, spread Tate apart, and swiped his tongue along the narrow channel of his ass.

The pleasure-filled moan that filled the barn was like music to Logan's ears as he did it again, and this time when he raised his head, he eased his thumb deeper inside the tight muscle, loosening Tate up.

When Tate's hips bucked again, Logan knew exactly what he wanted, and removed his hand so he could lower his head and get his tongue in on the action. He licked, sucked, and tongued his way along the shadowy cleft that the scent of their soap still clung to, and when he raised his head and eased one of his fingers all the way inside, Tate

frantically pumped his cock and started to curse up a storm.
Damn, Tate was a greedy fucker when it came to
getting eaten out, and Logan never would've guessed that to
be something he would end up loving the most. But hell if
he hadn't been pleasantly surprised to find that out about
Tate. His guy was as dirty as he was, and that pleased him
down to the very corners of his kinky soul.

"Logan... *God*. Again. Fuck. I *need* something."

Logan slowly withdrew his finger, licked over the
stretched hole, and then sucked two digits into his mouth,
got them good and wet, and eased them into Tate. A low
growl left the man who was bent at the waist, braced naked
against the truck, and Logan finger-fucked him until Tate
was demanding he get up there and get his cock inside him.

Quickly, Logan turned and reached for Tate's
discarded jeans, knowing he kept his wallet in there, and
when he dug it out and—*yes, there you go*—located a small
packet of lube, he patted himself on the back for always
teaching Tate to be well prepared. Both for life in general
and for living with him, the man who always used any
excuse to get inside Tate.

Getting to his feet, Logan tore open the packet with
his teeth, squeezed most of it on him so he could lube up his
cock, and slid his fingers in the hole so nicely waiting for
him. Then he put his hand on Tate's waist, bent over, and
said in his ear, "Put your hand out." And when Tate offered
up his left hand, Logan squeezed the rest into his palm.

Things were about to get real hard, real fucking fast.

* * *

WITH ONE HAND on the edge of the truck, Tate wrapped his slick palm around his dick and braced himself the best he could. Logan's hands were spreading him apart, and he could feel him teasing his hole with the head of his cock.

"You ready?"

Fuck, am I ever, Tate thought, but talking was proving a little too difficult for his brain right then. It was too busy trying to remind his heart to beat and his lungs to breathe, because Logan had him so wound up he was stunned to be functioning at any kind of capacity.

"Tate?" Logan asked again, and smoothed a hand midway up his back, and when Tate nodded, the hand left his spine, grabbed on to his hip, and, finally, Logan slid inside him.

He moaned as the pleasure of being so unbelievably full overtook him, and Logan growled, "Fuck," as his fingers dug into Tate's waist.

Tate's knuckles turned white where he gripped the truck's side, and as Logan's body stilled for a moment, he could hear him saying, "Damn, Tate. Fucking *damn.*"

Tate's head hung forward as the hot throb of Logan's erection pulsated inside of him, and as the rush he always got from being taken started to wash over him, Tate began to pump his cock.

As his hips began to move, sliding off Logan, he felt Logan grab hold and pull him back, tunneling into him as deep as he could get. Then Logan came down over the top of him and whispered, "Hang on."

That was all the warning Tate got. After that, Logan went at him like a savage. Teeth bit into his shoulder. Fingernails made marks in his skin. And with every forceful thrust, Tate shouted out for more.

He loved being taken like this.

Loved the man doing the taking.

And he fucking loved that Logan understood everything about him and loved every part of it.

Logan was his person. Just as he was his.

And as they both came hard in the heat of the afternoon, Tate had never been more content in his life.

Chapter Twenty-Five

LATER THAT NIGHT, after they'd showered and eaten, Logan headed into the living room with a bottle of wine and two glasses to see that Tate had opened up the glass sliding doors that led out onto the balcony.

If the day had been beautiful, then the night was magnificent. With nobody even remotely close to their cabin, one of the things that made this getaway perfect was how quiet it was. In the evenings, especially. There was no hustle and bustle of the city, and when you were constantly surrounded by that, it was nice to just turn it off and have a change of pace.

Logan also loved how they didn't have a TV or computers up there—unless they chose to bring a laptop. He'd offered to get both when they started coming up there more often, but Tate had been in total agreement that this was the one place they should just unplug and be together, and Logan loved the nights in this cabin with no one but the two of them for miles.

After pouring them each a glass of Merlot, Logan placed the bottle on the side table by the end of the couch and walked to where Tate was standing out on the balcony.

After his shower, Tate had pulled on a pair of loose linen lounge pants and nothing else, while he'd gone for his grey fleece cut-off sweats and a white tee. When Tate turned to see him standing there, he flashed that pearly grin Logan loved so much and then reached for the glass he offered.

"It's a beautiful night," Tate said, leaning over to rest his forearms on the railing.

"It is," Logan agreed, and took a sip of his wine. Then he mirrored Tate's pose, standing close enough that he could feel the heat emanating from his body. "I love it here."

"So do I. I have ever since that first time you brought me here." Tate gave a tight smile. "You were so mad at me that night."

Logan nodded and gave a crooked grin. "I was. You'd broken my heart."

Tate turned toward him and moved in close so he could lay a hand over Logan's chest. "I know. I'm sorry."

"Tate," Logan said around a chuckle, "that was a long time ago. Stop apologizing for it."

"I know, but I didn't know all the details back then, and ever since I talked to Jill—"

"It's brought it all back?"

Tate sighed and turned around to look out into the darkness again. "Yeah, I suppose that's it."

"Listen to me," Logan said, and when Tate didn't look at him, he reached for his chin and turned his face. "We've been through so much since then. That was just one of the *many* bumps we ran into at the beginning of our relationship, but Tate?"

"Yeah?"

"That's water under the bridge. Stop worrying over it. I'm not."

Tate nodded and slowly smiled. "You're a pretty amazing guy. You know that?"

"I mean, I've always suspected it. But feel free to tell me whenever you think I need reminding."

Tate chuckled. "I'll do that."

"Good. And for the record, you're pretty wonderful yourself. What you did this week? Going to see your sister? I'm not sure I could've done that after what she did."

"Yes, you would've," Tate said without hesitation. "You and Cole have one of the strongest relationships I've ever seen, and that didn't start off easy."

"No, it didn't. But that's because he's a pain in the ass."

"Mhmm, I'm positive *that's* the reason why," Tate said. "But...speaking of Jill."

Logan's heart clenched at those words. They hadn't really talked much about Tate's meeting with his sister. He knew she'd apologized and asked for Tate's forgiveness, but beyond that, Tate hadn't said much more.

He was thinking on it. Like he tended to do over things that troubled him. He took them inside of him to reflect. It was Tate's way. And whenever he got quiet, Logan knew to let him be, and eventually he'd talk when he was ready.

So he'd known this was coming. And while he'd given Tate the time he needed to process, Logan had never pushed it far from his mind. There was something Tate hadn't yet told him about that meeting.

"What about her?" Logan said, trying to appear open and...calm.

"She had a lot to say the day we sat down." When Tate stopped talking, Logan knew he was trying to find the right words to say whatever it was that had been bothering him, so Logan waited.

He took a large gulp of his wine, and when he lowered the glass, Tate turned to look at him, and the expression on his face had Logan's heart racing.

Whatever it was, it didn't look like Tate wanted to say it, and didn't that make his anxiety triple. *Just spit it out,* Logan thought.

"She wants to meet you."

* * *

TATE KEPT A close eye on Logan's face for his initial reaction, and the shock that flashed into his eyes was definitely better than what Tate had thought he would see.

"She wants what?"

"To meet you," Tate said again, trying for a smile.

Logan blinked a couple of times and then started to shake his head. "Uhh, I don't think—"

"Logan?"

"Yeah?"

"If I didn't think she was sincere about this, there's no way in hell I would ask you, or put you through this, again."

Logan pinched the bridge of his nose and blew out a breath. Tate knew he was asking a lot, but he also felt this was something he needed to do. Something he owed to himself. The opportunity to have the family dinner he'd wanted to have all along with Logan.

But if Logan wasn't on board, then he wasn't going to force his—

"Okay."

Hang on. Did he just say what I think he said?

"I'll meet her," Logan said. "If that's what you want."

"You'd do that? For me?"

"Tate, I would do anything for you. But I'm not going to lie. I'm not excited about the idea. Nor am I going to hold my tongue if she behaves like she did the first time around."

Tate walked into Logan's space, put a hand on his chest, and kissed him slowly. As Logan relaxed under his touch, Tate said, "I wouldn't want or expect you to. But to make sure shit doesn't go south, I made a stipulation before telling her I would ask you."

"Oh? And what was that?"

"It's going to be at Dad's," Tate said, and Logan's shoulders instantly relaxed. "Yep. If she wants to meet, it's going to be on my terms, and this way she'll see we have an ally. Dad loves you."

"As long as *you* love me, I don't care about anything else," Logan said. "But that was a smart move, having it at your dad's."

"Thank you. And thank you for saying yes."

"Don't thank me until *after* the dinner. God knows how that will go."

"No matter which way it goes, I'll be leaving Dad's place with you, so I'm not worried."

Logan linked their fingers together. "I'm sure it'll all be just fine."

Tate laughed at Logan's less-than-convincing smile. "That was the worst attempt at encouragement that I've ever heard." When Logan shrugged, Tate held up his empty glass, deciding to let him off the hook for the rest of the night. "I think we could both do with another glass of wine. What do you think?"

Clearly relieved by the change of subject, Logan plucked his empty glass out of Tate's hand and said, "I think that's a great idea." Then he headed back inside to the living room, leaving Tate standing there wondering how he'd been lucky enough to wind up with a man as understanding as

Logan.

As Logan settled into the end of the couch, he crooked a finger at him, and Tate knew how.

He'd gotten lucky because four years ago Logan happened to pick the bar he worked at, sat down opposite him, and was just...himself. And there'd been no way Tate couldn't see that man *or* fall in love with him.

* * *

AS TATE CAME inside, Logan tracked his movement, enjoying the way the soft glow of the lamp made his skin look warm to the touch, because it was a true representation of how it actually felt under his fingers.

When he stopped beside the couch, Tate frowned and pointed to the purplish mark on Logan's leg. "You have a bruise on your shin."

Logan glanced down at it. "I know. It's from that damn wine box last week. Our place is too small. There are boxes everywhere. In the hallway. In the study, which isn't even a study anymore."

Tate picked up his refilled glass and took a sip. "You're right. But the loft is no bigger. I mean, this place is great, but it's too far away from everything. So, unless you plan to sell the condo..." Tate's words faded off, and he shrugged as if to say, *What other options are there?*

But Logan cocked his head to the side and said,

"What if we *did* sell the condo?"

Tate's arm froze where he'd been raising the glass back to his lips. "What? You love that place."

"I did. I mean, I do," Logan said, putting his glass on the table and scooting to the edge of the couch. "It was great when it was just me. And then when you moved in it was..." He paused and took a breath, remembering that day not long after Tate had gotten out of the hospital. "That was one of the best days of my life. But with two of us, things have accumulated over the years and it's just too small. There's shit everywhere."

Logan looked up at Tate, who had walked forward to stand in front of him. "You're serious. You want to sell the condo? And what? Move into a house in the suburbs with a dog and a white picket fence? That doesn't sound like Logan Mitchell."

Logan screwed his nose up, horrified at the thought. "Who said anything about the suburbs? *Or* a white picket fence?"

Tate chuckled and reached out to run a hand through his damp hair. "But the dog's open for negotiation?"

"That would be a negative. I do not want some slobbery four-legged animal running around our place chewing the furniture and leaving hair all over my clothes."

"Of course you're worried about your clothes."

"Why wouldn't I be? I pay good money for what I wear. What? Do you *want* a dog?"

Tate started laughing at that question, hard.

"What's so funny?" Logan asked, grabbing Tate's hips and pulling him in between his legs.

Tate cupped the back of his head so he could angle Logan's face up to him, then leaned down and kissed him. "You. Worrying over some imaginary dog while we're sitting here—"

"Well, technically you're standing," Logan pointed out.

"Okay, smartass. While we're *discussing* a really big and important decision."

Logan shrugged as Tate straightened, and then he let him go and sat back on the couch. Tate put his glass down and came over to lie down beside him, resting his head on Logan's thigh.

As they sat there in comfortable silence, Logan allowed himself a moment to really think about what he was suggesting. The two of them house-hunting. They hadn't done that before. Yeah, they had places they lived in. His condo and this cabin he'd already owned, and Tate had picked out The Popped Cherry, and the loft came along with it.

But this? This would be *them* going out and finding a house that they both wanted to live in and own forever. Or at least for a long while. It was a huge commitment.

Ahh, there's that word again. It was one that he kept coming back to over these past few months. A word that hadn't even entered his mind until he'd caught that blasted bow tie and Tate had given him a look that had made Logan stop and think twice about who they were to one another.

And where that idea, the prospect of committing legally to another, had once scared the shit out of him, as he sat there in the quiet of the night playing with the soft curls brushing over his thigh, Logan no longer felt that sense of panic at the possibility.

Instead, that possessive side of him, the one that recognized Tate as his match, his equal in all ways he ever could have imagined, stirred to life, as he acknowledged the possibility of being bound to this man forever, in *every* way he could be.

Curious to know what was running through Tate's mind as he lay there, Logan asked, "Do you not want to move?"

"You know, until right this second, I'd never even thought about it," Tate said as he tipped his head back and looked up.

"Me neither," Logan said, a grin crossing his lips. "But I like the idea. Looking for a house with you."

"Do you?"

Logan nodded as he stroked Tate's hair. "I do."

"Me too. You know, it's funny, but it feels like things are shifting lately, doesn't it?"

"Shifting?" Logan asked.

"Yeah," Tate said, and reached up to stroke his

fingers along Logan's jaw. "Not in a bad way. I just mean with our jobs, this, and Jill."

"I don't know," Logan said. "Maybe it's just the next stage."

"The next stage?" Tate chuckled. "In what? The evolution of us?"

Logan leaned down and brushed a gentle kiss over Tate's lips. "Hmm, something like that."

"I like it," Tate said, grinning against Logan's mouth.

"So do I," Logan said as he settled back into the couch. *So. Do. I.*

As Logan stared down at Tate, who'd now shut his eyes, he memorized the thick eyelashes that kissed the top of his cheekbones and the damp curls that were all over his lap. Tate looked relaxed and beautiful, and suddenly the words *settled, domestic,* and *committed* no longer sent warning bells off in Logan's head.

No, suddenly they had him thinking of other bells...wedding bells.

But no—that would mean a church. And that would mean marriage. What the...? Am I really thinking about—

"Logan?"

As Tate's voice cut through his unbelievable thoughts, Logan looked down to see sleepy eyes focused on him and a breathtaking smile aimed his way. "I love you."

"I love you too," Logan said, and as Tate shut his eyes, he knew without a doubt that, yes, he really was thinking it. Now it was just a matter of where and when he would ask Tate Morrison to marry him.

Special Thanks

"Special Thanks" are always difficult, and not because you don't want to thank everyone, but because it's so incredibly hard to find the right words to express how thankful and grateful you are to have these people take part in such a special thing as creating a book.

When I went into this project—the second installment of The Temptation Series—I knew without a doubt it was going to be a project that took some time and planning to have it done exactly the way I wanted it. Because not only did I want to re-launch the original three books TRY, TAKE, and TRUST with a stunning new makeover, but I also wanted to announce that I was ready to write the final three books in Logan & Tate's story.

The first stop in this journey was, of course, to run the idea by my awesome BFF and co-author, Brooke Blaine. I know it has been said many times before, but I couldn't do this without her. I actually have an anxiety attack if she hints she might be busy the week I hope she can read my final work. Seriously…an anxiety attack.

BUT...she is never too busy, and is *always* there for me whenever I have doubts, ideas, or need her to check anything and everything for me. And when I came to her with this idea, not only was she excited, she was so supportive and helpful in listening to my thoughts and outline for these next three books that I count myself extremely fortunate to have such a friend who will convince me to tackle my fears and pursue my dreams. And who has the strongest strength of character in a person I have ever seen.

I couldn't have done this without you, and these boys wouldn't be the *same* without you! No one knows them as well—and sometimes better—than I do but you. <3

Then I wanted to see what my fabulous agent, Kimberly Brower, thought about the idea. Was this smart after three-four years?? And as she always is, she was one hundred percent supportive. I can't thank you enough for talking with me about this idea and encouraging me to go forth! Your advice and complete accessibility (pretty much instantly LOL) makes you invaluable. And I can't tell you how much better I felt having your eyes on my lawyer. Thank you!

Oh, and when you all get your brand new beautiful paperbacks, we can thank Kimberly for helping me switch over to EverAfter Romance publishing. They make a beautiful book!

The next stop was finding the perfect Logan and the perfect Tate for these gorgeous new covers.

I knew exactly who I wanted for Logan. There was no one else for me, and I was determined. I was lucky enough to be able to track down the wonderful Chris Davis at Specular Photography who I knew had photographed the man I was after, and then, well, Brooke and I had the oh-so-difficult task of picking three photos of the extraordinarily handsome Adam Cowie. I am thrilled to say I got some of the most stunning photos ever, and that is due to the talent of Chris. What magnificent photos you take, sir.

Then it was a matter of tracking down a Tate. He was a little harder because I had a vision in my head for so long. But then I came across a photo by Fred Goudon of the beautiful Clément Becq (the cover photo on Try) and it was as though Tate stepped out of my head and came to life on my screen. He was perfect. I reached out to Fred and crossed all my fingers and toes he had more of Clément, and luckily for me, he did!

So, that was the photos secured…that took a couple of months and happened at the end of 2016. I have to say, I am terrible at keeping secrets so sitting on this was agonizing! I would open the photo files and just want to show everyone—BUT NO. I waited.

And I HAD to wait because Shannon at Shanoff Formats had to go in and create some magic with these bad boys— and BOY DID SHE EVER! Have you seen these covers??? Damn girl. Not only did you brand them perfectly, but you made them so beautiful I literally couldn't have seen them any other way.

Words cannot express how much I love the re-vamp of TRY, TAKE, and TRUST. Then TEASE came along, and I can't wait for everyone to see the final two!

Thank you for working with me on these, and for all of your talented work for the teasers. You're awesome, and I hope I have communicated this clearly. (See, Shannon? I'm working on it!)

And wait... there's someone else... someone I'm trying to put my finger on but it's difficult because she is never in one place for too long. She is elusive...Jenn Watson. You know that's you, lady!

This wonderful woman and owner of Social Butterfly PR is an insanely busy human who never actually sleeps—of this I am convinced. She is, however, dedicated to her clients (and friends) and does everything in her power to help facilitate the best release for each and every one of us.

I love how easy it is to communicate with you, Jenn. I love having you to ask advice and bounce my ideas off when it comes to go time, and I can't wait to see you at Shameless this year! Big hugs coming your way!

Oh Arran. I always say this while shaking my head because I'm convinced when I read some of your comments that that is what you're doing. Case in point "MATCHBOX AND HOT WHEELS ARE DIFFERENT BRANDS ENTIRELY, GOD!"

Consider me schooled LOL. But seriously, your sarcasm and dry wit makes the editing process much less painful— for me, anyway. I'm sure it's horrible for you. Hahaha! Are you thinking YES as you read this right now? Are you? Thank you for being awesome! And I'll be emailing you again soon! Aren't you excited?

To my two wonderful proofreaders: Judy at Judy's Proofreading & Alison at Red Leaf Proofing. Thank you for being my fresh, and final, set of eyes on this project as we got Tease ready and pretty for the public. I was so pleased to get a chance to work with both of you, and I can't wait to do it again. There's no one I trust more.

To the four ladies of the Naughty Umbrella who gave me the names of the drinks that Logan ** cough cough ** swallows. Ahaha. THANK YOU. I love them! They were fun, creative, and cheeky! A great tribute to our guys and so very fitting IMO.

- The Cherry Banger - Tessa Parke
- The Tongue Twister - Gina Olivieri
- The Throat Tickler - Julie Covington
- The Ivy League - Lisa VanHollebeke Howell

To every single blogger who originally picked up TRY and had faith in me: Thank you for supporting my journey into a genre I adore and have only grown to love even more with every single book I have read, and written, within it. You are the people who helped spread the word about Logan and Tate. And you are who helped me convince others to give it a "try."

To my ravenous readers: YOU are the reason Logan and Tate are back in your hands and YOU are the reason that I get to spend more time with these two phenomenal men. You trusted my vision, took a chance on me, and thankfully fell in love with these men just as hard as I did.

I can't wait to continue their journey later this year, and I thank you for all the emails, all the love, and the constant support of these men. I can't ever begin to tell you just how much it means to me.

And finally, to my husband: Thank you for putting up with me and my moody writing ways. Thank you for being supportive of everything I write. And thank you for never complaining when I do my out loud reads with Brooke. You are a trooper, and so patient and unbelievably supportive, and I couldn't ask for anyone more understanding than you. <3 <3

Much love to everyone, and until next time...

Xx Ella

About the Author

Ella Frank is the *USA Today* Bestselling author of the Temptation series, including Try, Take, and Trust and is the co-author of the fan-favorite contemporary romance, Sex Addict. Her Exquisite series has been praised as "scorching hot!" and "enticingly sexy!"

Some of her favorite authors include Tiffany Reisz, Kresley Cole, Riley Hart, J.R. Ward, Erika Wilde, Gena Showalter, and Carly Philips.

CPSIA information can be obtained
at www.ICGtesting.com
Printed in the USA
BVOW03s1520040917
493890BV00001B/63/P